TEARS OF Salvation

USA Today Bestselling Author

MICHELLE HEARD

Cover Designer: Cormar Covers

TABLE OF CONTENTS

Dedication

To the best Beta team in the world.
Thank you for all the support and for putting up with my crazy deadlines.

Songlist

Click here - ***Spotify***

Arsonist's Lullabye – Hozier
The Devil Within – Digital Daggers
Take Me to Church – MILCK
Shadow Preachers – Zella Day
Losing My Religion – BELLSAINT
Raise the Dead – Rachel Rabin
Day Is Gone – Noah Gundersen, The Forest Rangers
Behind the Mask – Ivy & Gold
Between the Devil and the Deep – XYLO
Devil Side – Foxes
Born Ready – Zayde Wolf
Shoot To Kill – Tommee Profitt, Quivr
Save Yourself – Claire de Lune
The War – SYML
I Fell In Love With The Devil – Avril Lavigne
Salvation – Gabrielle Aplin

Synopsis

ISABELLA

I was the party crasher.
He was the Devil.

Three months ago, I suffered a moment of insanity and had a one-night stand without even knowing who the man was.
It was hot and unforgettable.
I tried to forget him, but there are moments I swear I can still smell his aftershave.

Little did I know he's the head of the bratva.
Alexei Koslov.
My family's worst enemy.

There's a thin line between love and hate,
and I'm straddling it.

ALEXEI

There's an even thinner line between the truth and a lie.

As the head of the bratva and the best assassin,
I'm the devil everyone fears.

I get more than I bargained for when I come face to face with Isabella Terrero.
Instead of the *Princess of Terror*, she might just be the embodiment of the goddess of mischief and chaos.

For her, I broke all my rules.
For her, I burned down the world.

TEARS OF SALVATION

Mafia / Organized Crime / Suspense Romance
COMPLETE STANDALONE.

Tears of Salvation is part of the Underworld Kings Universe. A multi-author series of standalone books filled with mafia families waging war, danger and violence, arranged and forced marriages, angst, love, and everything in-between.
Light or dark, twisted or sweet, the Underworld Kings has something for every reader.

Also part of The Saints series of standalones.

WARNING:
18+ only.
Please read responsibly.
THIS NOVEL CONTAINS TRIGGERING CONTENT RELATED TO SEX SLAVERY AND VIOLENCE.

Family Tree

ALEXEI KOSLOV

↓

HEAD OF BRATVA.

32 years old.

Father: Marko Koslov (Deceased)

Brother: Carson Koslov

Best Friend & Partner: Demitri Vetrov

ISABELLA TERRERO

↓

PRINCESS OF TERROR
25 years old.

Mother: Sonia Terrero – Queen of Terror (Head of Terrero Cartel)

Friend & Partner: Ana Sofia Rojas

Chapter 1

ALEXEI

(Alexei; 32. Isabella; 25)

"Let's drink," I say to Demitri as I turn away from the drug dealer we're interrogating.

Since I've taken over as head of the bratva, it's been one shit show after the other. The past year, I've been focused on instilling fear in my enemies and solidifying alliances while building the bratva back up from the ashes.

Demitri, my right-hand man, has been by my side every single day during the past ten years. He's my custodian, but if we're honest with each other, I don't need him to protect me.

No, he's not just my custodian. He's so much more.

Demitri's my partner. My best friend. He's the only person on the face of this planet I trust.

Leaning back against the armored SUV, I pull a flask from the inside pocket of my coat and take a sip of vodka. Handing the flask to Demitri, I let out a sigh as my eyes settle on the Columbian. *Diago*. I only know his name. The fucker is more resilient than a cockroach.

"You think he's going to talk?" Demitri asks.

"I'll make him talk," I murmur while I take in the broken state of the man.

Like I don't have enough shit to deal with since becoming the head of the bratva, now there's a new cartel trying to worm their way into the underbelly of crime. They made the mistake of moving into the area I've made my home.

Everyone knows to stay out of California.

"You sure he's not one of Terrero's?" Demitri asks as he hands the flask of vodka back to me.

Fucking Terrero.

Sonia, the *Queen of Terror*, is the bane of my existence. She deals in human trafficking and drug smuggling. Flesh peddling is something I hate with a vengeance, thanks to my father.

Tilting my head, I stare harder at the man.

Also, there's an unspoken line drawn between Terrero and me. She rules over South America, Africa, and Asia, where North America, Europe, and Russia belong to me. It's a line she'd be stupid to cross.

The only reason I haven't killed her yet is that she's fucking powerful. She's the only one who'd be able to cripple the empire I've built. And vice versa. Hence the unspoken truce.

If Terrero's stepping over the line, I'd have to call in every favor owed to me. It will be a fucking war between the north and the south.

It will be a massacre.

Letting out a sigh, I tuck the flask back in my pocket and push away from where I'm leaning against the SUV. Diago tenses when I stalk toward him.

Coming to a stop in front of him, I tilt my head and lock eyes with him. I've been beating the shit out of him in this warehouse where I have him hanging like a carcass.

The black eyes staring back at me are empty.

He's willing to die.

I take a deep breath and let it out slowly. Lifting my left hand, I wrap my fingers around the side of his neck, and then the corner of my mouth lifts.

"Diago, let me make myself clear." I lean in, my features settling into a coldblooded expression. "I will hunt your family. I'll hang them from bridges for all of Columbia to see."

It's not how I do things, but the cartels love displaying the mangled bodies of those who crossed them. It's a language Diago will understand.

There's a flash of anger and fear in his eyes.

Finally.

"But I won't kill you. I'll let you go, so there's someone to bury your family as I kill them one by one."

"Everyone knows you don't kill the innocent," Diago sneers at me, the fear starting to take root inside him.

People love getting that fact wrong about me. I let out an amused chuckle. "We must have different definitions of innocence." Shaking my head, I say, "Your family is part of the cartel, Diago. They're not innocent." My smile widens as doubt joins the fear on his face.

Good.

Taking a step back, I let my eyes drift over the blood and gashes covering his body. "As entertaining as this has been, I'm growing bored. Which cartel? Tell me, and I won't touch your family and put you out of your misery."

His lips part, and I slowly shake my head in a silent warning for him to think twice before he answers me. "Refuse, and you're free to go. I'll give you a head start of seventy-two hours before I start hunting your family. Those are your only choices."

I didn't become as powerful as I am by showing mercy. Yes, I have moments where I'll help someone, but only if I'll gain from it. Everyone knows this about me.

Mercy is for the weak.

Diago realizes this fact, and I watch as the last of his fight drains from him. "Terrero."

The single word explodes in the air.

Fuck, I was hoping to hear Gaviria. It would be easy to take out Pablo Gaviria's cartel. Child's play compared to Terrero.

"Why is she moving into my territory?" I ask as I pull my gun from behind my back. My fingers flex around the engraved steel of my Heckler & Koch's handle while I wait for Diago's reply.

The last of the strength flows from his body until he hangs limply from the hook I have him tied to.

"I don't know. We were just told to expand into the US."

Nodding, I lift the gun and train the barrel between his eyes. "Your family is safe from me."

Diago lets out a burst of humorless laughter, and then I pull the trigger.

Demitri immediately makes a call to Mr. Wan, my cleaner, who'll dispose of the body and take care of removing any trace we were here.

I stare at Diago's body, feeling nothing for killing the man. Instead, anger begins to simmer in my chest.

Sonia Terrero, you made a big mistake. I'm going to tear your world apart.

Demitri ends the call, then looks at me. "How do you want to handle Terrero?"

"Same as any other hit," I murmur, my anger shimmering through in my tone. "We'll watch her for a while before we plan the attack."

Demitri places his hand on my shoulder, and letting out a sigh, he says, "We knew this day would come."

Slowly, I nod, and then I tuck the gun behind my back.

It was inevitable.

Just like with my father, it's time to end Terrero's reign of horror.

ISABELLA

I learned at a young age, everyone wears masks. For example, take my mother, Sonia Terrero. She's known as the Queen of Terror, violent and cruel. She tortures and kills without blinking an eye. She takes pleasure in destroying things.

But when she's with her custodian, Hugo, she becomes nothing more than another love-starved woman, and it's given Hugo more power than he should have.

Then there's me. The Princess of Terror who's expected to follow in her mother's footsteps.

Stepping into a pair of *Stuart Weitzman* stilettos, I check my reflection in the full-length mirror. I look like the perfect socialite in a shimmering black, backless gown with a plunging neckline. It's a risqué dress with a split skirt and cut-away sides.

It fits my act as the silly little Princess of Terror who likes to dress up in the most expensive clothes.

That's if anyone recognizes me at the party I'm planning on crashing at the exclusive club. Thanks to it being Halloween and the sugar skull makeup I have on, I doubt I'll be caught. If I was in Columbia, my so-called friends might recognize me, but here in California, I'm just another girl with too much money looking for some fun.

A slow smile curves my lips.

It's all about the risk for me. The adrenaline rush of walking into the unknown and not knowing what the next second holds in store for me.

I live for the rush.

It's the only thing that makes me feel alive in the cesspool of death and depravity I'm stuck in.

No, not stuck. I'm no one's prisoner.

I can walk away right this second, but I won't. I'll keep playing the dutiful socialite. The selfish and stupid heir to the Terrero cartel who spends her mother's bloodstained money on all the luxury life has to offer.

It's all for *them*. The girls and boys the cartel keeps luring and snatching off the streets. I don't care about the drugs my mother floods the world with.

I only care about the innocent lives she destroys.

My smile grows as I lift my chin, my brown eyes filled with the courage it's taken to become my own mother's worst enemy. I'm destroying her from within. I'm the Trojan horse she never saw coming.

She's never abused me. Never sold me. I was sent to the best private schools in the US. I attended St. Monarch's in Switzerland for the best training. It would be natural to follow in my mother's footsteps.

Only it isn't. Not for me. I've seen too much horror. Too many children broken and used until they were killed. Seeing an innocent being torn apart leaves a stain on your soul, and I've seen enough to coat my soul crimson.

I'd like to think I take after my father even though I don't know who he is. When I used to ask about him, my mother would just say she was with too many men to know which one was the father.

The anonymity gives me the hope that somewhere in my ancestral line, there was a good person. Someone I take after and that this evil isn't the only blood flowing through my veins.

I'm expertly skilled in both masks I wear. The Princess of Terror – who only cares about the luxuries the cartel can give her.

Then there's Isabella Terrero – the woman who spends her nights freeing slaves. The trained fighter who never misses a shot. The daredevil who knows no fear.

During the day, I drive around in my Audi R8 Spyder, and at night I go against the cartel with my Yamaha motorcycle.

Like I said, everyone wears masks.

Turning away from the mirror, I pick up my *Jimmy Choo* clutch that holds my credit card and phone. Walking out of my hotel suite, I take the elevator down to the lobby, leaving my two so-called bodyguards behind, blissfully unaware of my plans for the evening.

They're probably stuffing their faces with food in their hotel room, thinking I'm tucked safely in bed. Jorge and Rico aren't the best guards. Far from it. They're more for show than anything else, which makes it easy for me to come and go as I please. My mother figures if I get myself kidnapped or killed, I don't deserve to be her heir.

As I make my way to the exit with the grace of a princess, eyes follow me. The women watch me with envy and the men with lust.

The hotel arranged a limousine for me, and as I step out of the building, the chauffeur hurries to open the back door. Elegantly, I slip inside, and a couple of seconds later, I'm driven to the club.

I have no idea whose party I'm crashing. During lunch, I overheard two women my age gushing over this party being an event not to miss.

If it turns out to be boring, I'll leave early. Hopefully, it won't be a waste of time but an exciting thrill.

When the limousine pulls up to the club, I wait for the chauffeur to open my door, and then I step out right in front of the entrance. I don't bother looking at the line snaking along the front of the club but walk toward the bouncer, who looks more like an ape than a man.

His eyes scan over me, and then he unclips the golden rope and nods at me. Inside, tiles gleam beneath my heels as I'm stopped and searched before being allowed to enter the first floor, where the elite are getting drunk and rubbing more than just shoulders. Music makes the air tremble, and colorful lights flash over the interior. I glance at all the tables, most already occupied.

Lifting my gaze to the second floor, where the VIP area has been cordoned off for the party, I watch as a woman dressed as a vampire hugs another woman who looks like an Egyptian princess.

I don't see any bouncers vetting the guests, and it makes the corner of my mouth lift into a pleased smile.

Glancing to the right of the second floor, I take note of the narrow hallway that's been decorated for Halloween.

I walk toward the stairs that go up to the second floor and fall in behind a group of four people. When we reach the top of the stairs, the four begin to greet their friends, and it gives me the perfect opportunity to slip past them.

I make my way to the bar and order red wine. When the bartender slides the glass over to me, I take hold of the stem and then turn to look at the private dance floor where a group of women my age is dancing and laughing.

Just as I take a sip and the wine bursts over my tongue, the hair on the back of my neck rises. I feel a strong presence coming from my left as someone stares at me. Slowly turning my head, I keep my demeanor calm. Then my eyes collide with dark ones, and the immense intensity coming from them delivers a punch to my abdomen.

The man is also wearing sugar skull makeup, sitting like a king at what seems to be the main table.

The music instantly fades, and my heartbeat begins to speed up as I meet the gaze of the thrill I've been craving.

You'll do.

Chapter 2

ALEXEI

Sitting at a table, I glance to where Ariana's hugging Hana. Demitri's fiancée wanted a party at a club, and what Ariana wants, she gets. Not because she's entitled, but because Demitri will move heaven and earth for the love of his life.

The corner of my mouth lifts when my eyes land on Demitri, where he's hovering between Ariana and me. Ariana has him looking like a vampire, so they match for the party. When his gaze flicks to me, I indicate for him to come to the table.

Reaching me, he raises an eyebrow.

"Relax, brother. Enjoy the party with Ariana. I'm fine," I say to put him at ease.

Shaking his head, Demitri's mouth lifts a little, and then he walks to Ariana.

I let out a chuckle, knowing he's not going to listen. It's ingrained into Demitri's DNA to protect me, and nothing will change that.

My other business partner, Tristan Hayes, takes a seat at the table. I started a company with him a couple of years back, and he's basically been running it on his own because I'm too busy taking over the world.

Tristan's amused eyes land on me, and then he chuckles. "I almost didn't recognize you. I seriously can't believe you sat still so Ariana could put makeup on you."

"Never let it be said, miracles don't happen," I mutter.

It's Ariana's first birthday with us, and after all the shit she's been through, I'd fucking dress up as a clown if it would make her happy. She might be Demitri's fiancée, but she's also the most important woman in my life, seeing as Demitri and I are inseparable. She makes my friend happy, and at the end of the day, it's all that matters.

I glance to where Ariana's greeting more of our friends who have just arrived, and a pair of long legs catch my attention. My gaze follows the woman as she walks to the bar. Tilting my head, my eyes snap up to her face, and then a slight frown forms between my eyebrows. I scan over the VIP area, looking at our friends and acquaintances, and then I glance back to the woman as she takes a sip of the drink she just ordered.

She doesn't belong up here.

Her makeup matches mine as if we made plans to come as a couple, and the thought is a bit unsettling.

I don't do the couple thing. Ever.

Casually, turning her head in my direction, her eyes lock with mine, and then all my senses go on high alert. There's something about her that screams danger.

The predatory look in her eyes.

As if I'm the prey.

I let out a burst of soft laughter at the thought.

Slowly my gaze roams over her body and the revealing dress she's wearing. I'll admit she's fucking hot but still, she has no place being up here.

My eyes stay locked on her with an impassive look as she continues to slowly sip on her wine.

One wrong move and I'll end you.

The only reason I'm not throwing her out of the club is that I don't recognize her, so I doubt she's a threat. She's probably a socialite who's trying to mingle with Tristan and Hana's families.

A hand lands on my shoulder, and when I glance up, it's to find Demitri staring at the woman by the bar.

"Do you know her?" he asks.

"No." Looking back to the woman, I add, "I'll keep an eye on her. Don't worry. Enjoy the party with Ariana."

Demitri nods before he heads back to where Ariana's sitting with Hana. It's good to see Ariana making friends.

My attention returns to the woman by the bar as she sets down her wine glass. Then she walks to the dance floor, her movements confident and elegant. The dress is cut at the sides of her hips, leaving a fuck-ton of skin on display and giving me and every other man a perfect view of her toned legs.

Even though the beat is fast, the woman begins to dance at a slow sensual pace, and it somehow fits.

Fuck does it fit.

Her movements are smooth, like flowing water, and loaded with sensuality. My skin prickles at the sight of her, and it feels as if she's dancing for me.

Then her eyes lock on mine, and the corner of my mouth lifts.

Now, this is what I call entertainment.

My friends laugh and party around me. The music makes the air tremble. And all I can do is watch the show this Aphrodite is giving me. As if she's casting a spell around us.

There's a moment where my blood rushes faster through my veins at the thought that she doesn't know who I am. And I don't know her.

It's been years since I felt exhilaration.

Getting up, I walk to the bar, and hardly giving the bartender a glance, I order, "Vodka. *Stoli.*"

"Yes, sir."

When the bartender slides the tumbler over to me, I take a sip and turn my attention back to the dance floor. While I enjoy the drink, she dances for me, and soon the only thing I can think of is taking her right here.

After more time has passed, I set the tumbler down and walk toward the restrooms. I stop by a vending machine and grab a condom, and then I feel her presence behind me.

She stops next to me, and glancing down at the foil packet, she murmurs, "I hope you're planning to use that on me."

The corner of my mouth lifts, and I gesture for her to lead the way. My smile grows into a smirk when she heads to a short hallway overlooking the VIP section and the floor below. It's only used for Halloween décor. Spiders and cobwebs are wrapped around two pillars, and pumpkins rest on the chrome railing.

It's public enough to add to the thrill while offering us some privacy.

I follow her past a luminous skeleton, and then she stops in the corner next to one of the pillars. I come up behind her, noticing she's not much shorter than me. Then again, she's wearing high heels. Without them, the top of her head would probably only reach beneath my chin.

Placing her hands on the railing, she looks at the dancing crowd below, and then her body begins to move, drawing me back under her spell.

I step closer until her bare back brushes against my shirt. Leaning down, my mouth skims over the shell of her ear as I say, "Your name."

She shakes her head, keeping her gaze on the people below. "I'm just a party crasher."

Like I thought.

"You?" she asks.

The corner of my mouth lifts again.

Baby, you don't want to know who I am.

"The Devil," I murmur as I let out a breath of air against her ear, which makes her shiver.

"You better fuck like one."

Christ, I'm starting to think I actually managed to get drunk for once, and I'm hallucinating her. There's no way she's real.

Placing my hands on her curvy hips, my body begins to move in sync with hers. I relish in the feel of her smooth skin as my palms slip beneath the glittering black fabric, and then satisfaction roars through me.

Fuck, her ass is perfect.

My party crasher leans back against me, her head resting on my left shoulder as she keeps dancing. Glancing down, I have a perfect view of her cleavage and part of her toned stomach.

She's nothing short of a dream.

A fucking fantasy.

With the railing giving us some privacy, I move my left hand to her pussy, and I almost groan when my fingers brush against the thin silk covering the intense heat coming from between her legs.

Soon my lungs are filled with a decadent explosion of flowers, vanilla, and something earthy. I've never smelled anything like her before, and it's intoxicating.

As I begin to rub her clit through the silk, she moves her hands to my thighs.

Our dance takes on a life of its own, and I'm so fucking focused on her, I barely hear the music. Her palm covers my hard as steel cock, and through the fabric of my suit pants, she strokes me like a fucking expert, making my heartbeat speed up.

Fuck, yes.

I'm pretty sure I'm about to have my mind blown in a way that won't have me forgetting her any time soon.

ISABELLA

He's everything I've been craving.

The Devil.

God, I hope so.

He knows what he's doing as he rubs my clit until I'm seconds away from shattering with pleasure. Exhilaration floods me as if I'm riding my motorcycle at top speed. As if I'm leaping from building top to building top, or I'm almost caught while freeing slaves.

The rush of adrenaline makes me lightheaded, my body craving the pleasure I know he can give me.

It's moments like this that keep me sane. They're scarce, and I lose myself entirely in the intensity building between us.

I barely take in the moving bodies below as his cologne's woodsy scent, smoky and sultry, envelops me.

Through the fabric of his pants, I'm pleased to feel how well-endowed he is.

Our bodies move as one as he dances in perfect sync with me.

God, he feels incredible behind me. Unlike any other man I've been with. The power coming off him in waves calls to the strength surging through me.

My devil moves his hands, and he brushes my palm away from his cock. I feel as he unzips his pants, and he takes a moment to sheath himself with the condom.

My blood rushes in my ears as the anticipation in me reaches breaking point, and then he pushes the dress away from my ass, and I feel his cock brush against my heated skin.

Resting my hands on the railing again, I spread my legs and lift myself onto the tip of my toes to give him better access.

He doesn't waste time and moving my g-string to the side, he positions his impressive head at my entrance. He surges into me with a long, hard thrust that makes my body bow forward from how good it feels.

Mother of God. Yes.

A satisfied moan escapes me as he fills me completely.

He takes me the same way I've been dancing for him, slow and torturously. I feel every inch of him as he pulls out and thrusts back inside me.

My fingers curl around the chrome railing, my sight blurring until all I see are the flashing lights. My mind goes blank, all my worries forgotten in this blissful moment of lust and ecstasy.

I grind my ass back against him as he enters me again, and shivers of pleasure rush over my skin.

The silence between us. The anonymity. The intensity. It all turns me on like I've never been turned on before.

It's the perfect thrill.

He moves his left hand back to my clit, and the way he rubs the sensitive bundle of nerves makes me unravel at the speed of light. Not even I have been able to touch myself like this. It's as if he knows exactly what to do to make me come apart at the seams.

God, it's a pity this is only a hook-up.

Closing my eyes, I lean my head back against his shoulder, and then I feel his other hand's fingers skim over my neck and down to my cleavage.

"So fucking beautiful," he breathes against my jaw. "Are you real?"

Turning my face toward him, I answer honestly, "No."

I'm only the real me when I'm risking my life to free those who've been stolen by my mother. Anything else is an act to divert everyone's attention, so I won't be found out.

Our eyes lock, and our breaths mingle as he slams harder inside me. Sighs and moans begin to spill from my lips, mixing with the beat of the music pulsing around us.

His muscled chest is solid against my back, and the power radiating from his body as he fucks me makes me feel drunk.

So good. God, so good.

He pinches my clit, and it instantly sends me spiraling with pleasure as an orgasm crashes through my body. Every muscle in my body tenses as I begin to convulse.

His lips brush over the sensitive skin beneath my ear. "Christ, milk my cock."

My body listens to his order, and my inner walls clench hard around his impressive girth, drawing a deep groan from him.

Pleasure keeps hitting me in paralyzing waves until there's a real threat I'll sink to the ground from my legs going numb.

Wrapping his left arm around my waist, he holds me pinned to him as his pace becomes forceful. I have to tighten my grip on the railing because it makes my orgasm so much more intense.

By the time he finds his own release, I'm struggling to take a breath of air, my body nothing more than spasms of bliss.

His thrusts slow down, and gradually the pleasure ebbs away. The music returns. My sight focuses on the VIP section on the other side of the club. I become aware of the fine coat of sweat covering my body.

Then he pulls out, and after tucking his cock back into his pants, he straightens my g-string and dress.

I keep still as he presses a kiss to the side of my neck, and then his knuckles brush down my back before he walks away.

Slowly, I turn my head, and I watch as he makes his way to the restrooms, his strides filled with power and confidence.

There goes the best sex of my life.

I take a moment to find my composure and to make sure my dress covers everything it should. When I'm sure my legs won't give way beneath me, I walk toward the stairs, and without glancing back, I make my way to the exit.

With every step, I still feel him between my legs, and his aftershave clings to my skin.

Outside the club, I only wait a minute for the chauffeur to bring the limousine. Once I'm sitting in the back, and we're heading to the hotel, a smile forms around my lips.

That was everything I needed.

The craving in me has been satisfied. It will help me get through the next six weeks of social events and fundraisers hosted here and in Europe before I can return home and to my role of saving lives.

Chapter 3

ALEXEI

Two months later…

We've set up cameras near Terrero's mansion and places she tends to use to bring in new shipments of slaves.

The first two months, I watched her from LA, gathering as much information as possible on her. We arrived in Columbia yesterday, and keeping a low profile, Demitri arranged a place for us to stay with one of our contacts. It's a simple-looking house, squashed into an overcrowded area, that won't attract any attention.

My gaze flits over all the screens, and not seeing anything of value, boredom begins to weigh down on me.

This is the part I hate most. Waiting for the right moment to strike.

I'm tempted to call my brother and every other favor owed to me so I can just get the attack over with. But acting out of boredom would be stupid.

"It's been two months," Demitri mutters. "Either Sonia never leaves the compound, or she's coming and going without us noticing."

"Wouldn't be surprised if she crawled through tunnels like the rat she is. See if you can get a map of what's beneath the property."

Taking my phone out of my pocket, I begin to check my bank accounts. Call me materialistic, but seeing what I've worked my ass off for calms me.

"Is that…?" Demitri murmurs as he leans closer to the screen showing the front of the mansion. "Is that the daughter?"

My eyes lift to the screen, and I watch as Isabella Terrero comes out of the mansion. She looks like any other socialite as she walks to the Audi parked by the foot of the steps.

Resting my elbow on the armrest of my chair, I rub my thumb over my bottom lip. "Yeah. That's the princess."

"We could take her to lure Sonia out," Demitri mentions.

I shake my head. "Sonia won't do shit to get her daughter back. We'd stand a better chance of getting her attention by taking a shipment."

Demitri lifts an eyebrow at me. "Why don't we do that?"

"Because it will only get her attention. There's no guarantee it will draw her out of that fucking fortress."

"True." Demitri relaxes back in his chair.

My gaze goes back to the screen showing Isabella steering the Audi away from the mansion. An SUV follows behind her. Probably her guards.

With nothing else of interest happening on the screens, I spend the rest of the day making business arrangements with Semion Aulov and Lev Petrov. They're part of the bratva and stationed in Russia, so I allow them to handle things on that side of the world.

After having an early dinner, I catch up on some sleep before relieving Demitri so he can rest. It's just past midnight, and I'm staring at the screens showing all angles of the compound when a black figure scales one of the side walls.

The person is small enough to be a woman.

Fuck, please let it be Sonia.

I'm up from my chair in a second, and grabbing my backpack that holds my rifle, I leave the house. I send Demitri a message letting him know I'm out scouting, and I activate the tracker in the tag hanging from the chain around my neck. That way, Demitri will be able to find me if something goes wrong.

A moment later, Demitri responds.

Demitri: I'm going to fucking kick your ass.

Alexei: I activated the tracker. I'm just scouting.

Demitri: Don't do anything else without me there to back you.

Alexei: And people wonder why I don't do relationships. You're clingy enough for me.

Demitri: Fucker.

Demitri: Be safe.

Alexei: Always. I'll be an hour at most.

Bringing the camera feed up on my phone, I steer the unmarked SUV I'm using while in Columbia in the direction of my target.

I reach a safe spot to follow the person from, and taking a pair of binoculars from my backpack, I get a closer look at the target. When the figure stops and glances behind them in the direction of where I'm parked in the shadows, a frown forms on my forehead.

A street light sheds some light on her features, and I feel a flicker of disappointment that it's not Sonia but Isabella. She's dressed in workout gear. As if she's out jogging.

Which isn't fucking weird at all, seeing as it's past midnight.

The frown remains on my face, and out of curiosity and boredom, I watch as she crosses a street.

There's something familiar about her movements, but before I can try to figure out what it is, Isabella walks to a shed that's on the side of a vacated house. The property is worse for wear and wouldn't attract any attention.

Interesting.

She's in there for a while, and my eyebrow lifts when she pushes a motorcycle out of the shed. She's changed out of her workout clothes into black leather pants, a jacket, and boots. She's also grabbed a backpack that's snug on her back as she climbs onto the machinery that's nothing short of a masterpiece.

She's got taste. I'll give her that.

When she steers the motorcycle onto the street, I pull the unmarked SUV away from the curb and follow at a safe distance.

I don't know much about Isabella Terrero. Only that she trained at St. Monarch's and that she's the same as any other socialite. Up until now, she's done nothing to make me think she'll even take over from Sonia. So my focus has been on the mother instead of the daughter.

Okay, little princess, you've got my attention. What are you up to?

ISABELLA

Reaching the shed, I check in with my partner, Ana, before changing into my usual outfit I wear when freeing slaves. Throwing my leg over my motorcycle, I head in the direction of the junkyard where a shipment of four girls is being held.

Ana was the first girl I helped when I returned from my training in Switzerland. She had nowhere to go and was angry over what happened. At first, I used her anger to my advantage, but during the past two years, we've grown close. We have the same goal – to destroy my mother.

We set up a safe house on the outskirts of the city where Ana works from. Whenever I free a shipment of girls, I tell them to wait in front of a specific hospital if they need help. Ana watches them before she makes contact.

The longest a girl or boy has stayed with Ana has been a month. We try to move them quickly to lessen the chances of my mother finding out about us.

I park my motorcycle down the road from the junkyard and glance around to make sure I haven't been spotted. Sticking to the shadows, I begin to jog toward the side of the junkyard.

This will be an easy job because there are many places to hide with all the junk and scrapped vehicles.

Reaching a wall made of metal sheeting, I quickly hoist myself over it and drop to a crouching position behind a stack of crushed steel that used to be cars.

I listen for any movement as I pull a ski mask over my head so I won't be recognized. Cautiously, I make my way to the main gates, and pulling a bolt cutter from my backpack, I cut through the chain, so the girls will be able to leave the property once they're free.

After securing an exit for them, I sneak to the office. I pull my Glock from behind my back and check how many men there are. As expected, I only have two to worry about.

One's asleep on an old chair, his feet propped up on a desk that's littered with takeaway containers and empty beer bottles. The other guy's watching a rerun of a football game.

The lack of guards tells me the girls I'll set free tonight are meant to work in the whorehouses. They're not of much value to my mother.

There would be a small army guarding a virgin.

Checking the area, I move to the side of the office, and pressing my back against the wall, I carefully glance through the window.

The tiny hairs on the back of my neck rise, and I peer into the darkness around me for the source of my uneasiness. Not seeing anyone, I dismiss the eerie sensation. It's probably because it's been two months since I've freed a shipment.

Ducking low, I creep toward the door. As I straighten up, I take a deep breath, and then I kick the door open. Training the barrel of my gun on the guy that's awake, I bury a bullet between his eyes. The other guy startles awake just as I pull the trigger, silencing him before he can make a sound.

I hurry inside and pat both bodies down for the key to the storage room where the girls are. Finding a set of keys, I rush out of the office and run toward the door that's secured with a padlock. Taking a flashlight from my backpack so I can see the lock clearly, it takes me precious seconds to find the right key, and then I yank the door open.

I shine the flashlight over the empty space and find the girls huddled in a corner. The room reeks of urine, but I ignore it as I move closer. Two stare at me with terrified eyes while the other two startle awake.

"I'm here to help," I offer them some reassurance. "Are any of you hurt?"

One of the girls shakes her head as she cautiously climbs to her feet, and then the other three do the same. Assuming she's taken the role of leader in the group, I focus on her. I take a slip of paper with the hospital's address from my pocket and hold it out to the leader. "You have to run. If one of you needs help, go to this hospital and wait out front where there are people. Only wait twelve hours. If a woman doesn't come for you by that time, you're on your own."

"How will we know the woman was sent by you?" the leader asks.

"She'll give you a password. Nightbird."

The leader nervously licks her lips, and then she glances at the door.

"I've unlocked the main gate. Just run straight ahead and get out of here." They all blink at me. "Run," I hiss, injecting a bite into my voice.

The leader of the girls grabs the paper from me and then hurries out of the room with the other girls following behind her.

Hopefully, they can manage on their own because this is the best I can do for them.

Rushing out of the storage room, I head to the side of the yard, and tucking my gun behind my back, I climb over the wall. As soon as my feet hit the ground, I break out into a sprint toward my motorcycle. Just as I reach it and I'm about the pull on my helmet, a familiar scent grabs my attention.

Woodsy. Smoky and sultry.

Impossible.

Now's not the freaking time to think of the hook-up I had in LA!

I pull the helmet over my head, and climbing onto my motorcycle, I let the engine roar to life. Racing away from the junkyard, the corner of my mouth lifts when the rush of a successful operation finally hits.

Once I'm done hiding my motorcycle and weapons in the shed on the property I purchased under Ana's name, I quickly change back into my leggings and t-shirt I usually wear for jogging before heading back to the mansion.

It's already two am. Knowing where every guard will be, I climb over the back wall and creep toward the side of the house, where I scale the wall to the balcony of my bedroom.

Only when I'm safely inside my bedroom suite do I take a deep breath of relief.

I hope the girls will be safe.

Walking to my bathroom to take a quick shower, my thoughts turn to the one-night stand I had in LA.

What I wouldn't give to hook up with my devil again.

Chapter 4

ALEXEI

After watching Isabella sneak back over the mansion's wall, I steer the SUV toward the safe house.

What the fuck did I witness tonight?

It's rare for something to catch me by surprise. Isabella freed a shipment of girls. I was prepared for anything but that.

It's also rare for anything to impress me.

And fuck, did Isabella Terrero impress me tonight.

She was nothing like the socialite everyone thought her to be. Far from it. She was badass and expertly trained, in and out of that junkyard in less than an hour.

Holy fuck.

Parking the SUV in front of the house, I get out. Still stunned, I walk toward Demitri, where he's standing by the front door.

He looks pissed as fuck as he snaps, "Two hours?"

Stopping in front of him, I lock eyes with him. "You will not believe what I saw tonight."

A frown forms on Demitri's forehead as he moves to the side so I can enter the house. "What?" he asks while following me to the security room.

I drop my backpack next to the chair, and sitting down, I shake my head as I lift my eyes to Demitri's. "Isabella Terrero freed slaves."

Demitri takes a seat on the other chair. "Was that her sneaking into the mansion?" He gestures at the screens, where he must've seen it.

"Yes." I let out a deep breath, then shake my head again. "I wish you were there to see her in action. She was fucking badass."

"So…? Are you telling me she's working against her own mother?" Demitri asks with a skeptical expression.

"Yes, but we'll watch her for a while to make sure," I reply, needing to make sure this wasn't just a once-off thing for Isabella.

I doubt that's what it was. Isabella was too comfortable… as if she's done it a hundred times.

"Then what?"

Relaxing back in the chair, I shrug. "Then we can use Isabella to get to Sonia."

"Or…" Worry flickers in Demitri's gaze.

"Or what?"

"They know we're here, and Isabella's a distraction to get you out in the open."

Resting my elbow on the armrest, I stare at Demitri for a while before I say, "I don't think that's the case."

"How do you know?"

"The same way I know everything. I'm God, remember," I chuckle at Demitri before I grow serious again. "Gut instinct."

"Okay." Demitri glances back at the screens showing all the cameras. "You're not tailing Isabella alone again. Just in case."

"I planted a tracking device on her motorcycle," I mention as I take my phone out of my pocket. "I'll get an alert if Isabella's on the move." I bring up the phone number for St. Monarch's, then look at Demitri. "Time to find out everything we can about the Princess of Terror." I press dial, and a couple of seconds later, Madame Keller answers her private line.

"Mr. Koslov, to what do I owe the honor?"

Madame Keller is the architect behind St. Monarch's, where most of us received our training. It's also neutral ground where people like me can hide if we need to.

"I need everything you have on Isabella Terrero."

Madame Keller lets out a chuckle. "Miss Terrero is high-value. It will cost you fifteen million."

Information is one of the most expensive things in my world.

I glance at Demitri. "Make a transfer of fifteen million euros to St. Monarch's."

I watch as he carries out my order, and when he nods at me, I say, "Payment made."

"I assume you know the basics for Miss Terrero?" Madame Keller asks.

"Tell me about her training."

"Sonia Terrero sent her daughter to learn the fine art of sex slavery and drug smuggling, but Isabella wasn't interested in any of that. Instead, she requested to be privately trained as a custodian. We were ordered to not inform Sonia of the change in training."

"Did she mention why?"

"No. Isabella kept to herself while she was visiting with us. But, I will say this… she was exceptionally good at her training."

"Exceptionally good?"

Madame Keller hesitates for a moment, then she admits, "Same level as the Vetrovs."

Fuck.

My eyes dart to Demitri's. If Isabella is on the same level as him, we're in for a rough time unless we can get her to join us.

"Thank you," I murmur absentmindedly as I cut the call.

"What did she say?" Demitri asks, worry etched on his features.

"Isabella's apparently as good as you."

Demitri's right eyebrow lifts. "She trained as a custodian?"

I nod, processing what I just learned. "Sonia doesn't know her daughter trained as a custodian." I consider the important fact. "Adding that she freed slaves earlier, I'm certain Isabella is trying to take Sonia down from the inside."

"If that's the case, do you think we can get Isabella to side with us?"

I shake my head. "It depends on her reason for sabotaging Sonia. If she's attacking Sonia so she can take over the cartel, we're still her enemy."

"How do you want to handle this?" Demitri asks as he glances over all the screens.

"Let's watch them for a while and see what the queen and princess are up to. With a little luck, we might not have to do anything, and they take each other out."

My thoughts turn to earlier when I watched Isabella free the girls. There's something familiar about the way she moves, but I still can't figure out what it is.

She showed no fear and took out the two guards without any hesitation. It was well planned and executed.

If Isabella tries to overthrow Sonia to take over the cartel, she will be a bigger threat than her mother. But… if she's destroying the cartel from the inside out… she might just be the alliance of a lifetime.

Fearless. Dangerous. Beautiful. Isabella will make the perfect partner.

That's if we can get her to work with us.

"What are you thinking?" Demitri asks.

Taking a deep breath, I let it out slowly, and then the corner of my mouth lifts. "How everything went from boring as fuck to fun in a matter of an hour."

ISABELLA

Wearing a bikini, I'm lying in the shade near the pool, pretending to scroll through my friends' social media accounts.

Their Instagram pages all look the same. Always showing off their latest purchases and how social they are.

My mother stalks out of the house, and with a sigh, she sits down in one of the plush chairs. A servant rushes to bring her a glass of juice and a fruit salad for lunch.

I keep scrolling through the posts, my attention focused on my mother.

"Is that all you plan on doing with your life?" Mother asks, her tone tight with disapproval.

I let out a lazy chuckle. "Yep." Knowing it will annoy her, I let the 'P' pop.

"You're a disgrace to the Terrero name," Mother mutters before she takes a sip of her beverage. "You need to start learning the business."

I let out a bored sigh. "Why? Hugo can take over. I have no interest in dealing with the filth you sell."

"But you love spending the money?" Her tone is now ice-cold.

Giving her a wide grin, I get up from the lounge chair and walk toward her. "I'm only doing my part to support the economy." Taking a seat at the table, I steal one of the grapes from my mother's salad and pop it into my mouth. "Besides, you know all the killing and torturing freaks me out."

Mother's eyes lock on me, emotionless and laced with a deadly poison. "It's my legacy."

"I'm thinking of becoming a model," I flippantly change the subject.

"Over my dead body," she hisses.

Soon.

I relax back in the chair and cross my legs. Just then, Hugo walks out onto the patio, and I give him a smile. "Hugo, you wouldn't mind taking my place in the cartel, right?" My voice is sugary sweet, and it earns me a possessive death glare from my mother.

Hugo will never betray my mother. He ignores me as he sits down next to my mother, and leaning into her, he whispers, "We lost another shipment."

Mother's eyes snap to his. "Which one?"

"The one meant for the Soacha."

Surprise.

I bring up the summer catalog for *Chanel* and scroll through it, pretending not to care about their conversation.

"What are you doing to find out who's behind it?" Mother asks, doing her best but failing to remain calm as her cheeks flame up and her mouth settles in a grim line.

Hugo brushes his hand over her long black hair to soothe her. "It's one person. Some vigilante. Don't worry, we'll catch him."

Sure you will. Idiot.

I got the same training as Hugo at St. Monarch's, only I'm a hell of a lot better than him. The poor bastard doesn't stand a chance against me.

It's fun watching them worry, not having the slightest clue the person is right under their noses.

"Double the security on all the shipments," Mother orders.

Double the fun.

"What about the shipment for the auction?" Hugo asks, and it takes a lot of effort to not glance up.

The auction will be for virgins. It's held once a year, and I almost got caught last year. I need every bit of information I can get my hands on.

"I'll have the shipment come through Cali instead of Medellín," Mother replies.

The shipment is scheduled to dock in three weeks, and then the girls will be brought here, where the auction will take place. I can either free the girls at the docks or en route from Cali to here. Both will be risky as hell.

"Have every man we can spare guard the shipment," she orders.

Hugo leans into Mother and presses a kiss to her cheek. "I'll take care of it."

I peek up, and for a moment, Mother's features soften as she looks at Hugo.

Four years ago, she bought Hugo during an auction at St. Monarch's. Even though he's twenty years younger than her, it was love at first sight, which was totally weird and out of character for my mother. They must be made of the same thing because they fit perfectly together. He's also the only person who's managed to get any kind of affection from the Queen of Terror.

As I said, it's weird and sometimes downright creepy.

"Ooooh," I coo, and then I hold my phone, so they can see the dress I'm looking at. "Isn't this pretty? It will be perfect for Nadia's party tomorrow night."

"Isabella," Mother snaps angrily. I can see it's taking all her self-control to not slap me. "I don't have time for your shit." I watch as she gets up and stalks away to deal with business.

Hugo gives me a look of warning which would strike fear in most men. "Don't you think it's time you grow up and join the business?"

I smile my sweetest smile. "You do a much better job than I'll ever be able to. You don't mind, do you?"

My words stroke his over-inflated ego. He lets out a sigh as if it's such a burden dealing with me, but then he admits, "Of course, I don't mind."

I'm sure you don't. You better enjoy being at the top of the food chain while you can.

We stand up at the same time, then I say, "I have shopping to do." Faking excitement, I hurry into the house to change out of the bikini.

Three weeks until the shipment docks. I have a lot of work to do. Luckily Nadia's party will be held on her father's superyacht, so I'll be able to check the shipyard and surrounding areas then.

Sometimes I wish I had enough power to overthrow my mother and Hugo, but seeing as it's just Ana and me, freeing the slaves is all I can do at the moment.

Chapter 5

ALEXEI

Watching Isabella attend a party on a yacht, she's so fucking good at the act as socialite, she has everyone believing it.

Through my night vision binoculars, I follow Isabella as she moves between the other attendees. She smiles at something a woman is saying to her, and then she nods.

Isabella and the other woman walk to where a group is already dancing and join them.

"Have a drink," Demitri says.

Setting the binoculars down on the table, I take the tumbler from him. After taking a sip, I ask, "How's Ariana doing?"

Demitri checks in with her every couple of hours.

"Good," he replies, a grin tugging at his mouth. "She misses me."

I let out a chuckle. "Probably not half as much as you miss her." My friend fell fucking hard for Ariana.

Demitri glances out over the water. "I need to get Ariana a new car."

"What are you looking at?"

He shrugs. "Probably a Mercedes or Audi."

I take another sip of vodka, then say, "We should build another house on the property so you and Ariana can have privacy. Either that or you should find your own place."

Right now, Demitri and Ariana live with me in the mansion I have in LA. Demitri's stubborn as fuck, though. I know he won't move into his own house. The fucker thinks the second he turns his back, I'll get myself killed.

"I like the idea of building another house on the property. That way, I'm still close by," Demitri relents.

Chuckling, I shake my head. "You do know I can take care of myself, right?"

He nods but then mutters, "Still my job to keep you alive."

We stare at each other for a moment. "I want you to be happy, brother. Build a family and future with Ariana."

The corner of his mouth lifts again. "Family. Never thought I'd consider having kids."

"I'll teach them how to shoot a gun," I joke.

Demitri's smile widens. "You better, seeing as you'll be their godfather."

Our eyes lock again as emotion washes through my chest. "I'd be honored."

Fireworks explode in the air, and laughter flows from the other yacht, pulling my attention back to Isabella.

Picking up the binoculars, I search for Isabella, finding her where she's still dancing, her movements slow and sensual.

Again, there's a niggling familiarity, and then a frown forms on my forehead when I realize who she reminds me of.

The party crasher.

Isabella moves like the party crasher did the night of Ariana's party… like flowing water.

What are the odds?

My gaze is glued to Isabella as she loses herself in the music, and my thoughts return to the woman I fucked. The woman who cast a spell on me until I was solely focused on her.

I'll never forget how she felt, a mixture of danger and sensuality. Her skin was softer than the silk panties she wore. I can almost smell her perfume, flowers, vanilla, and something earthy.

Christ, it felt like I was on a high as I buried my cock deep inside her. Her moans as she orgasmed and her pussy clenching hard around me were enough to make me lose control.

I'm starting to grow hard just at the memory and quickly shove the erotic memory aside, focusing on Isabella again.

The party lasts until the early morning hours, and only then do we head back to land. As soon as we reach the harbor, Demitri and I step off the yacht, and we find a safe spot we can watch the other vessel from. As the party-goers head to their vehicles, Isabella pauses to take photos of the harbor. Her friends join in, and the act fits, but I get a feeling Isabella's here to look around the harbor.

"What do you think she'd do if I walked up to her?" I ask as I watch Isabella head to where her limousine is parked. She gets in, and a moment later, the vehicle drives away.

"Probably kill you," Demitri replies.

Shaking my head, I smirk at him. "She can try."

He lets out a chuckle as he nods toward our unmarked vehicle. "Let's get out of here."

Once we're both seated in the car, I say, "There must be a shipment coming in soon. She took those photos so she can get familiarized with the layout of the area."

I start the engine and steer the vehicle towards the airfield where our private jet is waiting to take us back to Bogotá, where Sonia's compound is situated.

"I'm curious as to why Isabella frees the slaves," Demitri mutters as he glances around us, always on guard for an attack.

"That makes two of us."

I'm curious about a lot of things when it comes to Isabella Terrero. She's an enigma, one I'm dying to figure out.

I wonder what her reaction would be if we came face to face.

ISABELLA

It's after midnight when I walk out onto my bedroom's balcony. I always keep the sliding door open so it won't look suspicious on the nights I head out.

I wait a little longer before climbing over the balcony and dropping to the lawn below. Then, staying low, I hurry toward the wall, and without much effort, I hoist myself over.

I jog to the vacated house and first change into my leather outfit before shrugging my backpack with my tools and weapons onto my back. After pushing my motorcycle out of the shed, I throw my leg over the seat and get comfortable. When the engine roars to life, a smile forms around my lips.

I drive the distance to the safe house, enjoying the feel of the wind rushing past me. The streets are quiet as I leave the city, and another twenty minutes later, I pull up the gravel driveway of the safe house. I park my motorcycle, and when I get to the side entrance, the biometric scanner scans my face and unlocks the security door.

The front and back doors are only for show. Besides the security entrance, there's a tunnel beneath the house that leads to a nearby field. I've spent a lot of money to make sure Ana's safe.

Stepping inside the house, it's dark and quiet. I walk through all the rooms, checking that everything's okay before I go down to the basement. I find Ana behind the computer.

"Hi," I say as I sit down in the chair next to her.

"I've looked at the photos you sent me last week," she gets right to work.

Before I managed to free Ana, she was raped and tortured. The only way she's able to cope is by losing herself in the work we do. I've tried talking to her about what she endured, but she made it clear the subject is off-limits.

"Are you okay coming with me?" I ask again.

Ana nods, and then she turns her face to look at me. She's shorter and skinnier than me, but her features are striking and feminine. Ana's so beautiful it still catches me by surprise at times.

"Yes. I'll take the van down to Cali in case there's a couple of girls who need help."

I turn my attention to the photos and look at each one. "I think entering from the containers' side will be best. It'll give me the cover I need."

Ana points to the warehouse section of the harbor. "Or here."

"Both could work."

"How many men is Sonia sending?"

"A lot. Usually, I'd only have a dozen or so to worry about, but she's sending every available man. I'm prepared for a small army."

"Let me be your backup," Ana says for the hundredth time.

Even though I taught her how to handle a gun, I shake my head hard. "No. I'm not putting you in that kind of danger."

Ana's eyes narrow on me. "I can't just sit and watch as you get killed, or worse… taken."

A soft smile curves my lips up, and I gently place my hand on Ana's forearm. She used to cringe whenever I touched her, but that stopped a year ago.

"I won't let myself be taken," I try to offer her some comfort. "I'd kill myself before I allow that to happen."

Ana shrugs my hand off and scowls darkly at me. "Don't say that."

Tilting my head, I take in the worry in her eyes. I lean a little forward. "Ana?"

Her features tighten until it looks like she's about to cry. With a quivering voice, she says, "I can't lose you, Isabella. You're my family."

Slowly, I reach for her and pull her into a hug. At first, Ana stiffens, but then she relaxes in my embrace.

"Promise me you'll get out of there if things become too dangerous," she whispers.

I brush a palm over the back of her head, the short strands soft. “I promise.”

Ana pulls back, and she gives me a rare smile. “Let’s get back to work.”

We turn our attention to the photos, examining the harbor until I can walk blindfolded through the area. Ana goes to make us both a cup of coffee while I check the weapons I keep at the safe house.

The shipment is coming in next week. My mother and Hugo are under the impression that I’ll be in New York for a fashion show. Fooling them is the least of my problems right now. The harbor will be heavily guarded.

I glance to the stairs leading up to the first floor and let out a heavy breath.

There’s a good chance I won’t be able to keep my promise to Ana. I have a safety fund set up, which she has access to, so at least I know she’ll be taken care of should I die.

Chapter 6

ISABELLA

Two years ago, when Isabella saved Ana.

I've been back from St. Monarch's for two weeks when the yearly auction is held.

The mansion is draped in luxury, servers scurrying everywhere to prepare for the guests. I glance at the elevator that leads beneath the house. That's where the girls are being kept in rooms and where the auction will take place. I've only been down there twice before, but it was enough to see what horrors take place beneath the house I call my home.

"Don't embarrass me tonight," Mother suddenly says as she comes up behind me.

I turn to face her and let out a sigh. "Do I have to attend?" I whine like a spoiled brat.

She gives me a cold glare. "Yes."

I shrug and walk toward the elevator with her. "I'd rather go clubbing with Nadia and Gloria."

Mother puts in the key, activating the elevator and the doors slide open. Once we step inside, her gaze sweeps over the revealing red dress I'm wearing. "Now that you've completed your training, I expect you to get involved in the business."

"Nope." I give her a sweet grin. "I plan on making up for the lost time. The training was tedious. I feel I deserve a couple of years off for the torture you had me endure."

Mother's eyes narrow on me. "How did I manage to raise a spoiled daughter? I despise that you don't take after me."

The elevator doors glide open, revealing a chamber with an octagon-shaped stage in the middle of the room. Chairs with bidding stations form a half-moon circle around the podium where the girls will be paraded.

Shrugging carelessly, I walk into the somber space. "You should've thought about that when you fucked my father."

Mother's face tightens with anger, and then she sneers, "You're right, I should've. But, like you are now, I was young and stupid."

I grin at her again. "See, I'm like you after all."

I'm given a look of warning, and then the guests start to arrive, escorted down by Hugo, my mother's lover and right-hand man.

My features turn to solid steel as I watch one depraved person after the other fill the room. Watching as the cesspool of humanity gathers, hatred begins to tremble in my chest.

I wish I could end them all with one blow, but knowing that's an impossible task, I play the role of the Princess of Terror and dutiful daughter.

Soon the bidders take their seats, and then the auction begins. My heart bleeds as the young girls and boys are paraded, but it's when the last girl is offered for auction that my muscles tense.

She's fairy-like, giving me the impression that she could be killed by a simple slap, never mind whatever the winning bidder has planned for her.

My heartbeat speeds up as I listen to the bidding climb higher until she's sold for one point two million dollars. Then, my focus turns to the man who just bought the girl, and stepping closer to my mother, I ask, "You must be happy with the price he's paying?"

She hardly spares me a glance as she sneers, "You'll probably spend it all in the next two weeks."

I let out a fake amused chuckle. “Don’t mind if I do.” I let my gaze roam over the attendees. “Who are these people?”

“Mostly businessmen and bored wives of millionaires.” Luckily, Mother gestures to the man who just purchased the girl. “Mr. Sawiris is in construction. He’s been known to bury his slaves under the latest building he’s constructing.” Mother smiles at me. “Once he’s done with them, of course.”

The blood chills in my veins, but somehow I manage to keep up my act.

I’ve followed Sawiris to Medellín, where he’s spending the weekend before heading back to whichever hole he calls home.

I only have two days to free the girl. After that, she’ll be lost forever.

My heart is thundering in my chest as I climb over the wall of the mansion where Sawiris is staying. I’m dressed in black pants, a long-sleeve shirt, boots, and gloves, blending in with the dark night around me. I also have makeup on that makes me look like I’m in my fifties, with a grey-haired wig, so I'm not easily recognizable. Creeping toward the back of the house, my mouth goes dry from the adrenaline pulsing through my body.

You can do this, Isabella. This is what you trained for.

My muscles tense when I spot the two guards stationed outside the patio's sliding door.

Once I'm close enough, I burst into action, darting forward. Jumping into the air, my legs wrap around the first guard's neck, and as I flip him, I hear the satisfying crack. His body drops to the gleaming tiles as I land on my feet.

The second guard pulls out his gun, and I dart to his left as he fires off a silenced shot. The palm of my hand meets his nose but not hard enough to shove the bone back into his skull. He stumbles but catches his balance just as I deliver a solid punch to his jaw. Another shot is fired, missing my right leg by an inch.

Grabbing hold of his shoulder, I use his solid frame to swing my body behind his, and then I wrap my arm around his throat and my legs around his waist. I tighten my grip, cutting off his air supply. With grunts, he drops to his knees, and then he slams me back against the tiles. The force vibrates through my body, but I don't loosen my hold.

It takes a moment before his grunts grow quiet and his body goes limp. Then, shoving the bastard off me, I grab his gun, and training the barrel on his forehead, I pull the trigger. I pick up the other guard's weapon and shove it behind my back.

Opening the sliding door, I step into the living space. A guard comes running from a hallway to my right, and I quickly fire a shot that hits him in the neck. Then, swinging around, I plant another bullet in a guard's chest as he comes racing down the stairway.

I check the clip, taking note that I have seven bullets left. Shoving the clip back into place, I stalk to the stairs and swiftly make my way to the second floor.

I search through the rooms, thinking how stupid Sawiris is for only having six guards. The remaining two are stationed at the front of the house, and I know it's only a matter of time before they realize something is wrong if they haven't been alerted by the gunfire yet.

Reaching the main bedroom, I kick the door open just as Sawiris is busy choking the girl.

The sickening scene shudders through me. The girl's naked and beaten, which tells me I'm too late.

Sawiris glances over his shoulder, irritated that he's disturbed while raping and abusing a girl that doesn't look much older than eighteen.

His eyes widen, and then I pull the trigger, burying a bullet between his eyes. His body slumps over the girl that's in too much shock to even make a sound.

Rushing to the bed, I grab hold of Sawiris' body and toss him to the floor. For a moment, bile builds up in my throat when I take in the broken state of the poor girl.

I'm so sorry I didn't come earlier.

"We have to get out of here." My words don't seem to register, and I can't blame the traumatized girl.

I grab some of Sawiris' clothes, quickly dressing her in a button-up shirt just so she'll be covered. "We have to go. Come on," I say as I pull the girl to her feet.

Grabbing hold of her arm with my left hand, I pick up the gun from where I set it down on the bed, and then I drag the girl out of the suite.

The moment I step out into the hallway, I'm prepared to kill anyone who gets in my way of saving this girl.

I pull her behind me as we begin to walk to the stairs. When we reach the front door, I murmur, "Stay behind me. If anything goes wrong, just run."

I feel her shuffle a little closer to me, and I give her arm a comforting squeeze.

Opening the front door, my eyes search for the other two guards. The one's taken partial cover behind a pillar slightly to my right, and as he glances from behind the pillar, I pull the trigger.

I yank the girl out of the house, and as we race down the stairs to the driveway, I spot the other guard up ahead by the gates.

That's the mistake many wealthy people make. They hire idiots.

I fire two shots, and as his body drops to the ground, I throw the gun to the side and pull the other weapon from behind me. Rushing to the guardhouse, I press the button for the gates to open, and then I drag the girl off the property to where the unmarked van I bought two days ago is parked.

I shove her into the passenger seat, and once I'm behind the steering wheel and we're driving back to Bogotá, I take a couple of deep breaths.

I glance at the girl who's cowering against the door.

"You're safe now. I'm taking you to a house where you can recover. After that, you can go home."

Finally, she lifts her eyes to me. "Who are you?"

"A friend."

"Why did you help me?"

"I hate sex slavery." I keep my answers short, not wanting to give her too much information about me.

Silence falls between us, and I can feel the pain she's in, trembling in the air.

Halfway to Bogotá, she whispers, "I'm Ana."

Chapter 7

ALEXEI

Present day.

We've followed Isabella back to the harbor, and just like I thought, she's here for another shipment.

Only this time, there are men swarming all over. The shipment coming in must be of high value for Sonia to guard it so heavily.

"There's no way Isabella will be able to pull this off on her own," Demitri whispers next to me where we've taken position on one of the warehouse roofs. I have my rifle out, and lying down, I use the scope to survey the area below.

"There are easily over a hundred men down there," I mutter.

Demitri gets his own rifle ready, then asks, "Do you plan on helping her?"

"Yes." I grin at him. "That way, she'll owe me."

I turn my scope to where Isabella's taken cover on one of the containers. I can barely make out her black-clothed figure as she lies dead still.

"Movement on the ship," Demitri says.

"You watch the shipment. I'll keep my eye on Isabella," I instruct him.

Slowly Isabella gets up, and then she jumps to another container. I watch as she stealthily moves closer, and it makes the respect I already feel for the woman grow.

When she's close to the first line of guards, she jumps to the ground, and I lose sight of her for a moment. Then, seconds later, she creeps into the open, holding a gun in each hand.

"The moment she takes down the first man, all hell will break loose," I voice my worry.

"I have the left side covered," Demitri whispers, his voice tense with focus.

Isabella moves into action, and it's fucking breathtaking as she raises both her hands and opens fire on the men. I train my sights on the men nearest to her and begin to take out the ones that are the biggest threat to her.

Isabella's head snaps in our direction as I drop another body for her.

You're welcome, little one.

I take another shot, and it has Isabella jumping back into the action.

Demitri begins to fire off shots, but too many men have broken away from the left side, and they're moving in on Isabella's position.

"I'm going for her," I say as I get up.

"I've got your back," Demitri replies, and then I'm running toward the side of the warehouse. Jumping onto the aircon units and then a stack of crates, I reach the ground in a matter of seconds.

I break out into a flat-out sprint, firing shots as I move in Isabella's direction. Bodies drop around me as Demitri covers me. I come up to the side of the containers and weave my way through them, not wanting to face Isabella head-on.

Right now, she'll see me as another target.

As I move around a set of containers, I come up behind Isabella. She's being forced back by the men, and then Demitri's voice sounds up in the earpiece I'm wearing, *'Reinforcements arrived. Get out of there.'*

"Not without Isabella," I grind the words out as I walk up behind her, firing shots at the nearest threats.

Isabella darts to the side, trying to stay focused on Sonia's men while glancing at me.

"This place is about to be overrun. Reinforcements just arrived," I shout at her as I keep firing shots. I'm on high alert that she can turn on me at any second.

'Get the fuck out of there,' Demitri hollers in my ear as he keeps dropping one body after the other, giving us a moment of reprieve.

With my free hand, I grab hold of Isabella's arm, and shaking my head, I say, "You can't free them. You're outnumbered."

Isabella looks back to the war Demitri's waging against the men running in our direction, and then I yank her into the maze of containers.

For a moment, she comes with me, but then she yanks back against my hold and assumes a fighting stance. "Who the hell are you?" she demands, warning lacing her voice.

She'll probably kill me the moment she hears my name. The corner of my mouth lifts. "The Devil."

Isabella's eyes widen behind the ski mask she's wearing. "What did you just say?"

A man comes up behind Isabella, and I just react. Planting three shots in his chest, I grab hold of her arm and yank her against my body.

There's an explosion of flowers, vanilla, and something earthy. For a moment, I'm caught off guard as my eyes lower to the wide gaze staring up at me.

Holy. Fuck.

I recover quickly. "Nice seeing you again," I say, amused by how this is all turning out.

'Fucking move, or I swear I'll shoot you myself!' Demitri hollers in my ear again, yanking me back to our present predicament.

"How about we kill each other later and first get out of this mess alive?" I ask, the corner of my mouth lifting higher from learning the identity of the hook-up I had a couple of months back.

The hook-up that's turned out to be a mischievous goddess of chaos, taking blow after blow at the cartel.

Isabella recovers from the shock, and we begin to move deeper into the containers until we break free on the other side of the harbor.

"Where are you?" I ask Demitri.

Isabella's eyes snap to me as Demitri answers, *'To your right.'*

Turning my head, I see the SUV coming my way. But, when I glance back at Isabella, I come face to face with the barrel of her gun.

She begins to back away from me, slowly inching in the direction of her motorcycle.

I hear the SUV come to a screeching halt and hold up my hand, so Demitri doesn't shoot Isabella.

"When you're ready to talk, let me know," I say to her.

"Who are you?" she bites the words out, her body tense as she keeps moving backward.

My mouth lifts into a smile again. "Alexei Koslov."

Isabella freezes for a moment, shocked at hearing my name. Then she spins around and runs toward her motorcycle.

I'll see you soon.

ISABELLA

Shock waves keep shuddering through me as I make my way to where Ana's waiting.

Tonight was a failure of epic proportions.

Shit.

The girls.

Pulling over the side of the road so I can take a moment to process my failure, I climb off the bike, and then I let out a frustrated scream.

I yank off my helmet and ski mask and throw them to the ground.

Alexei Koslov.

My God.

The freaking devil I had sex with turned out to be the head of the bratva.

My God.

I breathe through the rampant emotions waging war in my chest. My disappointment for not being able to free the girls. My shock of having Alexei freaking Koslov help me get out of there.

I wouldn't have escaped alive otherwise.

When the bodies started dropping around me, I was totally caught off guard. But there were too many men for me to fight on my own.

God, my mother sent an army.

I stop moving, and feeling drained, I suck in deep breaths of air as I stare into the darkness around me.

Just then, the unmarked SUV I saw at the harbor pulls up a couple of yards behind me.

He knew I'd be at the harbor.

My eyes dart to my motorcycle.

Shit, he's been tracking me, which means he might know everything about the double life I've been leading.

There's a sinking feeling in my chest as everything I've worked so hard for begins to crumble around me.

Knowing I have to face off with Alexei at some point, I pull my Heckler & Koch from behind my back and train the barrel on the SUV. Alexei and his custodian, Demitri, climb out of the vehicle, looking every bit like the powerful duo they are.

Demitri Vetrov. I think I can take him.

But I can't take them both.

I have no idea how good Alexei is. If he's better than Demitri, I'm dead.

I move my aim to Alexei, the uncertain threat.

"You have a tracker on my motorcycle?" I ask as they come to a stop.

"Of course," Alexei answers. It's too dark to make out his features clearly, but I can hear the amusement in his voice. "My turn," he says as he takes another step closer to me. "Why are you freeing the slaves?"

"They're not slaves," I bite the words out. "They're innocent people."

I can make out as Alexei nods. He moves a little closer, and my finger tightens around the trigger as a wave of danger washes over me. The power this man holds radiates into the night.

Unlike where it was a turn-on the night of the party, the tiny hairs on the back of my neck now rise in apprehension.

Alexei Koslov is known to be unpredictable and ruthless. He's deadly and the most feared man. Those facts alone should make me take the shot while I can, but for some unknown reason, I don't.

He's also my mother's biggest enemy.

He can destroy her.

"Why are you watching me?" I ask.

"Actually, I'm watching Sonia. Discovering you was a pleasant surprise," he replies.

Another step from Alexei has me biting out, "That's close enough."

"So you're the party crasher?" he asks.

Goosebumps spread over my skin, as a flash of him thrusting inside me throws me off balance for a moment.

Keeping my voice neutral, I reply, "It was a moment of stupidity."

Alexei lets out a sexy chuckle. "It's too late for lies, little one." *Little one.* It sounds more like a term of endearment than a derogatory pet name.

Demitri keeps still, but I can feel his presence.

"What do you want from me?" I demand.

Another sexy chuckle from Alexei sends a tremble through my body. "I wouldn't say no to a repeat performance, but for now, I'd like to offer you an alliance. Of course, that's assuming we have the same goal."

"What goal?"

"Taking down your mother."

"What makes you think I'll work with you? You're no different from her."

Alexei slaps a hand to his chest. "That hurt. I'm nothing like Sonia Terrero."

It's my turn to chuckle. "Right. You don't kill while ruling the world with a ruthless fist."

Alexei shakes his head, and ignoring my warning from earlier, he takes a couple of steps closer to me. I fire off a shot in the ground by his feet, but he doesn't even flinch. Instead, he lets out a burst of amused laughter.

Demitri has his gun trained on me so fast that I didn't even notice him moving.

Alexei doesn't even bother looking at Demitri as he says, "Lower your weapon, brother."

Demitri listens, but his body is wound tight and ready to explode into action at any moment. Looking at him, a smirk forms around my lips as I say, "You're no match for me, Vetrov."

"Want to put down your gun so we can find out how good you really are?" Demitri asks.

"Another time. I have a mess to clean up," I answer before turning my attention back to Alexei. He takes a final step closer, which will make it easy for him to try to disarm me, then he tilts his head and says, "I don't kill innocent people."

I've heard people say that about him.

Now that he's closer, I can make out his features. He's attractive if you're into being devoured by a wolf.

Like I was.

I lower my gun a couple of inches until it's no longer trained on his chest but instead on his cock.

Again Alexei laughs. "Do you really want to deprive the world of the ecstasy you felt when I fucked you?"

My left eyebrow shoots up. "Vain much?"

"No, just confident."

Lowering my weapon completely, I'm still on high alert as I ask, "What's your proposal?"

"We take down Sonia."

Cynical laughter bursts over my lips. "And then? What guarantee will I have you won't kill me after I've helped you?"

"You'll have my word," he states as if it should actually mean something to me.

Giving him a condescending smirk, I shake my head. "Thanks for the offer, but I work alone."

Alexei crosses his arms over his chest, looking more like a god than a man. "It's only a matter of time before your cover is blown."

"Is that a threat?" I bite the words out, taking a threatening step toward him. Our eyes lock, and for a moment, there's a power struggle between us before he lets out another bark of amused laughter.

"Fuck, are you real?"

He asked me the same thing while we were hooking up.

This time the corner of my mouth lifts with confidence. "Yes."

Alexei meets my smile as he looks at me with admiration. I've never had anyone look at me like that, and it makes a weird sensation ripple through my chest.

His expression turns serious, then he says, "Join me, Isabella. Together we can take down Sonia. I'll owe you a favor."

A favor from Alexei Koslov? Damn, that's tempting.

I actually take a moment to think about it but knowing this man is still my enemy, I shake my head. "As I said, I work alone. Thanks for the offer, though."

I take a couple of steps back, raising my weapon on Alexei again. "You can leave."

Alexei stares at me a moment, then he says, "Until we meet again."

Which will hopefully not be any time soon.

I watch as they walk back to the SUV, and only once they're driving down the road do I shove my gun behind my back and pick up my helmet and ski mask.

As interesting as that was, it's time to get back to Ana so we can decide where to go from here.

Chapter 8

ALEXEI

I'm still fucking grinning by the time we get to the house we're staying at.

I definitely got more than I bargained for when it comes to Isabella Terrero. Christ, the woman is one of a kind.

A fucking masterpiece.

The way she stood her ground in front of me was one hell of a turn-on. Usually, people cower in fear before me, but not Isabella. There wasn't an ounce of fear between us.

Isabella Terrero is a goddess if ever I saw one.

"She smirked at you," I taunt Demitri, and then I let out a burst of laughter at the memory. "You're no match for me, Vetrov," I mimic what Isabella said to him, only to crack up laughing again.

"You really enjoyed that moment, didn't you?" Demitri asks, shooting a glare my way as we walk into the house.

"More than you'll ever know." When we get to the security room, I drop down in one of the chairs, then grin at Demitri.

He shakes his head at me, the corner of his mouth lifting. "You're that impressed by her?"

My grin grows into a wide smile. "You have to admit, Isabella Terrero is… fucking exhilarating."

Demitri's expression grows serious, and then he stares at me.

Knowing what he's thinking, I say, "I just admire the woman."

He raises an eyebrow at me.

Giving him a look of warning, I add, "You know I don't do love and relationships. Let's get back to work."

I check the tracker on Isabella's motorcycle and notice she's at the safe house on the outskirts of town.

I wonder if she's going to remove the device so I can't track her motorcycle anymore?

Then Demitri mutters, "But it's okay when you play matchmaker to everyone?"

"I don't play matchmaker." Letting out a sigh, I glance at my friend. "I just nudge people in the right direction."

“Okay.” Demitri gives me a cocky grin. “Let me nudge you in the right direction then. What about a marriage alliance between you and Isabella?”

Laughter bursts from me. “You saw the same woman as me tonight, right? She’d probably castrate me the moment I mention a wedding between us.”

My comment makes Demitri chuckle. “I’d actually like to see her try.”

“So much for keeping me alive,” I chastise him.

Demitri shrugs. “No one said anything about protecting your manhood. You’re on your own when it comes to your cock.”

“Fucker,” I grumble playfully as we get back to work.

We check the screens, and seeing there’s no activity that’s worth our attention, Demitri asks, “What do you want to do now?”

I think for a moment, then reply, “There’s no use in waiting much longer. I think we should attack after the auction. Security will be high until then.”

“I’ll handle Damien while you take care of Carson,” Demitri says as he pulls his phone from his pocket to call his brother.

Taking my own phone out, I bring up my little brother’s number and press dial.

"Hi," Carson answers a couple of seconds later. He's one of the best assassins in the world, living in Switzerland with his girlfriend, Hailey. It's been almost a year since I've seen him when he helped me secure the position as head of the bratva.

"How are things there?" I ask.

"Good. Quiet," he replies. "What's up?"

"I need you in Columbia. I know you hate the heat, but I'm taking down Sonia and can't do it without you."

"Fuck, you had to choose the middle of summer to attack?" he grumbles. "When do I need to be there?"

"As soon as possible," I chuckle.

"Send me the details of the airfield."

"Will do."

Carson takes a deep breath. "So you're really going after Terrero? Why?"

"She moved into my territory," I explain.

"Fair enough. I'll be there tomorrow night."

We end the call then I glance at Demitri. He tucks his phone back in his pocket as he says, "Damien will be here tomorrow night."

"Send them both the airfield's details."

Demitri nods then he turns his attention to the screens. “Oh, by the way, there’s no map of what’s under Terrero’s compound.”

“If I were her, I’d have a fuck-ton of tunnels. There’s no way she doesn’t have another escape route.”

Demitri points to the screen showing the mansion. “She has the helicopter, but that thing hasn’t moved since we got here.”

“There’s something under that house. I’d bet my life on it,” I murmur as I look over every inch of the property.

It’s a pity Isabella declined to work with us.

ISABELLA

Ana and I have been sitting in silence for the last hour. I keep replaying the failed operation over and over in my mind.

Letting out a sigh, I shake my head for the hundredth time.

“There were too many men,” Ana whispers. She’s just as disappointed as me that we couldn’t free the girls.

"It makes everything a million times harder," I mutter before letting out another sigh.

We're avoiding talking about the next step because it's exactly what happened to Ana. I have to wait until after the auction, and there's no way I'll be able to get to all the girls before they disappear, which means I'll have to choose who to save and who to leave.

My eyes drift shut at the thought.

How do I choose?

For the first time ever, Ana places her hand on mine. My eyes snap open, and I stare at where she's touching me before slowly lifting my gaze to hers. She tilts her head, the pain that's ingrained into every fiber of her being, clear on her features. "We help who we can."

Shaking my head, I ask, "What about the ones we don't rescue?"

Tears well in Ana's eyes, then she repeats, "We help who we can, Isabella."

This is the first time we've failed so badly, and it's weighing heavy on us. The ones we can't rescue will be subjected to rape and torture until they're killed.

Lifting my other hand, I rest my forehead in my palm and close my eyes again.

What am I going to do?

Ana pulls her hand away from mine, then says, “We can’t avoid it.”

Nodding, I lift my head, and then I swallow hard and meet Ana’s eyes. “We’ll wait until after the auction.”

“Save the youngest first,” she says, and I grab onto the out she’s giving me of making the decision.

“Okay.” My tongue darts out, wetting my lips. “I’m going to need you close by. As I free the girls, you need to pick them up so I can go after the next one.”

Ana nods. “I’ll be there every step of the way.”

I stare at my friend for a moment then ask, “We can do this, right?”

The corner of her mouth lifts slightly. I’ve never seen her smile. I’ve never seen Ana happy.

“You can do this, Isabella,” she offers me the encouragement I need.

Feeling emotional from the failure, I lower my gaze from Ana’s, then I whisper the words I’ve never said out loud to her, “I’m sorry I didn’t get to you in time.”

Ana quickly shakes her head, and then she gets up from the chair and hurries toward the stairs. I stare after her, wondering if I’m even making a difference in this depraved world.

Just like with all the other auctions, I'm wearing a red dress. It's my silent way of protesting the blood that will be spilled and the innocence that will be stolen.

My mind keeps racing, trying to come up with a way I can free all the girls tonight. But there's no way, and it makes me feel frustrated and worried, which are emotions I'm not used to.

Coming down the stairs, I hear Hugo talking to my mother. "It was definitely a woman who's been attacking us, but there's more. Look."

Walking into the living room, I see as he turns his phone so my mother can see the screen, and then her eyes widen as she hisses, "Alexei Koslov."

I sit down on one of the plush couches, faking boredom while my attention is one hundred percent focused on Hugo and my mother.

Hugo grins at my mother. "The woman could be Winter. She's trained."

Shit.

Winter Vetrov is the Blood Princess and married to Demitri's younger brother, Damien. The last thing I want is for my mother to go after Winter.

If there's a woman I respect, it's Winter. It's because of her that I'm fighting back against my mother. When I saw Winter training at St. Monarch's and how she faced off against her enemies, it made me want to do the same.

Then again, Winter has all the Vetrovs and Koslovs behind her. My mother won't stand a chance against those two families.

The thought has me relaxing, and pulling out my phone, I pretend to check my social media accounts.

"It would make sense," Mother says, anger lacing her words. "Which means Alexei's declared war."

"Probably because we're moving into his territory," Hugo reminds her.

Which was a stupid move, if you ask me.

"Let's focus on the auction, and then we'll form a plan of retaliation," Mother says, too confident. Yes, she's powerful, but taking on the Vetrovs and Koslovs is just reckless.

"Do I have to attend?" I mutter, injecting a world of boredom into my voice.

She waves her hand toward the elevator, impatience tightening her features. "Don't start, Isabella."

Letting out a huff, I get up and follow my mother into the elevator while Hugo stays behind to welcome the guests.

Fifteen minutes later, I watch as the *guests* start to fill the chamber, and it feels as if a tight fist is gripping my heart.

Youngest first, Isabella.

I keep reminding myself of what Ana said, trying to detach myself from the moment. It doesn't help because as the bidding starts and the first girl is led onto the stage, I feel my heart crack.

Once again, regret bubbles up in me from failing to free the girls at the harbor.

I'm so sorry.

I stare at the pale face framed by black curls. The girl stumbles to the side as she's forcefully turned for the bidders to see all of her naked body.

I swallow the bitter taste down that the sight leaves in my mouth, and lifting my chin, I take a deep breath.

Keep your shit together. You're of no use to these girls if you're dead.

Time crawls by, and as each girl is put on display and sold, the weight on my shoulders increases until it feels like the world is bearing down on me.

The last girl is brought onto the stage, and seeing how young she is, makes my fists tighten by my sides.

God, single digits?

My eyes dart to my mother. She has a pleased smile on her face as she watches the bidders go crazy, and the amount rockets through the thousands and well into the millions.

Looking back at the little girl, I think about the offer Alexei made. It will get rid of my mother, stopping the terror she's spreading instead of me trying to save one girl at a time.

Shoving the idea to the back of my mind, I focus on the girl.

'I'll save you first.'

I turn my gaze to the bidders, and when the girl is sold for three million, my eyes settle hard on the man who just bought her. He also purchased another girl, and clearly, he likes them way too freaking young.

If I go after him, I'll be able to save two girls at once.

Chapter 9

ALEXEI

With Damien and Carson joining us, the space is a little cramped in the security room.

We're all watching as people arrive at Sonia's mansion for the auction.

From the underground chatter, we've learned there are four virgins up for sale. There's no way Isabella will be able to get to all of them before they leave Columbia.

I've reached out to one of my contacts from *The Ruin* – a syndicate in Desolate, New York, to get more information on the virgins for me.

I check my phone, and not seeing a reply from my contact, I impatiently shake my head. I hate waiting for information.

"What are you thinking?" Demitri asks.

"Isabella won't be able to free all the girls," I murmur.

Carson shakes his head. "I'm still trying to process the fact that Isabella's working against Sonia. I seriously never saw that coming."

"If she's as good as us, she might be able to free all four," Damien voices his opinion. "But she'll have to move fast with absolutely nothing going wrong."

I glance from our brothers to Demitri, then say, "Unless we help her."

"We don't know who she'll be going after first," Carson says, shaking his head.

"She hasn't disabled the tracker on her motorcycle." My eyes find Demitri's. "And she'll probably go for the youngest two."

"That's what I'd do," Damien agrees.

I nod, then say, "We'll go after the oldest two of the group."

Just then, the message I've been waiting for finally comes through, and I hurry to open it.

Thank fuck. It's everything we need.

I sync the information up to one of the bigger screens, and seeing the faces of the four girls makes anger start to simmer in my chest.

If there's one thing I hate, it's people preying on young girls.

Just like my father preyed on my mother.

It's something I've kept from Carson in an attempt to protect him from our sordid past.

Demitri points to one of the girls. "Damien and Carson can follow this girl while you and I take the other one."

I glance at the younger two, hoping Isabella will be able to get to them in time. Then, getting up from the chair, I say, "Let's get ready."

It only takes us five minutes to gear up, and then we leave the house. We test the earpieces we're wearing before Carson and Damien head to their SUV.

When I slide behind the steering wheel of our vehicle, I wait for Demitri to shut the door behind him, then say, "Hopefully, we'll gain some ground with Isabella by helping her."

He pulls on his safety belt then chuckles, "Yeah, I wouldn't hold my breath."

As I steer the SUV onto the road, Carson follows us. We head toward Sonia's compound and park the SUVs down the street. Then, bringing up the camera's footage of the grounds and entrance of the mansion on my phone, we wait for the bidders to leave with their purchases.

Demitri has the camera showing the back of the property on his phone. "Isabella just snuck out. Reckless with all the guards."

I glance at his phone and then look up the street, just in time to see her running away from the compound.

You can do it, little one.

My lips tug up into a smile as another burst of admiration for her fills my chest.

"Get ready," I say, so Carson and Damien will hear.

I watch the entrance, and a couple of minutes later, people begin to leave the mansion.

"Your girl is in the white Maybach," I say to Carson. Then, as the Mercedes nears the gate, I murmur, "In three… two… one."

'Got it,' Carson replies as he pulls away and begins to tail the girl they need to save.

"There's our girl," I say when she's led to a G-Wagon. I start the engine, and as the vehicle comes through the gates, I steer our SUV after them.

When we head in the direction of one of the private airfields, Demitri says, "Just as well we're helping. They'd have the girl out of the country before Isabella could even think of trying to help her."

"How are you doing, Carson?" I ask, checking in with my brother.

'Looks like we're heading into the city,' he replies. *'The fucker probably plans on getting his money's worth from the girl tonight and then leaving her body in Columbia.'*

"Be safe," I mutter.

'Always.'

When we near the airfield, Demitri says, "Lean forward." I do as he says, and he pulls my gun from behind my back. I settle back against the seat again while Demitri checks my weapon even though I've already done it.

"Ready?" I ask as the G-Wagon comes to a stop near a private jet.

"Yes."

I floor the gas, and as we speed toward the men climbing out of the G-Wagon, Demitri opens his window. I turn the steering wheel hard to my right while pulling up the hand brake, and it gives Demitri the perfect angle to take down two of the guards.

The moment I bring the SUV to a screeching halt, Demitri hands me my gun, and we get out of the vehicle.

The remaining guard fires shots in our direction, but Demitri drops him with a bullet to the head. The bidder looks torn between shoving the girl toward the private jet and leaving her behind to save his own ass.

"You'd think the fucker would have more protection," I chuckle as we close in on him.

"Idiot."

The man places his hands behind his head in a surrendering motion, only making me shake my head before shooting him in the right knee cap. He sinks to a kneeling position with a cry. "That's better. If you're going to beg, do it on your knees." I smile at the man, shaking my head at him again while I wait for Demitri to pull the girl out of the line of fire. Training my barrel on the man, I say, "Picking flowers before they've even had a chance to blossom? Tsk." I pull the trigger, and without any emotion, I watch as the body slumps to the tarmac.

'We're moving in on the target,' Carson suddenly says over the earpiece.

"We already have our girl. You're losing your touch," I taunt him.

'Fuck off,' my brother grumbles, earning a chuckle from me as I turn toward Demitri and the girl.

I glance over her for any bruises or wounds, and not seeing any, I hide my gun behind my back as I lean down to catch her eyes. "Are you hurt, little one?"

Fearfully she shakes her head.

"What's your name?"

"Paola," she whispers with a quivering voice.

"You're safe, Paola. We're going to take you to a woman who will help you get home. Okay?"

It doesn't look like she believes a word I'm saying, but still, she nods.

Demitri gently takes hold of the girl's arm, then says, "Let's get out of here."

When we get to the SUV, Demitri gets into the back with Paola, so she doesn't try to throw herself from a moving car. It's only natural that she doesn't trust us.

I start the engine, and as I steer the SUV away from the private jet and bodies, I pull my phone out and check the tracking device on Isabella's motorcycle. It shows she's on a highway heading out of the city.

'Got our girl,' Carson's voice comes over the earpiece.

"Meet you at Isabella's safe house," I reply as I drive in the direction of it.

A half an hour later, we come to a stop a safe distance from the house, so we don't spook Isabella. It takes Carson another fifteen minutes before he pulls up behind us.

Getting out of the SUV, I walk toward the other vehicle. Carson rolls down his window when I reach him, then asks, "Aren't we dropping off the girls?"

I gesture down the street to where the house is. "Doesn't look like anyone's home. Bring your girl to my SUV. Demitri and I will wait for Isabella to get here with the other girls. You and Damien can head back and start preparing for the attack."

I walk back to the SUV, and when I climb into the driver's seat, I say, "We're going to stick around with the girls. We can't just leave them on the doorstep."

"Okay," Demitri replies, glancing at Paola, who's still in shock from everything that's happened.

Carson brings the other girl, and Paola seems to relax a little when she gets to huddle with her friend.

As we wait, my thoughts turn to the impending attack. We'll strike at the crack of dawn.

ISABELLA

Jorge Dos Santos.

That's the name of the man I've been following back to his house for the last hour. After parking my motorcycle, I pull on my ski mask and then jog toward the side of the villa. Hoisting myself over the wall, I crouch down the instant my feet touch the ground and quickly move to behind a tree.

Quietly, I pull my binoculars out of my bag, and then I canvas the area, taking in the positions of the guards stationed around the mansion.

Dos Santos has half a dozen men, which means I'll have to move as quietly as I can. At the first gunshot, all hell might break loose.

Pulling my KA-BAR from its holder, my fingers tighten around the knife, and then I keep low as I creep toward the back of the house that's less guarded than the front.

Reaching the sidewall, I glance at the pipe and windows that I can use to scale up to the second floor. I bite onto the handle of my knife and grab hold of the pipe running up to the second floor.

I keep my breaths slow and deep, focusing on not making a sound as I pull myself up the pipe. When I reach the second floor, I have to swing my body toward the balcony, almost missing grabbing hold of the ledge. My fingers tighten around the wrought iron of the railing, and I let out a slow breath. When I hear movement inside, I hold still, my arms straining from hanging off the side of the balcony.

I hear a girl sniffling, and then a slap rings from the room. Slowly, I pull myself up until I'm able to climb over the railing. I quickly press my body against the wall then take the knife from my mouth. Cautiously, I lean forward until I have a view of the inside of the room through the glass doors.

Dos Santos is alone in the room with the two girls, and he's currently unbuttoning his shirt.

Fucker.

My muscles tighten from having to hold back because if I move now, he'll definitely see me coming. The last thing I need is for him to alert his guards that I'm here.

It feels as if a fist is tightening around my throat, and my breaths grow shallow as I watch Dos Santos undress.

The youngest girl stands rooted to the spot, silent tears falling over her cheeks. The older one stares at the carpet, her face expressionless as if she's mentally left the room.

I'm here.

Dos Santos slaps the older girl, which only makes the younger one sob. The bastard is mentally playing them up against each other.

When he's focused on the youngest girl, pretending to console her while groping her chest, I slowly inch forward until I'm able to take hold of the door lever.

Don't let it be locked.

Little by little, I press down on the lever, and when the door softly clicks open, I say a silent prayer of thanks.

Moving fast, I come up behind Dos Santos, and before he can realize I'm here, I drag the blade of my KA-BAR across his throat. I cover his gaping mouth with my hand to muffle his garbled breaths and plunge the knife into his heart to finish him off. I lower his body to the carpet and then look at the girls. Bringing my finger to my lips, I show for them to not make a noise.

They're still dressed in the white cloaks my mother had them wear for the auction.

I crouch down in front of the girls, then whisper, "Hold hands and stay behind me. I'm going to get you out of here."

The older girl's eyes flick to mine, then she whispers, "You're helping me?"

"Both of you. Stay behind me at all times. Okay?"

When she nods, I add, "Take her hand and don't let go. If anything happens to me, you take her and run as fast as you can."

The older girl nods again, emotion returning to her face. It makes her eyes shimmer with unshed tears.

"You're so brave. You can do this. Okay?" I try to offer her some encouragement.

She nods as she takes hold of the younger girl's hand in a tight grip.

I turn my focus to the youngest, then say, "Don't make a sound."

She nods quickly, and then I get up and walk to the door.

I press my ear to the wood, listening for any movement outside the room, then I take a fortifying breath before I yank it open.

Darting into the hallway, there are two guards. I manage to plunge my knife into the one guard's eye, and then the other one's fist connects with my left ear. I stumble to the side, then swinging around, I bring my right leg up, slamming the heel of my boot against his temple. The kick sends him sprawling onto the tiles, motionless. Pulling my knife from the dead guy's eye socket, I walk to the unconscious one and slit his throat open.

I glance at the girls as I rise to my feet and begin to move down the hallway. The older one drags the younger girl behind her as she follows after me.

Reaching the top of the stairs, I become aware of my heart pounding against my ribs as I cautiously lean forward to see what's on the first floor.

Two guards are stationed at the foot of the stairs.

I inch back behind the wall, and taking off my backpack, I pull a silencer from it and attach it to the front of my Heckler & Koch.

I take five seconds to even my breathing and to calm my racing heart.

Focus, Isabella.

Slowly, I suck in another deep breath of air, and then I move. As soon as I have a clear shot at the guards, I pull the trigger. As the first guard falls, I bury a bullet in the temple of the second one as he begins to turn.

Moving down the stairs, I hear hurried footsteps coming from the left, and as the men appear, I begin to fire shots. I'm aware of the girls behind me as I keep taking one guard after the other down. While I'm reloading the clip of my Heckler & Koch, the front door bursts open, and a bullet clips my right arm before I can take out the man shooting at us.

Too close.

I move toward the open front door, every single one of my senses on high alert. I keep checking behind us, so I'm not caught off guard as we step out of the house.

Holding the Heckler & Koch in my right hand, I pull my Baretta from the side of my left boot, and then I open fire on the remaining guards.

A bullet slams into my left shoulder, and I clench my teeth at the sharp pain while not losing my focus. I keep pushing forward until the last man drops.

Putting my Baretta away, I yell at the girls, "We have to run!" I hurry them toward the main gates as I pull my phone out, calling Ana.

"Are you okay?" she answers, her voice strained with worry.

"I'm bringing them out. Meet me at the front of the house."

"Okay."

Ending the call, I rush to the security booth and open the main gates. Seconds later, Ana pulls up, and I herd the girls toward the van. Ana stays behind the steering wheel as I open the side door, and then I shove the girls inside.

I spare a second to say, "You're safe now." Slamming the door shut, I pound a fist against the metal so Ana will leave, and then I run toward my motorcycle.

Following behind the van, I escort Ana and the girls back to the safe house so I can protect them should there be a hit while we're on the road. Luckily nothing happens, but I only feel a sliver of relief when we pull up the driveway.

My thoughts turn to the other two girls I couldn't save as I become aware of the pulsing pain in my shoulder.

As I climb off my motorcycle and remove my helmet, movement from the street grabs my attention. I drop the helmet and have my gun drawn and ready within the next second.

My breath shudders from me when I see the two older girls running toward me.

Oh. My. God.

My eyes instantly begin to burn as intense relief washes through me. I'm only overwhelmed for a moment before I dart forward to make sure there's no one behind the girls that's a threat.

When the street is clear, I turn back to the girls, then ask, "How did you get here?"

"Men brought us. They said you'd help us get home."

Nodding, I gesture toward the house, still holding my gun ready in my right hand. "Let's get you inside where it's safe."

I glance up and down the empty street again and then back to the girls.

I can't believe it.

Thank God.

There are only two men I can think of. Alexei and Demitri.

Alexei Koslov helped me?

Why?

Probably so I'd owe him a favor and help him take down my mother.

Then it really sinks in – all the girls are safe with Ana and me, and it doesn't matter what I owe Alexei.

Emotion bubbles in my chest, and I bite back the thankful tears knowing all four girls have been saved from a horrendous life as sex slaves.

Chapter 10

ALEXEI

Besides the four of us, I have another ten highly trained men to attack Sonia.

I'm worried about Isabella, but I hope she'll make a run for it the moment we strike.

Everyone's wearing an earpiece and is heavily armed. Carson's taken position on the roof of a nearby apartment block from where he'll offer cover. Damien will breach the front with a group of men, while Demitri and I will enter from the back of the property with the remaining four men.

It's judgment day, and I'm confident that I'll remain standing while Sonia falls.

"Ready?" I ask.

'Ready,' Carson answers.

'In position,' Damien's voice comes over the earpiece.

"Time to hunt," I chuckle, then I give the order, "Breach."

We scale the wall, and instantly rapid gunfire sounds from the front of the house, startling the men guarding the back. They spot us as we move in on them and open fire.

Lifting my sub-machine gun, I pull the trigger, and the weapon vibrates in my grip as one bullet after the other flies, riddling the guards' bodies.

As we push forward, moving in on the patio, one of the glass doors on the second floor opens, and Hugo Lamas steps out, opening fire on us. The fucker manages to take out two of my men before he darts back into the room.

Demitri and I split from the remaining two men, and I shout to them, "Breach through the patio. We're going for the second floor."

Demitri and I keep firing shots, moving fast to avoid being hit. When we near the back of the house, I sling the strap of my sub-machine across my shoulder and chest.

Running faster, I jump to the wall of the house, then use the momentum I've gained to push my body higher so I can grip hold of the balcony. Using all my strength, I yank my body up, and grabbing hold of the handrail, I swing myself onto the balcony. I quickly pull my Heckler & Koch from behind my back as Demitri lands next to me, and then we enter the room.

Just then, the sound of the helicopter's engine starting attracts my attention, and I dart back out onto the balcony. Glancing up to the side of the roof, I see the blades picking up speed.

"Fuck, Sonia's making a run for it!"

Running back inside the room, Demitri and I are met with some of Sonia's men as we burst into the hallway. It takes precious seconds to kill the men before we run up the stairs to where the exit to the roof hopefully is.

At the top of the stairs, I kick my way through the door. The downdraft from the helicopter taking off slams into me, ripping at my clothes, and as I lift my arm to aim at the aircraft, I say, "Carson, the helicopter can't leave."

'Got it,' his reply comes over the earpiece.

Surprise vibrates through me when I see Isabella run toward the helicopter as it lifts into the air. My heart stutters as she leaps into the air, grabbing hold of one of the landing skids. She swings wildly for a moment as the helicopter slants to the side, and then a bullet bounces off the steel body.

"Fuck, it's armored," I spit out, knowing that makes it almost impossible for us to take the helicopter down.

I take aim for the cockpit window as the helicopter turns, but then the side door slides open. As I move my aim, Isabella only hangs by her left hand as she pulls her gun from behind her back.

She fires a shot at Hugo, hitting him, but then she loses grip as he takes a shot at her, and my breath stalls in my throat as she falls.

Demitri and I open fire on Hugo, but for the first time in my life, I don't think and just react as I start to run for the back of the roof. I leap down to one of the balconies beneath, and grabbing the railing, I throw my body over the side, landing on the lawn in a crouching position. Darting up, I sprint for the side of the house where Isabella fell, and as I round the corner, I see her where she's lying in a courtyard. A wrought iron table is tipped over, which must've happened when her body hit it.

Fuck.

Reaching Isabella, I crouch beside her, and then there's a heavy sinking feeling in my gut. Blood's trickling from her slightly parted lips, and there's a gash on the left side of her temple.

"Is she alive?" Demitri asks as he comes up behind me.

"I don't know," I murmur as I glance up, in time to see Sonia's helicopter fading in the distance.

"Fuck," I curse as anger explodes in my chest. I look down at Isabella again.

What a fucking fuck up!

Demitri has two fingers to her neck, then his gaze meets mine. "There's a weak pulse."

Damien comes running around the side of the house. "We have to move!"

"Where are the rest of the men?" I ask when I notice he's alone.

He shakes his head, then stares down at Isabella. "What happened?"

"She fell," Demitri answers. "Go get me a towel."

While Damien runs for the entrance closest to us, Demitri says, "I want to brace her neck before we move her. Carson, bring the SUV as close as you can to the right side of the mansion."

'On my way,' Carson replies.

It takes another couple of seconds before my mind starts working again. Then, pulling my phone from my pocket, I call the private airfield where my jet is waiting and instruct them to get everything ready for departure.

"Can you keep her alive until we reach LA?" I ask Demitri.

"I'll do my best," he mutters as he begins to check her for other wounds.

Bringing up the number for Tristan, my business partner in LA, I press dial.

"Hey, it's been a while," he answers after a couple of rings.

"I need your help."

"Anything," he replies without hesitating.

"Dr. West. I need her. Take her to the underground hospital."

Tristan knows where it is, seeing as a couple of years back, we got equipment from it to help save Dr. West's daughter after she was kidnapped and almost killed. It's time for the world-class cardiothoracic surgeon to repay the favor she owes me.

I check the time on my watch, then say, "We'll be there in seven hours."

"I'll take care of everything on this end. Who got hurt?"

"A friend. No one you know."

Tristan lets out a relieved breath before we hang up.

Damien comes back with the towel, and Demitri carefully wraps it around Isabella's neck before taking off his belt to secure it in place.

A minute later, Carson jogs toward us. "Let's go!"

"Where's the SUV?" I ask, wondering how the hell we're going to move Isabella. Just picking her up might cause more damage if she hurt her back or neck with the fall.

He gestures behind him. "Just around the corner."

Locking eyes with Demitri, I ask, "How do we move her?"

He shakes his head, taking a moment to think, then he says, "I need something solid to carry her on."

"Will a door work?" I ask.

The moment Demitri nods, Damien says, "One door coming right up."

I'd chuckle if I wasn't so goddamned worried about Isabella.

My gaze drifts over her pale face, and then the memory of her falling flashes through my mind. It makes a weird sensation grip my heart in a merciless hold. It's almost similar to what I felt when Demitri got shot.

You're strong. You're going to be okay.

It's only after I think the words that I realize I'm trying to convince myself this is not how Isabella ends.

Coming to a screeching stop at the back of the underground hospital, I climb out of the SUV and run to the back of the vehicle where Demitri meets me. We open the door, and then I jump inside so I can pick up the door by Isabella's head.

We're careful as we move her out of the SUV. She survived the flight, and the last thing I want to do is lose her because we're reckless.

Dr. West and Dr. Oberio, a trauma surgeon, wheel a stretcher toward us, and we carefully place Isabella on it with the door still beneath her.

My eyes lock on the doctors, then I say, "Do your best to save her."

Dr. West nods, and then they're both wheeling Isabella down the hallway toward the surgery room.

Tristan glances at his aunt before the doors shut behind the doctors and Isabella as he walks toward me. He embraces me, and it's only then I feel how tired I am.

"You okay?" he asks as he pulls back.

Letting out a heavy sigh, I say, "Yeah. Just worried."

"Who's the woman?" he asks.

I don't know what to call Isabella and end up murmuring, "A friend."

I walk to the small waiting room with Tristan and Demitri following behind me, and when I take a seat, I pull my phone out and dial Carson's number. He stayed in Columbia with Damien.

"Did you make it?" Carson answers the call.

"Yes. They're working on Isabella."

"What do you want us to do on this side?" my brother asks.

"Clean out the house we were staying at." Then I remember Isabella's safe house and the girls we freed last night.

God, has it only been twenty-four hours?

"Also, go to the safe house where we dropped off the girls and check on them. If they're still there, we'll need to figure something out."

"I'll handle everything. Don't worry."

"Thanks, brother," I say with a heavy sigh.

We end the call, and then I slump back against the chair and take a deep breath.

Fucking Sonia got away.

I only manage to sit still for a minute or so before climbing to my feet. Walking out into the hallway again, I stare at the shut doors, worry for Isabella and how serious her injuries are whirling in my chest.

A hand falls on my shoulder, and I know it's Demitri without having to look.

"She's a fighter," he says, probably trying to set me at ease.

"I hope Isabella makes it," I mutter. "It would be a fucking waste to lose her."

"What are we going to do about Sonia?" he asks.

Glancing at my friend, I say, "Have our contact in *The Ruin* start searching for anything on Sonia's whereabouts." I take a deep breath, my eyes going back to the shut doors. "You might as well head home. Spend some time with Ariana and check the underground chatter for talk of Sonia."

"And you?" Demitri asks.

"I'll stay here with him," Tristan answers on my behalf.

Demitri locks eyes with me, waiting for the order. "I'm good here with Tristan. Don't worry."

Nodding, he gives my shoulder a squeeze before he heads to the back entrance where the SUV is.

"Want some coffee?" Tristan asks. When I scowl at him, he lets out a chuckle. "Sorry, brother, I don't have vodka on me."

I shake my head. "I'm good."

There's no way I'll have the usual celebratory drink after walking away from a battle alive before Isabella's out of the woods.

Chapter 11

ALEXEI

The wait brought back memories of when Demitri was shot a year ago. I lost a couple of years of my life from worrying whether I'd lose my best friend back then.

I'm standing in the hallway, leaning back against the wall and lifting my left arm, I check the time on my watch.

They've been working on Isabella for almost four hours.

Tristan walks toward me and holds out a bottle of water. "Drink something."

Taking the bottle, I twist off the cap, and then I chug down a couple of gulps. I place the cap back on the bottle then toss it to Tristan. "Happy now?"

He catches the water with a chuckle.

"You don't have to hang around with me," I say. "Go home to Hana."

Tristan shakes his head. "Demitri will kill me if I leave you here alone."

"Fucking babysitters," I grumble, only making Tristan chuckle again.

Just then, the doors at the end of the hallway open, and I push away from the wall as Dr. West comes out.

I stalk toward Tristan's aunt, asking, "How is she?"

"What's the patient's name?" Dr. West asks instead of answering me. The woman is a genius and way too fucking practical, which makes her forget about the emotional side of things.

"Isabella." Locking eyes with Dr. West, I ask again, "How is she?"

"The surgery went well. We removed a bullet. It entered through her chest but luckily missed her lungs and settled above her diaphragm. She also has a recent bullet wound to her left shoulder. A hack-job was done removing that bullet, so I cleaned the wound and stitched it up. Her left forearm has a small hairline fracture, and she has a head injury. Other than that, she's okay. Dr. Oberio will keep a close eye on her during the next twenty-four hours."

"So she'll be okay?" I ask to make sure.

"Isabella should make a full recovery."

Nodding, I let out a breath of relief. "Thank you."

"Can I go?" Dr. West asks.

"Sure."

She hesitates, then says, "I trust things are now settled between us?"

I nod. "Of course."

Dr. West turns her attention to Tristan, but then I think to ask, "Can I see Isabella?"

"Yes," she replies, gesturing to the doors.

Leaving Dr. West with Tristan, I quickly walk down the length of the hallway and push through the double doors. Dr. Oberio glances up from where he's making notes at a small nurse's station. There's only one nurse on duty.

There are only three rooms, all with glass partitionings, situated around the nurse's station. The underground hospital serves the purpose if one of us needs medical attention.

"Mr. Koslov," he says, a smile forming around his lips, and then he gestures to a room. "She's in there."

When I step inside the room, my eyes instantly fall on Isabella, where she's lying on a bed, hooked up to various machines. The beeping is incessant, and it has me asking, "Is she okay?"

"She will be. Obviously, she needs some time to heal," Dr. Oberio replies. "What name can I put on the form?"

"Just put down Koslov," I instruct, so there's no trace of Isabella being here.

I gesture to the machines. "It doesn't sound like she's okay."

"It's for us to monitor the patient's vitals. Normal procedure."

I fucking hate the noise but try to ignore it as I step closer to the bed. My gaze locks on Isabella's way too pale face, and the weird sensation shudders through me again.

Christ, this shouldn't have happened.

'She also has a recent bullet wound to her left shoulder. A hack-job was done removing that bullet...'

Isabella probably got shot last night, and knowing that she still jumped for the fucking helicopter.

Shaking my head, I reach for her hand. As my fingers close around hers, there's a sliver of relief when I feel her skin is warm.

"You're too brave for your own fucking good, little one," I whisper.

Dr. Oberio pushes a chair closer. "Sit, Mr. Koslov."

As I take a seat, I ask, "Do you know when she'll wake up?"

"We're expecting her to regain consciousness in the next couple of hours."

Nodding, I turn my gaze back to Isabella's face, and then I just stare at her. This is the longest I've been able to look at her, and I take in her beautiful Latino features. Her high cheekbones give her a regal look.

A fucking goddess.

I brush my thumb over the back of her hand, her skin silky soft.

My heart constricts, and I shake my head, but then I still, inspecting my emotions. I'm obviously attracted to Isabella and fuck, her strength demands my admiration.

My gaze drifts over her face again.

You're strong enough to survive at my side, but how the fuck do I capture someone as wild as you?

I let out a soft chuckle thinking she's probably going to lose her shit the moment she wakes up, and then drag her ass out of the hospital. She's stubborn enough to do it.

Movement grabs my attention, and my eyes dart to the doorway as Demitri comes in. "How's she holding up?"

"Okay."

"Come on. I'm here to take you home so you can shower, eat, and sleep. It's not negotiable."

I'm tired as fuck and in no mood to argue with Demitri. Letting out a sigh, I look at Isabella again before getting up. I follow Demitri out of the room, then stop by the nurse's station. "Call me if there's any change."

"Yes, Mr. Koslov," the nurse replies.

I couldn't sleep. After showering and changing into clean clothes, I grabbed something to eat and then came straight back to the hospital.

It's unsettling.

Fucking unsettling.

Demitri's sitting near the door typing a message on his phone. He's probably chatting with Ariana. I'd tell him to go home if only he'd listen.

Turning my attention back to Isabella, I stare down at her, wondering when she got under my skin.

And what the fuck does it mean?

Do I want this woman?

To fuck, yes. I'm always game for that.

But to keep?

Frowning, I let out a sigh as I take a seat in the chair next to the bed. Just then, a soft sound escapes Isabella, and her features tighten as if she's in pain. I dart back up, and placing a hand on the pillow next to her head, I lean over her.

"Isabella?"

She lets out another soft groan, and then her eyelashes flutter. When she opens her eyes, I glance at Demitri, "Get, Dr. Oberio."

When I look down at Isabella again, our eyes lock, and then a frown forms on her forehead.

"Welcome back," I say, the corner of my mouth lifting. "You're made of some tough shit, little princess."

Her lips part and she lets out an incoherent sound.

"How do you feel?" I ask.

Isabella keeps staring at me, the frown deepening on her forehead. "Who… are you?"

Everything stills inside me for a shocking moment. "Alexei… Koslov."

Her eyes widen. "What?… How?" She glances around the room, then asks, "Am I still… at St. Monarch's? What… happened?"

Just then, Dr. Oberio comes rushing into the room, and seeing Isabella's awake, he smiles at her as he starts to check her vitals. "How's our patient doing?"

"Confused," she mumbles, a guarded expression settling on her features.

Moving back, I frown because something's not right. "Isabella," I say to get her attention. Once she looks at me, I ask, "What's the last thing you remember?"

"Ahh…" Her tongue darts out to wet her lips, and her eyes drift closed as she tries to focus. "I think… I'm at St. Monarch's to train." She opens her eyes again then says, "Oh wait. There was an auction."

I let out a relieved breath, but then Isabella continues, "My mother bid on Hugo… Damien was bought by Mr. Hemsley. I remember the shooting. Chaos… Wait…"

She focuses harder and shakes her head. "The last I remember was hearing Winter killed Blanco." Isabella frowns at me. "You were involved." Then, shaking her head, she asks, "Why are you here?"

Holy fuck.

My gaze snaps to the doctor, and I bite the words out, "That happened four years ago. What the fuck is wrong with her?"

Isabella flinches as if she's in pain, and it has me asking, "Where does it hurt?"

"My head," she murmurs. She lifts her right hand only to drop it down on the bed again as if she has zero energy to move.

"The memory loss could be from the knock she took to her head. But, in most cases, the memory returns in a couple of hours." Dr. Onterio gestures to the door. "Can you give us some privacy so we can perform all the necessary checks, Mr. Koslov?"

Looking down at Isabella again, I say, "I'll be right outside, okay?"

She hesitates, then asks, "Did you try to assassinate me?"

I shake my head. "No, I'm on your side."

Relief washes over her features, and then she nods at me.

Leaving the room, worry gnaws at my insides as Demitri follows me to the waiting room. I stand and process what just happened, and then I turn to face my friend. "Isabella doesn't remember the past four years."

"It might be from the fall. Her memory can return at any moment."

"What if it doesn't?" I ask, my mind switching over to a higher gear, forming one plan after the other. "Or what if it takes a couple of weeks or months?"

He narrows his eyes. "What are you thinking?"

"This might be the perfect opportunity to bring Isabella over to our side."

"How?"

I think for a moment, then lock eyes with Demitri. "I could tell her we're engaged to be married. I can fucking tell her anything. Tell her Sonia tried to kill her because of her relationship with me, and get Isabella to trust me that way."

Demitri shakes his head. "You're seriously thinking of going through with a marriage to align Isabella with us?"

The corner of my mouth lifts, and I let out a burst of soundless laughter. "Like it would be a sacrifice on my part. Any man would be lucky to have a woman like Isabella."

"You're not just *any* man, Alexei," Demitri says, looking uneasy. "Isabella might not take after Sonia, but she's still the fucking Princess of Terror. If you somehow get her to marry you and her memory returns, she's going to fucking kill you."

I shake my head. "Not if I can make her love me."

He lets out a bark of incredulous laughter. "You have no history with her. If she does fall for you, she'll be falling for whatever lies you tell her. Isabella just has amnesia, she's not fucking stupid."

A slow smile spreads over my face. "Isabella was the party crasher at Ariana's party that I hooked up with. The attraction was there once."

"Okay," Demitri lets out a sigh. "Let's say she falls for you, and you marry her. What the fuck are you going to do when her memory returns?"

I shrug. "I'll let her take a swing at me, and then we can have angry sex."

Demitri shakes his head, glancing up at the ceiling as if he's saying a silent prayer, then his eyes settle hard on me. "And if she tries to kill you, what do you expect me to do? Just stand by and let her have her way?"

Taking a couple of steps closer to Demitri, I place my hand on his shoulder. "You worry too much. I'll deal with it when and if her memory returns. This might be the only chance I have to get my hands on Isabella, and it will be the biggest fuck you to Sonia."

Letting out another sigh, Demitri shakes his head. "You're making me old before my time."

Letting out a chuckle, I smile at my friend. "I keep your life interesting, you ungrateful fucker."

Chapter 12

ALEXEI

Staring at Isabella as she sleeps, the plan to tell her we're engaged keeps growing, taking root in my mind.

Dr. Oberio said the amnesia could be temporary or permanent. There's no way of telling how things will play out in Isabella's case, as the mind is a mysterious thing.

I'm going to fucking do it.

If her memory returns before I've managed to make her fall for me, I'll let her go. Maybe fate will be on my side, and it will only return after the wedding. After I've managed to form a solid bond with her.

Before that, there will be no way on god's green earth I'll be able to keep her. Isabella's too wild, and I refuse to break her. I'm not even sure if that's a possibility with the will of steel she has.

She begins to stir, and it has me leaning forward and taking hold of her hand. I brush my thumb over her soft skin and wait until her eyes open and focus on me.

Smiling at her, I inject tenderness into my voice as I ask, "How do you feel?"

"Ahh... alive." She swallows hard, and I quickly reach for a glass of water. Slipping my left hand beneath her head, I help her so she can take a sip, and then she murmurs, "Thanks."

Instead of moving back, I pull my fingers through the strands of her hair, and it has her asking, "Are we close?"

Locking eyes with Isabella, the lie spills effortlessly over my lips. "Yes. We're engaged."

Her eyebrows shoot up. "We are? When did that happen?"

"After I helped Winter, I stopped by the academy, and we just hit things off."

She blinks at me, then a frown settles on her forehead. "And how does my mother feel about that?"

Letting out a chuckle, I shake my head. "She wasn't happy." *Here goes nothing.* "She attacked us, and that's why you got hurt." *It's not that much of a stretch.* Meaning my next words, I say, "I'm sorry I wasn't able to protect you. I wasn't expecting things to turn out the way they did."

Isabella stares long and hard at me, then she asks, "So we just hit it off, and what… we're in love?"

Nodding, I soften my expression, hoping it looks similar to me being in love. I've never loved a woman, so fuck knows what that looks like. "It was love at first sight."

The suspicion doesn't leave Isabella's eyes as she watches me. "Then I should feel something if you hug me... right?"

I fucking hope so.

Sitting down on the side of the bed, I place my hands on the pillow on either side of Isabella's head. Leaning down until we're face to face, I lock eyes with her. "You're the most amazing woman I know, Isabella. A fucking goddess. Not only did I fall for you, but I admire you."

Her lips part as her eyes jump over my face, then she starts to look uncomfortable and mutters, "Fine, I feel it. Give me some space."

Smiling, I press a kiss to her forehead, and then I move back to the chair.

"Ah... so I lost four years?"

"Yes. You're twenty-five now."

"How long did we date before we got engaged?"

Fuck. I didn't think that part through.

"Three years," I answer, just winging it. "We've been engaged a year and would've gotten married in a month."

Not bad, Alexei.

"Did I complete my training at St. Monarch's?" she fires off another question.

"You didn't train in sex slavery and drug dealing." And that is why information is so damn expensive in my world. "You trained as a custodian, and you were just as good as Demitri."

Surprise flickers in her eyes. "Really?"

"Yes, since you finished your training, we've been working against your mother to free the slaves."

Isabella tries to sit up, and I quickly reach for her shoulders, pulling her toward me so I can adjust the pillows behind her before leaning her back against them. "I've been freeing slaves… with you?"

I sit down on the side of the bed. "Yes. It's something you're very passionate about."

Isabella stares down at the covers over her legs, and I can see she's trying hard to remember.

Bringing a hand up to her face, I tuck some of her black hair behind her ear, and then I palm her cheek. "Your memories will come back. Don't push too hard right now."

Lifting her eyes to mine, it feels as if she's searching for something on my face, and then she asks, "Do you love me?"

Ahh… what the hell, let's just go with it.

"Very much. You have no idea how important you are to me."

No idea at all.

"So, do we live together?" she asks another question.

I nod. "In LA."

I'll have to make space for her in my room and fill half the walk-in closet with clothes. Fuck, I have a lot to do before she's allowed to leave the hospital.

Isabella nods, and a slight frown line forms between her eyebrows. Her gaze darts around the room before settling on mine. "I don't think I can get married in a month. I know… we share a history, but… I need time to get to know you again."

"I can be patient." *Now that's the biggest lie I've told her. I'm as impatient as fuck.* The corner of my mouth lifts as I say, "I don't want you to worry about anything and to just take it easy so you can heal."

Her eyes search mine again as if she's weighing every word I say, then she murmurs, "Thank you." There's a moment's silence before she admits, "All I know of you is that you're the best assassin."

Moving back to the chair, I get comfortable. "I'm now the head of the bratva."

Isabella lets out a chuckle. "Ooh, I bet that pissed off my mother."

"A fuck ton."

The smile on Isabella's face draws my attention to her mouth, and then I say, "When you smile like that, it makes me want to kiss you."

Her left eyebrow lifts slightly. "Are you warning me or asking permission?"

"Oh, baby," I chuckle darkly. "I'm warning you." Pushing up from the chair again, I frame her face with both my hands and press a kiss to her mouth. Everything fucking stills inside me the same way it did when I fucked her at the party. Then, a weird mixture of instinct and need takes over, and my lips begin to move against hers.

I can honestly say I can't remember when I last kissed a woman. Fucked, yes. But kiss… I come up blank.

My heart actually skips a fucking beat at the intensity I'm hit with, and then I yank away from Isabella. Getting up from the bed, I wipe the pad off my thumb over my bottom lip as I stare down at her. "I should go home and… pack a hospital bag for you. Get some sleep while I'm gone."

Isabella clears her throat. "Remember a toothbrush."

Nodding, I head out of the room while it feels as if I've just been fucking tasered in the heart.

ISABELLA

God, nothing makes sense. Besides feeling like I've been hit by a bus, everything's foreign.

I keep trying to remember, forcing myself until it feels as if I have a second heartbeat pounding away against my skull.

But the last thing I remember clearly is wanting to talk to Madame Keller about switching my training. I didn't want my mother to know, and it all adds up with what Alexei told me earlier.

When he stared into my eyes and told me what he thought of me, and when he kissed me, I felt a strong attraction toward him. I can see why I fell for him even though I can't say that I love him. Maybe the emotions will come back?

I'm engaged to Alexei Koslov.

"I'm engaged to Alexei Koslov," I say the words out loud, but it sounds more like a question than a fact.

"I trained as a custodian, and I'm as good as Demitri." This time I feel the words settle in my heart.

Everything else Alexei said makes sense. I'm not surprised my mother almost killed me because there was never any love between us, and I planned to overthrow her.

Also, I respect Winter and everything she stands for. Last I heard, she married Damien Vetrov, so I can see how I'd be open to getting to know Alexei, seeing as they are practically family.

My thoughts turn back to when he kissed me, and I focus on how I felt. It was like a rush… an adrenaline shot to my heart.

Letting out a sigh, I close my eyes and try to relax, but I feel too wound up.

God, it's like my mind is filled with blank spots. I know they're there, but I can't figure out what's missing. It feels like I've forgotten something or someone very important. As if it's on the tip of my tongue, but I just can't… I let out a frustrated growl, pushing my hands into my hair and gripping fistfuls.

Maybe it's Alexei? Maybe this feeling is the love I felt for him?

I keep my eyes closed, the bright lights of the hospital room making my migraine worse.

"You okay?" Alexei suddenly asks, and my eyes snap open. I didn't even hear him come into the room.

"Bad headache," I answer as I watch him set down a bag on the chair by the door.

Alexei glances to where the nursing station is, and then he orders, "Give her something for pain."

"Yes, Mr. Koslov," the nurse quickly answers, and a moment later, she comes rushing into the room.

After she injects something into my IV, Alexei murmurs, "Thank you." He comes to stand next to the bed, and once the nurse leaves, he leans over me, pressing a kiss to my forehead. "Hopefully, you'll feel better soon."

My eyes dart over his face as he pulls back, and once again, I try to imagine us a couple.

God, it feels so foreign.

Shouldn't I have some sense that I loved this man enough to marry him?

Alexei's dark brown eyes lock on mine, and I instantly feel the intensity and power coming from him. He's attractive, his features strong and mercilessly cut from granite. The blondish-white hair gives him an edgy vibe.

He is my type.

I focus on my feelings and notice I don't feel any fear, which means I subconsciously feel safe with him.

Alexei tilts his head. "What are you thinking?"

"I'm trying to make sense of everything." Shaking my head, I let out a frustrated sigh. "Everything's confusing. I hate it."

His mouth lifts into a sexy grin. "You have this thing of always being in control. So it's normal that you'll feel out of your depth right now." He takes hold of my hand, his fingers feeling strong around mine. "Until you're back to your old self, I'll take care of everything. Try to think of it as a vacation. You deserve it after working your ass off and nearly dying."

"How long will I stay in the hospital?" I ask, needing to know how much time I have to prepare myself before going home with Alexei.

"Dr. Oberio said another three days."

Slowly, I nod, then I ask, "What's… our home like?"

Alexei takes a seat on the chair next to the bed, making the damn thing look like a throne. "Right now, Demitri and Ariana live with us at the mansion. We're actually going to build another house on the property where Demitri and Ariana can move to so we'll have more privacy." He takes a breath, then explains, "We met Ariana last year. Her father was the former head of the bratva. I took over from him after he passed away, and because we had to protect Ariana, she and Demitri hit it off."

"What's my relationship like with her?" I ask, actually relieved to hear it won't just be Alexei and me.

"You're friends," he answers, then he adds, "I've told Ariana what happened and that you don't remember her. Don't worry. We'll take things slow when you're home."

Nodding, I murmur, "Thank you." I glance down at our hands, and as Alexei brushes his thumb over my skin, it doesn't feel uncomfortable. Instead, it actually feels good, causing something to hum to life deep inside of me.

My gaze moves to my left hand, and then I frown. "If we're engaged, where's the ring?"

"You sent it in to be cleaned. I'll pick it up once it's ready," Alexei immediately answers.

Feeling a little uncomfortable, I ask, "Do you mind holding onto it for a while… just until I'm ready?"

He gives me a comforting smile. "Of course."

I stare at Alexei, and somehow I know I'm safe with him, and it's what I need most while I recover – just a place where I'm safe until my memory returns and I can figure out what's next.

Chapter 13

ALEXEI

I've called a family meeting so we can all get our stories straight for when I bring Isabella home.

So far, everything is playing right into the palm of my hand, and I'll be fucking pissed if anything ruins it.

My eyes go over Demitri and Ariana. Then I look at Nikhil and Sacha, the two men who mainly protect the women whenever Demitri and I have to take care of a job. Lastly, I glance at Tristan and Hana.

These are the six people besides me who'll have direct contact with Isabella.

All eyes are on me as I say, "My plan is not negotiable. If anyone lets anything slip to Isabella, there will be hell to pay." There's no argument from the people I consider my family. "Isabella's not stupid. Don't underestimate her just because she has amnesia. She's well trained and dangerous. If her memory returns, do not engage with her." I focus on

Nikhil and Sacha. "You won't stand a chance against her. Just let her go." They both nod in agreement.

Turning my attention to Ariana, I say, "I've told her the two of you are friends. I don't expect you to go out of your way for her, but try to make her feel at home."

"But will I be safe being alone with her?" Ariana asks.

"Isabella won't hurt you unless you're a danger to her. She's similar to me in a lot of ways."

Ariana rolls her eyes. "I don't think I can handle two of you. You're difficult enough."

I let out a chuckle. "I'm sure you'll get along with Isabella."

"So, what's the story?" Demitri asks.

"I told her we met at St. Monarch's while she was training as a custodian. I stayed as close as possible to the truth. The only thing I changed is that we dated for three years, we've been engaged for one year, and we were going to get married in a month. I also told her she got hurt during an attack from Sonia."

"Sounds easy enough to remember," Tristan says.

Which reminds me of Hana. I turn my attention to her. "I'll tell her you're an acquaintance."

"I'll just wing it," Hana chuckles.

"Isabella is high value, and this is my one chance to get her. Don't fuck it up for me," I warn them all.

Everyone nods, then Demitri says, "If this is what you want, we'll make it happen. Hopefully, her memory doesn't return before you're married."

Ariana frowns at me. "Taking advantage of a woman who has amnesia doesn't sit well with me."

I lock eyes with Ariana, and she's only able to hold my gaze for a moment before she glances at Demitri.

"I'm taking advantage of the situation, not of Isabella," I bite the words out. "Don't confuse the two. Isabella will still have her free will. I'm not going to fucking lock her in my bedroom."

Ariana takes a deep breath and lets it out slowly. "Fine."

Rising to my feet, I say, "I don't care what any of you think. I will have Isabella. Don't get in my way of making that happen."

Tristan lets out a chuckle to alleviate the tension in the air. "We all owe you, so we have your back."

"Now I need to go shopping for Isabella." I look at Ariana again. "If you're not too pissed off with me, would you mind coming along?"

"Of course, I don't mind," she replies as she gets up.

"Let's get back to work," I say.

While Nikhil and Sacha leave, Tristan comes to give me a hug before he and Hana head back to Koslov & Hayes to take care of our company.

"Let's make a list of everything Isabella will need so we don't forget anything," Ariana says, and then she pulls her phone out.

Fuck, I'm going to have to find the perfume Isabella wears even if I have to sniff every bottle there is on this goddamned planet.

ISABELLA

With my left arm in a brace, I'm dressed in a black pair of leggings and a t-shirt. Sitting on the side of the bed, my eyes are on Alexei's back, where he's talking to the doctor.

When he turns around and starts to walk toward me, it feels as if I'm being stalked by a predator. But, instead of feeling fear, it causes a fluttering in my stomach.

I climb to my feet, my body still weak. My left side aches, and I'm covered in bruises. Alexei said it's because I fell on that side and took two bullets.

A tender smile curves his mouth, softening his dark features. "Ready?"

"As ready as I'll ever be," I say.

Alexei holds his hand out to me, and I get a feeling he wants to make it feel like this is my choice.

My eyes lift to his. "If I wanted to leave on my own, would you let me?"

He turns and gestures to the door. "The choice is yours."

Just to test him, I walk past him and out of the room. I spare the nurse a glance, murmuring, "Thank you." I feel Alexei behind me as I open a door and walk down a hallway.

"Straight ahead. We use the back entrance," Alexei murmurs, sounding amused by my actions.

When I step out of the building and into the bright sunlight, I instinctively glance around, taking in the buildings, the windows, the rooftops – every single hiding place a sniper can use.

Familiarity shudders through me, making me gasp.

Instantly Alexei's by my side, looking at me with concern. "You okay?"

I lift my hand to my racing heart and press my fingers to my chest. "I just felt something familiar."

"What?" The worry etches deeper onto his face.

"The first thing I did was check my surroundings as if it's second nature."

Relief washes over his features. He must be glad that I recall something.

"It should be second nature with the lives we lead," he says, then he gestures to a black SUV. "So, what's your choice? Coming with me or taking a chance on your own?"

I let out a chuckle. "Of course I'm going with you. I don't plan on sleeping on the street tonight."

A wide smile spreads over his face, and then he walks to the SUV, opening the passenger door for me.

It's only as I climb into the vehicle that I think to ask, "Where's Demitri? I thought you were always together."

"He's impatiently waiting at home," Alexei answers before shutting my door and walking around the front of the SUV. When he slides behind the steering wheel and starts the engine, he says, "Do you want to move some of your things into one of the guest rooms when we get home?"

Oh shit. Right. I probably share a room with him.

When I don't answer immediately, Alexei gives me a comforting smile. "You don't have to decide now. See how you feel later. Okay?"

I nod, and then Alexei hands me a phone. "Your old one got crushed in the fall, so I got you a new one."

"Oh… thanks." I stare at the device for a moment and then glance out of the windows, taking in our surroundings as Alexei drives us home.

Home.

Still feels weird.

When we come to a stop in front of an impressive Mediterranean-style mansion, I can't help but admire it. Climbing out of the SUV, I glance around the landscaped garden and then turn to stare at the place I'll call home.

I'm surprised to not see any guards and glance at Alexei, where he's watching my reaction like a hawk. "No guards?"

My question makes him let out a burst of laughter. "We don't need guards."

True. A person would be stupid to try and attack Alexei in his home.

"You'll also meet Nikhil and Sacha today. They work for me and keep Ariana safe whenever Demitri and I have a job."

"Not me?" I ask.

"You don't need a bodyguard, little one," Alexei says, admiration shimmering in his voice. "You can take care of yourself."

I lower my eyes to my left arm that's stuck in a sling.

Alexei comes to stand in front of me, and lifting a hand, he places a finger beneath my chin. He nudges my face up, and when our eyes meet, he says, "Until you're healed, I'm not leaving your side. As soon as you're able to, we'll start training and get you back to your old self."

His words make me feel better, and this time when he holds his hand out to me, I take it. Our fingers interlink, and again something hums deep inside of me.

Climbing the steps, we walk into the mansion, and I glance around the interior of the home I share with the man next to me.

My fiancé.

Taking a deep breath, I look at the expensive art on the walls, the lavish décor, and then my eyes follow the stairs up to the second floor.

"Did I help decorate the place?"

"No." When I turn my gaze to Alexei's, he explains, "We were going to redecorate after the wedding."

Nodding, I begin to walk toward the stairs. "Why? I think it looks great."

Alexei gives my hand a squeeze. "You just wanted to add your own touch."

When we reach the second floor, I glance around us, then ask, "Which way is our room?"

"We're in the right wing. Demitri and Ariana have taken over the left wing."

"Okay," I glance to my left, but not seeing anyone, I follow Alexei down another hallway.

Stepping into a luxurious suite that's decorated in creams and blacks, my eyes go straight to the king-size bed.

Alexei notices what I'm staring at and says, "It's your choice."

Nodding, I glance around the suite. There's a dressing table, and I move closer to it. Reaching for a bottle of perfume, I squirt some into the air to sniff it.

"That's your favorite," Alexei murmurs as he comes up behind me. "Your scent is one of the first things I fell in love with."

I look at the black decanter and read the name, "Fucking Fabulous." A smile tugs at my lips. "I have good taste."

"You do," Alexei agrees.

Setting the perfume down, I begin to walk toward the closet. Stepping inside, my eyes scan over the right side where Alexei's clothes are, and then I look to the left.

There's a stark contrast between the expensive dresses and suits and the black combat wear.

I move closer, and taking hold of a leather jacket, I stare at it. There's a flicker of something familiar, and it has me asking, "What did I wear most?"

"During the day, you were the perfect socialite, and at night you wreaked havoc in black leather."

I let out a soft burst of laughter then glance at Alexei. "Kinda like the sound of that."

Chapter 14

ALEXEI

Fuck, I worked my ass off to get everything ready for Isabella. My eyes are glued to her as she looks through the clothes I got for her.

Seeing her move around in my personal space feels… right.

Because she's the one.

The only woman who can survive being at my side.

My breaths are slow and steady as I assess every facial expression from her.

Isabella glances at me, then she frowns. "Why are you looking at me as if you're about to attack?"

Relaxing my features, I say, "It's just good seeing you here."

She takes a deep breath then walks toward the bed. "Our bedroom." It sounds as if she's tasting the words. Isabella turns to face me. "I'll feel more comfortable using a guest room while I adjust."

Nodding, I begin to walk to the door, saying, "I'll have some of your things moved."

"Ah… no."

I stop and glance over my shoulder at her. She gestures at the dressing table and closet. "Leave everything as is. I'll just sleep in another room until I'm used to the idea of us being a couple."

A grin spreads over my face, liking the sound of that. "I'm putting you in the suite next to mine, so you're close to me."

Isabella follows me next door and glances around the room. "So if I scream, you'll come running?"

"Butt naked and armed, but I'll come," I joke, and it makes laughter burst from her. Closing the distance between us, I say, "And there you make me want to kiss you again."

Isabella lifts her right hand and places it behind my neck. Her fingers run through my short hair, her eyes locking with mine, and then she lifts onto her toes and presses her mouth to mine.

I let her control the pace even though frustration ripples through me when there's no tongue.

Pulling back, she stares at me. "I wanted to see if I'm comfortable initiating intimacy with you."

"And?" I murmur. "Are you?"

A pensive smile curves her lips. "I'm surprisingly comfortable."

"But?"

"I can't place my finger on it." Stepping away from me, Isabella walks to the expansive windows and stares out over the backyard. "It's just frustrating not remembering any of this. I feel strange."

I move in behind her, and careful not to jar her left arm and shoulder, I wrap my arms around her. I press a kiss to the side of her neck. "Just give it time."

"It's so weird. This feels familiar," Isabella murmurs. "Having you behind me."

I hold her for a couple of minutes as we stare out of the window, wanting her to become used to me touching her. Isabella leans back against me, resting her head on my shoulder.

So far, everything's working out exactly how I hoped it would. Now it's only a matter of time.

I'll make Isabella love me, marry her, and then she'll be mine. Together we'll rule the world.

After making sure Isabella eats something, I close the curtains while she climbs into bed.

I pick up on her frustration of feeling weak and say, "Your strength will return soon."

"I hate this," she mutters.

Walking to the side of the bed, I lean over her and press a kiss on her forehead. "Get some rest, babe. I'll be downstairs."

Isabella stares at me for a moment, then says, "Thank you for understanding… and everything you're doing for me."

"Of course." I smile at her. Placing a hand against her cheek, I murmur, "I'll do anything for you."

Our eyes remain locked as I straighten up, and then she watches me until I shut the door behind me.

I let out a breath, relieved I'm pulling off the act. Not that it's hard because it almost feels natural to show Isabella affection. I'm more worried about her figuring things out.

With a little luck and a lot of skill, that won't happen.

Heading downstairs, I go to the security room where Demitri's checking for any leads on Sonia.

"Anything?" I ask as I take a seat on one of the chairs.

The security system is rigged with state-of-the-art equipment. If Sonia pokes her head from whatever hole she's hiding in, I'll know.

"Yeah," Demitri murmurs, bringing up the underground chat screen where there's a message from our contact in *The Ruin*.

Mole: ST spotted in Ethiopia. No POL received yet. Will be in touch.

"It's something," I murmur. "The moment we get proof of life, let me know."

Demitri slants his eyes in my direction. "I really don't want to go to Ethiopia."

I let out a chuckle. "If she's there, we won't have much of a choice."

Getting to work, I check in with Semion and Lev to make sure things are still running smoothly in Russia. While I have my phone out, I dial the head of the mafia's number, wanting to touch base with my friend.

"Wow, and here I thought you dropped off the face of the planet," Lucian's voice comes over the line.

"You wish. How are things?"

"Good. Very good."

"And Elena and Luca? They're well?" Lucian and Elena named their son after Lucian's father, who was a great man. At least Lucian's following in his father's footsteps, making an empire of the Italian mafia.

"Luca's growing too fast. Also, I'd rather face a gun than one of his tantrums. Aunt Ursula and Elena let him get away with fucking murder."

I let out a burst of laughter. "I'm sure if I asked Elena, she'd say you're the one letting him get away with murder."

"Yeah-yeah. How's business? I heard you had an altercation with Terrero."

"Calling it an altercation is the understatement of the year. I lost ten men that day, and she got away. If you hear anything about her whereabouts, let me know."

"I will," Lucian assures me.

"I just wanted to touch base with you. Send my regards to your family."

"Thanks, it's good to hear your voice again. Next time answer the phone when I call."

"You'd be so lucky," I chuckle before ending the call.

"Everything good in Italy?" Demitri asks.

"Yes, Lucian's well."

Demitri climbs to his feet, making me ask, "Where are you going?"

"Ariana wants me to me prepare dinner to welcome Isabella." As he reaches his door, he adds, "I blame you. If you have nothing urgent to take care of, get your ass to the kitchen."

Shaking my head, I put on a serious face. "I have so much work."

"Sure you do," he mocks me, and as he leaves the room, I hear him add, "Fucker."

Chuckling, I turn my attention to the screens in front of me, and then I begin to search through all the information, hoping to stumble across something related to Sonia.

ISABELLA

After having a nap, I feel a little better.

I go to Alexei's suite where my clothes are, and taking a shower, I glance down at the left side of my body, where it's covered in bruises.

I must've taken one hell of a fall.

When I'm done in the shower, I try to pat my hair dry, using only my right hand, then give up and throw the towel against the wall. Frustrated, I glare at my reflection in the mirror, and then my eyes lower to the two gunshot wounds.

I wish I could remember what happened.

"Isabella?" I hear Alexei call.

"I'll be right out," I answer. With a huff, I grab another towel and pat most of my body dry. I clench my teeth and power through the pain in my left shoulder and arm as I do my best to wrap the fabric around my body.

As soon as I step out of the bathroom, Alexei's eyebrows shoot up, then he says, "It doesn't look like you had a relaxing shower."

"I didn't," I grumble as I start to walk to the closet. "Let me just get dressed while screaming in frustration, and then I'll be with you."

Alexei darts in front of me, and giving me a caring look, he says, "Let me help. You don't have to do this on your own."

"Help me get dressed? You?" I ask incredulously. "Yeah, I'm going to pass on the offer."

Instead of being upset because I'm declining the offer, Alexei grins at me. "You're hot when you're pissed off."

Letting out an annoyed huff, I shove past him and walk into the closet. "I get you've seen me naked a million times, but do you mind giving me some privacy?"

"Of course. Just shout if you need help." When I shoot him a glare, he adds, "Or don't."

I watch as Alexei leaves the room, and then I turn my attention to the rows of clothes. Frustration bubbles over in my chest, and I clench my right hand into a fist, needing to beat the shit out of something.

I hate feeling helpless.

God, I hate it so much.

Grabbing a pair of panties, I bite through the pain of using my left arm and drag them up my legs. I drop the towel and decide a bra isn't worth the amount of pain it will take to struggle through clipping it on.

Reaching for a black t-shirt, I pull it over my head, and then I take a moment to breathe before I carefully push my left arm through the sleeve. By the time I have the shirt on, my shoulder and forearm are on fire.

Closing my eyes, I try to control the anger and frustration swarming inside of me before I get overemotional.

"Alexei," I call out.

The door instantly opens as he comes in. I hear it shut, and a couple of seconds later, I'm pulled into a hug. I rest my cheek against his chest and just focus on my breathing.

"I hate this," I whisper. "I feel… weak."

"I know." Alexei presses a kiss to my wet hair. "But you're not, Isabella. You're a fucking force. Right now, you're just injured. There's a difference."

I nod and then pull back to look up at him. "Can you help me put on my leggings?"

Wagging his eyebrows at me, he grins. "Mhhh… that kind of thing is foreplay to me." His eyes sweep over my body. "I mean, you have killer legs."

"Shut up and help me," I playfully snap at him, appreciating that he's trying to make me feel better.

Alexei turns to my clothes and pulls a pair of leggings from the closet. When he crouches in front of me, I place my right hand on his shoulder to keep my balance as I step into the pants, and then he tugs them up my legs.

Alexei adjusts the hem of my t-shirt then tilts his head as his eyes meet mine. "That wasn't so bad, was it?"

I shake my head then take a deep breath. *I fucking hate this.* "Will you help me dry my hair?"

Alexei drags his bottom lip between his teeth then says, "I like this wet and wild look on you. It's sexy."

Letting out a chuckle, I ask, "Is everything a turn-on for you?"

"When it comes to you, yes."

Our eyes lock for a moment, and anticipation begins to build between us, dimming the anger and frustration I feel.

Alexei has been nothing but good to me the past week. From the moment I opened my eyes, he was there to make everything better.

I probably would've lost my shit by now if he wasn't around to calm me down.

Closing the distance between us, I turn my head and rest my cheek against his chest again. Alexei's arms wrap around me, and it makes me feel safe… as if I belong… as if this is how things were between us.

Lifting my right arm, I place my hand on his back, then I whisper, "I just need a moment."

"Take as long as you need, baby. I get to hold you so you won't hear any complaints from me."

Everything he says is perfect.

Everything he does is perfect.

Too perfect?

"I love you, Isabella," he murmurs, and it sounds like he means it.

Pulling back, I meet his eyes. "Why do you love me?"

A slight frown flits over his forehead before disappearing. "I love you because you're so fucking strong. There's not much you're afraid of. You're a fighter, intelligent, caring, breathtaking. Honestly, there isn't one thing I can say I don't love about you."

I can see he means every word, and it eases the worry that popped up.

"Come on. Let's dry your hair. Demitri made dinner to welcome you back home."

I follow Alexei to the dressing table and take a seat on the stool. My eyes track his movements as he pulls the hairdryer out of a drawer, and when he begins to dry my hair, it feels as if he's done it before.

I relax and use the time to watch Alexei, memorizing his movements as his fingers comb through my hair… and every inch of his face.

I can see why I fell for him. I don't think it will take much for me to fall for him again.

The longer I stare at him, the more familiar he becomes, and by the time he's done drying my hair and looking down at me with pride, I feel warmth spreading through my heart.

Chapter 15

ALEXEI

As we walk down to the dining room, I'm thinking I need to ease up on the sugar and add some spice.

At some point, I'm going to have to pick a fight with Isabella. I could fucking feel the suspicion coming off her in waves and just blurted out I love her.

I think I defused the situation. I fucking hope so.

Walking into the dining room, I gesture at the seat to my left instead of pulling out the chair for Isabella. As I sit down, Ariana comes in with two plates of food, and Isabella pauses.

Every muscle in my body tenses as the two women stare at each other. Then a wide smile splits over Ariana's face, and she comes to set the plates down where she and Demitri will be sitting.

"I'm so glad you're back." She begins to move in on Isabella, then asks, "Is it okay if I give you a hug?"

Isabella's eyes dart to me and seeing that she's uncomfortable, I jump in. "Maybe hold off on the hugs until Isabella's had time to settle in."

"Everything just feels weird," Isabella explains. "You're Ariana?"

"Yes. If you need anything, just let me know."

"Thank you." Just as Isabella sits down, Demitri comes in with two plates of food, and it has Isabella saying, "This wasn't necessary."

"Demitri's practically a chef," Ariana boasts.

Demitri places a plate in front of me, and leaning over the table, he sets the other one down in front of Isabella.

I glance at the pasta. "Looks good."

"You better eat everything," Demitri mutters.

"Yes, Daddy," I taunt him, making Ariana chuckle. I look at Isabella and notice a smile is tugging at her mouth.

For a moment, silence falls around the table as we all dig in.

After swallowing a bite, I ask Demitri, "Did you tell Ariana about the house we're going to have built for the two of you?"

"A house? Where? Why?" Ariana rambles the questions off.

"Slipped my mind," Demitri says, and then he smiles at his fiancée. "On this property. It's just so we'll all have more privacy, but I'm still close to Alexei if something happens."

"Yes!" Ariana exclaims, then she smiles at me. "Not that I don't like living in this house."

"Just want to see you happy, little one," I say, affection lacing my words.

"I want a room just for my makeup," Ariana demands.

"Only fair, seeing as I'll have one for weapons," Demitri replies before taking a bite of the pasta.

"You like makeup?" Isabella suddenly asks.

"I used to be a makeup artist. It's now more of a hobby since I started the charity," Ariana explains.

"Charity?"

Demitri and I continue to eat while the women talk.

"I'm more like a benefactor for the elderly who don't have anyone. Especially those with medical conditions," Ariana says. "My mother has Alzheimer's, so the project's close to my heart."

Isabella's features soften. "I'm sorry to hear that, but I think it's amazing that you want to help… others." A frown forms on Isabella's forehead, and she stares at the table.

When her eyes narrow, my heart kicks up a gear. "You okay?"

Slowly, she shakes her head, focusing way too fucking hard on something.

Fuck.

"Isabella?" I ask, leaning a little forward.

"It's weird. It feels as if it's on the tip of my tongue," she murmurs, deep in thought. "It's right there."

Reaching a hand out to her, I place mine on the back of hers. "It's probably the thing about helping others. It's something you and Ariana have in common. Where she helps the elderly, you help slaves."

"They're not slaves," she says, strength brimming in the words.

"The innocent," I correct myself.

Again the frown on her face deepens. "It feels like déjà vu."

A feeling that Isabella's memory might return sooner than I'd like has me thinking I'll need to speed things along. Somehow. Fuck.

Suddenly Isabella smiles. "Don't mind me. Crazy talk."

"Don't say that." Ariana gives Isabella a comforting smile. "It must be hard. We're here to help you through this."

The moment passes, and we resume eating.

When I'm done, I get up and walk to the side table. "Want something to drink, Isabella? It might help you relax."

"Sure."

I pour three tumblers of vodka and carry them back to the table.

Isabella glances at Ariana. "You don't drink?"

"Not that poison. I'm okay with a glass of wine once in a while."

Isabella picks up the tumbler. "Vodka?"

"The best." Holding up my glass, I say, "*Na zdoróv'je.*" I lock eyes with Isabella. "To your health."

I take a much-needed sip and then relax back in my chair.

As I enjoy the drink, I start thinking about speeding things up without making Isabella uncomfortable or suspicious. It feels like I'm stuck in a catch twenty-two, and I fucking hate it.

When Isabella glances at me, I smile at her. "You okay?"

She nods. "The first day wasn't as bad as I thought it would be. I expected a lot more awkwardness."

"That's good to hear. I want you to feel at home."

Demitri finishes his drink then gets up. "I'm going to check the security."

Once he leaves the room, Isabella asks, "Is Dimitri always so quiet?"

"Depends. Whenever I piss him off, he doesn't shut up," I joke.

"Which you do a lot," Ariana sasses me.

"I keep him on his toes."

Ariana chuckles, shaking her head at me.

ISABELLA

It's been a week since I got home, and I'm starting to feel more settled. Things don't feel as foreign anymore.

The pain is also more manageable with all my wounds healing.

But I'm bored.

Ariana tries to include me in many things, but they don't scratch the itch that's formed. It feels as if it's creeping beneath my skin, needing to burst into action.

I'm sitting outside, ready to bang my forehead against the table when Alexei comes out of the house. "Come with me."

Getting up, I ask, "Where?"

"You'll see."

When Alexei holds his hand out to me, I place mine in his and walk back into the house with him. We head down a set of stairs, and then I'm led into one hell of an impressive room.

I've explored most of the house, but I haven't been down here yet.

Glancing around the armory, I pull my hand free from Alexei's and move closer to the cabinets lining the walls. "You're well-stocked."

"I like to be prepared," he chuckles.

"For a war?" I tease him.

"Amongst other things." Alexei comes to open a cabinet and removes two Heckler & Kochs. He checks the clips then hands me one. Nodding to the other end of the room, he says, "Want to shoot some targets with me?"

"God, I love it when you talk dirty to me."

Alexei takes a step closer to me. "Hmm… wait until you see how I handle my gun."

My voice comes out low and sensual. "You better be good at it."

Just as my heart begins to speed up, Alexei moves away from me and walks toward the shooting range. "Best shot wins."

"Wins what?"

"What are you willing to bet?" he asks, giving me a mischievous look.

I think for a moment, and as we reach the shooting range, I say, "If you win, I'll move back into the bedroom."

Alexei raises an eyebrow at me. "There's no fucking way I'm losing now."

"But..." I go stand in one of the cubicles, "if I win, I can start training without you telling me it's too soon."

"Fair enough."

I watch as Alexei raises the gun, and then he begins to fire at the target. For a moment, I can only stare because it's freaking hot watching him handle a weapon. Then I glance at the target, and my eyebrow lifts.

Shit.

He's good.

Obviously, he's good. He's a trained assassin.

Every bullet hits the head of the target.

Taking a deep breath, I turn my attention to my own target, and raising my arm, I take aim. When I pull the trigger, there's a rush of exhilaration in my veins, and then I just keep firing shots until my clip runs out.

God, that felt amazing.

Letting out a satisfied breath, I glance at Alexei. He's smiling at me.

"Was that as good for you as it was for me?" I ask, my words brimming with double meaning.

"I think you got a little more pleasure out of it than me," he smirks.

Then we check the targets, and it has Alexei giving me a wolfish grin. "I guess you're moving back, babe."

"Best out of three," I begin to negotiate, not because I'm against sharing a bed with him, but because I'm really enjoying this.

Alexei pretends to think about it, then he says, "We can do best out of three, but I want payment for changing the rules."

"What kind of payment are we talking about?" I ask as I set the gun down on the counter.

"Nothing big." Alexei also places his gun on the counter then closes in on me. Lifting a hand to my jaw, his thumb brushes over my bottom lip. "Just a kiss."

Locking eyes with him, I murmur, "Deal."

Alexei's hand moves behind my neck, and I only have a second to suck in a breath before his mouth comes down on mine.

It's quickly clear he didn't mean a peck when his tongue drives into my mouth and his other hand grabs hold of my hair, tugging my head back to give him better access to me.

A rush of adrenaline hits me, and then I kiss him back, our tongues starting to war for control. It quickly turns hungry and downright erotic as Alexei's mouth devours mine, his teeth tugging until it's bordering on forceful.

So good.

God.

So good.

It feels as if I'm being drugged until all my focus is on Alexei. His power calls to the strength in me, the strength I haven't felt since I woke up in the hospital. And for a blissful moment, it reminds me of who I am. How Alexei sees me.

My body melts against his, and I move my right hand up to his jaw, my fingers drinking in the feel of the dark stubble dusting his skin.

Alexei breaks away from my mouth and presses hungry kisses over my jaw and down my neck, whispering, "Fuck." His teeth nip at my skin. "Fuck." And then he yanks away from me, hissing, "Fuck."

Our eyes lock as my breaths rush from me, my body still tingling from the shot of adrenaline that's Alexei.

He stands still, the predatory expression on his face telling me the last thing he wants to do right now is stop.

For a moment, I actually contemplate taking it further, but then I catch myself, and I clear my throat. "Price paid. Time to shoot."

"I'm going to fucking lose this round," he mutters as he walks to the other side of the room to get more clips for us.

Somehow I doubt that.

Chapter 16

ALEXEI

I've been wound tight since the kiss. I pride myself on always having control over everything. But as soon as it comes to Isabella, the intensity overrides any hope of me keeping control of the situation.

It's as if a primal instinct takes over, and all I want to do is claim everything she has to offer until I own her.

I'm standing in my bedroom, and with my hands in the pockets of my pants, I stare blankly over the backyard while trying to figure out how I feel.

I fucking want Isabella Terrero. Not only because she'll be a valuable ally, but because I'm falling for her.

I'm fucking falling.

I've teased my friends and brother when they fell in love. I helped them get the girl. I've watched them build lives with the women they love.

But not for a second did I think there's a woman out there who will make me want my own happily ever after.

I let out a burst of cynical laughter.

Fuck, how the mighty fall.

Isabella Terrero. The fucking daughter of my enemy. I did not see that coming.

My eyes narrow at the thought that her memory can return at any moment. I have no fucking idea what I'll do if that happens.

I'm not sure how Isabella will react. After all, we could've left her to die in Columbia. Hopefully, that counts for something. Also, I've gone above and beyond to make her feel at home.

Maybe she won't freak out.

Maybe luck will be on my side for a little while longer.

I hear the door open behind me and slowly glance over my shoulder. Isabella comes in and shuts the door before walking toward me.

I turn my gaze back to the view outside the window as she comes to stand beside me. Silence weaves around us as I wonder what the future holds for us. I've always been able to plan ahead, but that seems to be a thing of the past.

"I want to start training," she murmurs softly.

"Okay." Turning my face, I glance down at her. "Just take it slow."

She nods, lifting her eyes to mine, and then we stare at each other.

After a moment, Isabella asks, "Who are you, Alexei? What makes you tick?"

I turn my gaze back to the view, thinking how to answer her. "I'm a conqueror." I take a slow breath, then exhale.

"It's all about the power. I'm addicted to it." Turning to face Isabella, I stare deep into her eyes. "You're the first woman to make me tick. You're such a fucking challenge, and I love it."

A soft smile forms around Isabella's mouth. "I just need a little more time."

Time.

Nodding, I lift my left arm and wrap it around her shoulders, pulling her against my side. "As long as you fall in love with me." I make it sound like a joke even though I'm dead serious.

Isabella glances up at me. "That's the easy part… but it's only been two weeks… in my mind. I can't just get engaged and marry you based on what I've been told. I'm sorry we have to start over. I know it must be frustrating for you."

Lowering my arm from her shoulders, I turn to face her. “Setting love aside, would you consider a marriage to form an alliance?”

Isabella’s left eyebrow lifts. “With the world we’re born into, I always knew my mother would try and force the issue at some point. Not that I had any intention of just marrying whoever she tried to pawn off on me.” Isabella shakes her head. “I’m not a slave.”

It was worth a try.

“But I’m willing to consider it,” she says, surprising me. “After all, it will still be my choice and not my mother’s.”

The corner of my mouth lifts. “Marrying me would be the biggest fuck you to your mother. Keep that in mind.”

And making the announcement of our engagement public might be just the thing to draw Sonia out of her hiding place.

Isabella lets out a chuckle and walks toward the bathroom. “You make it sound very tempting.”

Hopefully, tempting enough for her to agree.

“I’m going to get ready for bed,” she adds before disappearing into the bathroom.

My eyes drift to the bed, and knowing sex isn't on the table, I'm mentally preparing myself for one hell of a long night.

Letting out a sigh, I walk to the closet and moving my suits out of the way, the biometric scanner verifies me before the vault opens.

Taking the engagement ring I got earlier today from my pocket, I place it in the vault before shutting the door, not sure whether I'll ever get to put the ring on Isabella's finger.

ISABELLA

It feels strangely intimate hearing Alexei take a shower as I slip beneath the covers.

But not awkward.

There's even anticipation growing in my chest. Gathering my hair, I pull it over my right shoulder, and then I lie down.

I can smell Alexei on the covers, and turning my head, I look at the right side of the bed where he'll sleep. The bathroom door opens, and my eyes flick to where Alexei comes out wearing only a pair of black sweatpants, steam billowing behind him.

My gaze drifts over his chest and abs, and the hot V leading to the low-hanging waistband.

God, I have good taste.

He stops next to the bed, and tilting his head, he stares at me. "You look good in my bed."

Things have been great between us, and the sexual tension is off the charts, but I'm still healing, so there will be no sex.

"Don't get any ideas," I warn him.

Alexei grins as he shakes his head. Switching off the light, he comes to throw the covers back and then lies down.

"You stay on your side, and I'll stay on mine," I say.

"Fuck that shit," he grumbles. "I'm already forgoing sex." Alexei reaches for me, and then I'm tugged over to his side until my body's pressed against his.

My left hand lands on his chest, and I feel the heat from his body seeping into mine. I can't keep a smile from playing around my lips as I rest my head against his shoulder.

We lie in silence, and I take a deep breath of Alexei's scent.

I love it.

I relax and close my eyes, focusing on how it feels to lie next to him. With things not feeling so new between us anymore, the emotions growing inside me don't seem weird or too fast, but instead, natural.

Also, there's no worry of having to wonder how Alexei feels about me, so I'm not burdened by the usual uncertainties when starting a relationship.

"What are you thinking?" he murmurs.

"How natural this feels," I answer honestly.

"Yeah?" He places a finger beneath my chin and nudges my face up so I'll meet his eyes.

A bubble of intimacy wraps around us, and it has me admitting, "You make it easy for me to get back to how we were before I lost my memory."

Alexei slowly begins to lean down until I feel his breath on my lips. His voice is a low rumble as he says, "Christ, I want to fuck you, but for now, I'll settle for your mouth."

Our mouths meet in a frenzy, and I feel Alexei's need spilling over into me as his lips knead mine until they're swollen and tingling. His teeth bites and his tongue soothes, working me up until I'm second-guessing myself.

I've healed a lot. Maybe the pain won't be so bad.

I should've taken painkillers.

God, there's no way I'm stopping him if he pushes for more.

My heart rate spikes, and my breaths come fast as I lose myself in the kiss, handing the control over to Alexei. It makes him growl, and he pushes me onto my back.

Alexei pushes a hand beneath my shirt, and I'm surprised when his touch is soft and not rough. It's in total contrast to the kiss, but knowing he's still keeping my injuries in mind, warms my heart.

When his palm covers my breast, my breaths speed up even more. I wrap my right arm around him, my fingers splaying over his muscled back.

Alexei's tongue thrusts forcefully, sweeping through my mouth as if he's branding me.

His hand moves away from my breast, and as he keeps himself braced on his left arm to keep his weight off me, he pushes the waistband of my leggings down until the side of my hip is exposed. When his fingers trail up and down the stretch of skin, he lets out a satisfied moan.

Pulling his mouth away from mine, his lips move over my jaw and down my neck. "Christ, I love the feel of your skin. Fucking silk."

Caught up in the moment, I'm a second away from begging him to fuck me.

Before I can voice my need, Alexei pulls entirely away from me and slumps onto his back beside me, taking deep breaths. "Now we're both frustrated."

"You couldn't just suffer in silence on your own?" I grumble, frustrated that we can't take it further. Two weeks after taking two bullets is a bit too soon.

Lowering his hand, he grips his impressive length through the sweatpants and lets out a chuckle. "Trust me, I'm suffering more. I just wanted company tonight, seeing as I won't be getting any sleep."

"Aww… poor you," I mutter. "While you're unable to sleep, can you go get me some water and painkillers?"

Alexei's eyes snap to me, and he instantly leans over me. "Did I hurt you?"

Shaking my head, I grin at him. "It's just tender enough to annoy me, and they'll knock me out."

Getting up from the bed, Alexei says, "Be right back."

When he leaves the room, I stare up at the ceiling, and my thoughts turn to the passionate moment we just shared.

Maybe a marriage to form an alliance won't be the worst thing. I can definitely learn to love Alexei.

I already like him, and the attraction between us is strong.

Deciding to take a couple of days to think about it, I actually feel better than I have during the past two weeks. It feels as if things are slowly falling back into place even though my memories are still missing in action.

Chapter 17

ALEXEI

The waiting and not knowing what Isabella will decide or when her memory will return is going to be the end of me. I fucking hate it.

It's been two weeks since I mentioned the marriage to form an alliance, and she hasn't said anything about it since.

Patience is not a fucking virtue. It's pure torture.

Walking into the gym, I find Isabella jogging on a treadmill. She's nearly regained her former muscle and strength. But then again, she's been working out like a demon.

Climbing on the treadmill next to hers, I set the pace for a slow jog so I can warm up.

"You're late," she says, sounding a little breathless.

I was on a call with Carson, who hasn't been able to find the girls. It's been a month since Carson and Damien were forced to breach Isabella's safe house, only to find it empty.

The girls we saved before Isabella got hurt just vanished, and I can only hope Sonia didn't get to them first.

Also, there's still no fucking trace of Sonia. She's too quiet, and I get a feeling she's planning an attack. Even though she was seen in Ethiopia, there's been no proof of life, and I think it's to throw us off her track.

"I had business to take care of," I reply as I increase my pace.

"Something wrong?" Isabella asks, sparing me a glance.

"Just frustrated," I mutter, increasing my pace until I'm running. "Sonia's nowhere to be found, and I don't like it one bit."

Isabella slows her treadmill down to a stop, and then it looks like she's deep in thought.

"You know where she might be hiding?" I've asked Isabella before, but all the places she mentioned didn't help to find Sonia.

"What about St. Monarch's?" Isabella turns her eyes to mine. "That's where I'd go."

A frown forms on my forehead.

Then it fucking hits me like a ten-ton truck. I should've thought of St. Monarch's. That's where we all go if we need medical care and to lay low.

Fuck!

Madame Keller knows I've been looking for Sonia.

Fuck.

Stopping the treadmill, I rush out of the gym and head straight for the security room, where I left my phone. Picking up the device, anger begins to bubble in my chest as I dial the number for St. Monarch's.

"What's wrong?" Demitri asks. I hold up a hand to silence him.

"Mr. Koslov, to what do I owe the honor?" Madame Keller answers.

"Is Sonia Terrero there?" I bite the question out.

Madame Keller doesn't answer immediately before she says, "You know I can't tell you if a guest is on the grounds. Especially if they're paying for the security St. Monarch's offers."

Motherfucker.

I end the call before I start a war with Madame Keller, and then I slam my fist into the desk. "Fuck!"

Demitri gets up from the chair. "Want to tell me what's going on?"

"Sonia's fucking hiding at St. Monarch's," I say, my voice deadly from the rage pulsing through my body.

I fucking should've checked St. Monarch's first. I've wasted so much time.

"Fuck," Demitri mutters just as Isabella comes walking into the security room.

She must've heard what I just said because she doesn't hesitate to remind me, "St. Monarch's is neutral ground. Going after my mother while she's there will take a hell of a lot of firepower."

Demitri shakes his head. "Not to mention, a lot of our allies won't have our back."

"Carson and Damien will," I state the obvious. "Also Winter and Lucian."

"That makes seven of us against a well-trained army," Isabella says.

Seven?

My eyes snap to hers. "You're willing to fight with us?"

A frown forms on Isabella's forehead. "With a little training, I'll be ready. I'm healed, so I don't see what the problem is."

Fuck. Right.

I almost slipped up.

Isabella lifts her chin, and it makes her look powerful as she says, "Besides, it's only right that I'm at my fiancé's side."

My heart literally stops for a moment before it starts to speed up. "Is that a yes?"

Isabella shrugs. "Ask me and find out." Then, turning around, she walks to the door. "The proposal better be romantic."

Even though I'm still angry from learning where Sonia's been hiding, a smile spreads over my face.

That's one win I really needed right now.

Turning to Demitri, I ask, "How am I going to make the proposal romantic?"

He gives me an incredulous look. "You're aware I don't have a romantic bone in my body? Go ask Ariana."

"Right."

I leave the security room to take care of planning the proposal so I can focus solely on Sonia.

One fucking mountain at a time, Alexei.

When I walk into Ariana's office, she gives me a startled look. "What? Did something happen?"

Grabbing a chair, I sit down, and then I lock eyes with her. "Give me an idea for a romantic proposal." Ariana blinks at me as if I just spoke a foreign language. "Want me to repeat it in Russian?"

She quickly shakes her head. "Oh no, I just never expected to hear those words from you. I thought you knew everything," she teases me.

I give her a scowl.

"Don't give me the look of death. If you want my help, ask me nicely."

Taking a deep breath, I smile. "Help me plan a romantic proposal, little one."

Ariana lets out a chuckle. "You don't know how to ask for something, but that will do."

She begins to tap her fingers on her desk, and when a solid minute has passed, I say, "Take your time. It's not like I'm in a rush."

She shoots me a glare. "I have a million ideas, and I'm trying to figure out which one Isabella will love. So sit quietly and let me think if you want my help."

Christ, this is going to take all day.

"What about a candle-lit dinner?" I ask.

"Boring," Ariana mutters.

I try to come up with something else, but I've got nothing.

I stare at Ariana until she lets out a huff. "You're putting a damper on my creativity." Another torturous moment passes, then she says, "You could take her to a field with pretty flowers. Maybe have lanterns hanging from trees to make it look mystical. You're going to have to write vows or something to win her over with. Just asking her to marry you isn't enough."

"Me writing something? You're kidding, right?"

Ariana frowns at me. "Figure it out, Alexei. I'm not helping with that. It has to come from the heart."

I let out a burst of laughter. "It's cute how you assume I have a heart."

Ariana leans over to me, patting my chest. "You forget I know you. Don't try and be all badass with me." Settling back in her chair, she says, "Just tell Isabella why you want to marry her. Tell her how you feel."

Damn, have I been so good at the act that even Ariana believes I love Isabella? Yes, I'm falling, but that's not the same thing as actually loving her.

As if Ariana can read my mind, she says, "Only you think it's an act. I've seen how you are with Isabella. You care more about her than you'd like to admit, and maybe you should accept that fact before you ask her to marry you."

Getting up from the chair, I look down at Ariana. "Caring is not loving, little one."

I stalk out of her office and find myself heading to one of the empty guest rooms. I shut the door behind me and then go stand in front of the window so I can think.

I've been so caught up in everything, I haven't really considered how I feel.

I remember the hook-up I had with Isabella. Seeing her in action and how she earned my respect. But, having her close to me the past month… yeah, I do care.

I love her bravery, her strength, her intelligence. Most of all, I love how she fought against Sonia to free the slaves. It shows Isabella has heart. When she cares about something, she's willing to die for it.

Closing my eyes, I bring up the image of Isabella. Her beauty, her sensualness, her scent – I love it all.

I fucking love her?

My eyes snap open, and I frown.

Is this what it's like?

Taking a deep breath, I bring up the memory of Isabella falling from the helicopter. Her almost dying.

My hands tighten in fists as a shudder ripples through my chest.

Okay. Deep breaths.

You love Isabella.

Christ, so much for thinking I was the one in control.

My breathing begins to speed up as I feel panic for the first time in my life.

What if her memory returns and I lose her?

What the fuck will I do then?

ISABELLA

After yesterday's shit show, when we found out my mother's been hiding at St. Monarch's all along, Alexei's been tense as hell.

He only came to bed in the early morning hours and was gone when I woke up. I'm trying to think of a way to help, but right now, I'm coming up empty-handed.

I grab a bottle of water from the fridge when Alexei comes stalking into the kitchen.

Giving me an impatient look, he says, "You better drink that quickly."

"Why?"

"I want to take you somewhere."

I take a couple of sips and then place the bottle on the counter while asking, "Where?"

Alexei grabs hold of my hand, and then he drags me out of the kitchen and up the stairs to our suite. Gesturing at the closet, he says, "Change into your leather pants and jacket. I'll wait downstairs."

I watch him stalk out of the room as if he's off to kill someone, then I pull clothes from the closet. I quickly change and put on a pair of boots, hoping whatever he has planned will help ease his stress level a little.

When I look at my reflection in the mirror, a familiar sensation flickers through me. I feel comfortable in the clothes as if they're a second skin.

Also, I look badass.

Walking out of the room, I head down the stairs and find Alexei standing by the open front door. His eyes lock on me, and then the corner of his mouth lifts as if he's satisfied with what he's seeing.

We step out of the house, and when I see the motorcycle, a smile spreads over my face.

Alexei climbs onto the metal beast then holds a helmet out to me. "Come."

I take the helmet and put it on, and then I climb onto the back of the motorcycle and grip hold of Alexei's sides.

He starts the engine, and when he pulls away from the house, I wrap my arms around his middle.

The moment he steers the motorcycle off the property, he opens the throttle, and we dart forward.

I let out a burst of laughter, feeling more excited than when I'm at the shooting range.

When we hit the highway, the wind rips at us. Exhilaration rushes through my veins, and I close my eyes, losing myself in the moment.

With my arms wrapped tightly around Alexei, and the motorcycle's power between my legs, the moment feels… perfect.

Losing track of time, I have no idea how long we're riding or where we're heading until Alexei brings us to a stop. Glancing around, we're near a cliff overlooking the ocean.

We climb off, and after removing the helmets, Alexei takes hold of my hand and leads me up a trail. When we reach the top, I stare out over the beautiful view, still smiling.

"Isabella."

I turn to Alexei, and seeing the serious expression, I give him a questioning look.

He takes a deep breath and then tilting his head, the seriousness makes way for a tender look that causes my heart to constrict.

"Whatever happens in the future, I want you to remember this moment. I mean everything I'm going to say."

"Okay." My tongue darts out to wet my lips.

Alexei takes another deep breath, and then his eyes lock with mine. "I love you."

The words hit me straight in the heart, which is weird because it's not the first time he's saying them to me. But this time, it sounds different… heartfelt.

He shakes his head, emotion tightening his features. "I fucking love everything about you. I could spend the next hour going into detail, but I won't. I want you. All of you. I want you next to my side. I want to wage wars with you. I want to build empires with you. I want you in every new memory I make because there isn't a woman on the face of this planet I respect more."

Alexei's words knock the breath from me, filling my racing heart with overwhelming emotions. Happiness. Comfort. Anticipation. But most importantly, affection… and the first glimmer of love.

"Isabella Terrero, will you marry me?" Alexei asks.

I stare at him for a moment, taking in the importance of what's happening on this cliff.

It's not just about love. It's us forming an unbreakable alliance for life. Together we'll fight. Together we'll die.

But first… together, we'll live.

"Yes, I will."

Alexei's eyes drift closed, and relief washes over his face. "Thank fuck." He lets out a chuckle then reaches into his pocket, pulling out a ring. "Give me your left hand."

"Who said romance was dead?" I mutter playfully as I offer my hand to him.

Alexei slips his ring onto my finger, and then his eyes lift to mine. "There's no going back now."

I lower my gaze to the princess-cut diamond. "An alliance between a Koslov and a Terrero, who would've thought."

When I meet Alexei's eyes again, he says, "I can't wait to change your last name to Koslov."

Isabella Koslov.

I inhale sharply from how powerful the name sounds.

A new name for a new life.

Alexei closes the distance between us, and lifting both his hands, he frames my face and stares at me with absolute devotion.

Raising myself on my toes, I press my mouth to his, and then I wrap my arms around him… the man I'm going to marry… the man I'll conquer the world with.

Chapter 18

ALEXEI

Standing in the bathroom, I stare at my reflection as I replay this morning in my mind.

We're engaged.

Thank God.

Isabella might not have said she loved me, but the fact that she accepted the proposal means more to me. The alliance has been formed, and there's no getting out of it. Not in our world.

Which means she's mine.

The Princess of Terror is mine.

The goddess of mischief and chaos is mine.

Even if Isabella's memory returns, there's no going back on the promise we made on that cliff. It's alleviated some of the pressure I've been feeling, and now I can fucking focus on Sonia and St. Monarch's.

Tomorrow we have to start planning the attack, and I'll find out who's really on my side.

But for tonight, I have only one goal.

The thought has the corner of my mouth lifting in a predatory smile. I walk to the door and opening it, my eyes instantly go to where Isabella's rubbing lotion on her hands while walking to her side of the bed.

She glances up and watches as I stalk toward her. Then, lowering her hands, she lifts her chin, her eyes locking with mine.

When I reach her, I lift a hand to her throat, and then I slam my mouth down on hers.

This time there's no holding back.

This time I'm taking what I've wanted since I got to fuck her five months ago.

My tongue drives into Isabella's mouth, and I fucking devour her. It's reckless and dirty, just like the world we live in. Wrapping my other arm around her, I yank her body against mine as my teeth tug at her bottom lip.

I pull back an inch, and my eyes capture hers. "I'm going to fuck you."

"After all the build-up, you better be good," she sasses me.

I let out a chuckle that sounds more like a warning as I grab hold of her shirt, yanking it over her head. I grip her hips, pushing her back onto the bed, and then I crawl over her, my eyes locking on her breasts.

The scar from the bullet she took draws my attention, and leaning forward, I press a kiss against it. I brush my lips over her nipple, then place another kiss to the scar on her shoulder.

Moving to her mouth, my lips nip at hers as I thrust my hand inside her leggings. I cover her pussy with my palm, letting out a satisfied moan while my tongue dives into her mouth.

I part her and rub a finger over her clit, and then I push inside her heat. "Fucking finally," I growl before my teeth tug at her bottom lip.

Isabella brings her hands to the sides of my neck, and as I let the kiss spiral out of control, her palms roam down my chest and abs.

I begin to rub my palm against her clit, loving how wet she is for me. Freeing her mouth, I push my finger deeper, and then I trail biting kisses down the column of her throat to her breasts.

My teeth feast on Isabella's nipples until they're pebbled, and her moans tell me how much she's loving it.

Pulling my hand from between her legs, I bring it to my face and deeply inhale her scent before sucking my finger into my mouth. The taste of her bursts on my tongue, and it makes everything but this moment fade.

Moving down her body, I grab hold of her leggings and yank the fabric down her legs. Placing my hands on Isabella's tanned thighs, I spread her wide, and then I bury my face between her legs, drinking her wetness while spearing her with my tongue.

Isabella's hips buck up, and she rubs herself harder against my mouth as moans begin to spill over her lips. I eat her out until her thighs clench around my shoulders, and her body convulses.

Not having the patience to step out of my sweatpants, I grab a condom from the bedside drawer, and freeing my cock, I roll the fucking latex on as fast as I can.

I take hold of Isabella's thighs, and opening her wider, I move between her legs. I grip hold of my cock and position myself at her opening. Only then do I lock eyes with her again as I take hold of her hip and thrust hard inside her, burying myself to the hilt.

Intense tingles race down my spine from how fucking amazing it feels to finally be buried deep inside her.

Isabella gasps, and lifting her hands to her hair, she grips fistfuls as her back arches and her inner walls clench around me. "Oh, God. Alexei."

My lips curve up, and then I pull out to the last inch before slamming back inside her, letting her heat engulf me.

I lower my eyes to her breasts, rising and falling with her quick breaths. "So fucking beautiful," I breathe, and then I begin to move, fucking fast and hard, taking her the way I've been dying to.

The sound of our skin slapping and how wet she is for me fills the air, and it makes me drive harder into her.

"Mother of God," she moans. "Yes."

I watch as goosebumps break out over Isabella's skin, hardening her nipples even more. She lets go of her hair and covering her breasts with her hands, she begins to massage them before moving her palms down her body.

Christ. So fucking erotic.

While my cock strokes her pussy relentlessly, I quickly grow addicted to the sound of her moans and cries, and each one makes my thrusts become more forceful until it feels as if we're becoming one.

I move my hands to Isabella's sides, and she instantly reaches down, grabbing hold of my wrists. Her feverish eyes lock with mine, and then she fucking whimpers as if she's begging me to tear her apart.

ISABELLA

When the needy whimper slips over my lips, Alexei's eyes darken until they're black.

He moves over me, and bracing a forearm beside my head, his mouth nips at mine as he pushes a hand between us. His fingers begin to work my clit expertly while he keeps powering into me as if he'll die if he had to slow down for a second.

The way he fucks me makes me feel drunk, causing shivers of pleasure to race over my skin. My mind is blank, all my focus on Alexei as he claims my body.

My hands find his shoulders, and drinking in the feel of his muscled back as he moves, I dig my nails into his skin.

Our eyes lock again, and the possessiveness shining from Alexei's makes me feel wanted, protected, loved.

"Alexei," I whisper breathlessly, my abdomen tightening with need.

He pinches my clit, and it makes my body come apart at the seams. The orgasm's intense, seizing my body until it feels as if I'm convulsing.

"Fuck," Alexei growls. "Fuck, your pussy clamps so tight around my cock when you come."

As the orgasm tears through me, my lips part in a silent cry because there's no way I can even get out a sound.

Alexei's chest presses against mine, and his mouth is so close to mine we're breathing the same air. Pleasure keeps crashing through my body as Alexei keeps filling me, and when I finally start to come down from the high, his thrusts become more forceful. My body jerks from how hard he takes me, and it makes my orgasm rush back with the intensity of a tidal wave.

I can only gasp for air as my eyes remain glued to Alexei's, then he lets out a satisfied moan as his body jerks hard against mine, ecstasy washing over his features.

"Fuck, baby." His arms wrap around me, squashing me to his body as he rides his orgasm. I press kisses to the side of his neck until his thrusts slow down to a lazy pace.

Lifting his head, his eyes find mine as he slowly fills me one last time. "Mine. A fucking goddess belongs to me."

My lips curve up as I shake my head, and framing his jaw with my palms, I say, "No, a god belongs to me."

A proud smile forms on his face, and then he presses a possessive kiss to my swollen lips.

Alexei slowly pulls out of me, and moving away from my body, he gets up to take care of the condom.

I push myself up and scoot off the bed. Ignoring my clothes on the floor, I walk to the windows and stare into the dark night.

The light in the room turns off, and glancing over my shoulder, I hear Alexei say, "I don't want anyone seeing you naked."

"Hmm… so you're not into sharing?"

"Fuck no," he grumbles as he comes to stand behind me, wrapping his arms around me.

I lean my head back against his shoulder, and then he lifts his right hand to cover my left breast. He moves his other hand down, palming me between my legs, and it makes me chuckle. "Okay, so no sharing."

"Unless you want me going on a killing spree," he warns.

I take a deep breath and let it out slowly, enjoying the feel of Alexei's solid chest behind me.

He presses a kiss to my shoulder, then says, "I need to make arrangements for the engagement party."

"Engagement party?" I ask, and turning around, I wrap my arms around his neck.

His hands grab hold of my ass, and he lets out a rumbling moan. Gripping me tighter, he tugs me closer, squashing my breasts to his chest.

"Of course," he answers my question, his voice deep and predatory. "I'm going to tell the whole fucking world you're mine."

"I love this possessive side of you," I admit. "It's a turn-on."

"Give me ten minutes, and I'll take care of that turn-on," he says playfully.

Raising on my toes, I press a kiss to his jaw, then I say, "Do you want me to take care of the arrangements for the party?"

Alexei shakes his head, his hands gripping my ass tighter. "Don't worry about it."

I bring a hand to his face, trailing my fingers over his stubble. "You have a lot on your plate right now. I want to help take the edge off."

Alexei begins to move slow and sensually, and my body automatically follows his lead as we sway. "Okay. I'll handle the invites, and you can take care of everything else."

"What color scheme do you want?" I ask, my voice low as desire for this man trickles through my veins.

"Black and silver."

"I like those colors," I whisper, and then Alexei begins to lean down, our eyes never breaking contact.

"What do you want as an engagement present?" he murmurs, his breath fanning over my lips.

"A motorcycle," the answer comes easily.

Alexei grins at me. "And?"

I think for a moment. "A gun."

He lets out a chuckle as he moves a hand to my front, and then his middle finger slowly starts to tease my clit.

"What do you want?" I ask, intimacy weaving a spell around us.

"You naked every night."

He pushes a finger inside me, and a moan spills over my lips, then I breathe, "And?"

"You by my side forever."

As Alexei's mouth takes mine, my heart fills with warmth, and it slowly spreads through my body.

Today I made the right decision when I agreed to marry Alexei.

I have no regrets.

Chapter 19

ALEXEI

Half of me is happy, and the other half is murderous.

St. *fucking* Monarch's.

The air is tense in the security room as we stand by a round table, putting a map together. Demitri, Isabella, and I are trying to remember the layout.

Isabella points to the south side. "There's a courtyard here. Guards patrol every five minutes."

Demitri gestures to the west. "The outdoor shooting range. It's too close to the armory to breach from there unless we blow it up."

"Isabella," I say as I grab a pencil and lean over the map, "How many guards are on the south side?"

She thinks for a moment. "I'd guess between ten and fifteen."

I write down fifteen, then glance at Demitri.

"Stationed near the shooting range?" he asks. "Easily double. I'd prepare for thirty guards."

Then he shakes his head, and it has me asking, "What?"

"The guards aren't the problem. We'll be able to get through the first line of defense." His eyes lock with mine. "It's the custodians I'm worried about."

"Two always follow Madame Keller," Isabella mentions.

"And there's Miss Dervishi and Mr. Yeoh, the instructors," Demitri adds. "They trained us. They'll be able to anticipate our moves."

Fuck.

"Where would the other custodians be?" I ask.

The last time I was at St. Monarch's was almost two years ago, and I didn't pay attention to the guards.

"Two in the hallway leading to Madame Keller's office and two near the armory."

I write the numbers down. "When we breach, we'll have three highly fucking skilled people to deal with stationed by the armory, then two outside the office, and two on the inside."

"And Madame Keller," Demirtri adds. "Don't underestimate her. She might be old, but she can still fire a gun just as good as any of us."

I take a deep breath and let it out slowly.

"Besides the first line of defense and the nine skilled people, we'll have to find a way to get through the fucking vault door that will seal them in the office." I think for a moment, then say, "Unless we just blow that part of the building. Would the walls be steel-reinforced?"

Demitri shakes his head. "Maybe the back of the office where the cabinets with weapons are, but not the sides."

Nodding, Isabella agrees, "Demitri's right. After remodeling the castle, they kept the walls intact because of the historical artwork. The ceilings as well."

"At least we have that counting in our favor," I mutter. I stare at the map. "First line of defense will easily be sixty men. Second line, I'm guessing twenty."

Demitri lets out a sigh. "Final line of defense seven and a vault door."

"Nine," Isabella corrects Demitri. "Counting my mother and Hugo."

"You shot Hugo during the attack, and I'm pretty sure Demitri and I got shots in as well, so he might be out of the picture," I say.

"Let's count him just in case," Isabella replies.

Lifting a hand to my face, I scrub my knuckles over my jaw. "And that's not adding the custodians and assassins in training."

"We'll have to take Nikhil and Sacha."

I glance at Demitri and see the worry for Ariana's safety if they're not here to protect her. "We'll send Ariana to the island."

Demitri nods.

"I'll leave Tristan with her," I add to set his mind at ease.

"What about MJ?" Demitri asks.

MJ is Hailey's custodian that my brother got her for protection. From what Carson's told me, she's good. "I'll talk to Carson. Hailey can join Ariana on the island."

"Maybe we should leave them on Damien and Winter's island. Cillian and their guards will be able to protect them better than Tristan."

I begin to nod, knowing Winter's personal guard, Cillian, is good and tough as nails. "Good idea." I let out a heavy breath. "Now to figure out what kind of weapons we're looking at."

"A lot," Isabella chuckles, shaking her head at the map.

Ariana comes into the security room. "Time for a break, guys. Come eat."

I drop the pencil on the map, and when Demitri and Isabella follow Ariana, I glance back at the numbers I wrote down.

Worry gnaws at my insides like a fucking rat.

I'll be risking everyone who means something to me. My friends. My brother. Demitri. Isabella.

There's a chance some of us will die.

Closing my eyes, I contemplate calling the whole thing off and waiting Sonia out. She can't live there forever.

Demitri comes back into the security room. "What?"

I shake my head. "I'll be risking everyone I love. Sonia's not worth it."

Demitri places his hand on my shoulder, and we just stare at each other for a moment, then he says, "We don't back down, Alexei. If we do, Sonia wins. It will make her stronger and you weaker."

I let out a slow breath and lift my chin. "We don't back down."

ISABELLA

"Harder," Demitri orders.

I shake my head. "I'll hurt you."

"That's the point, Isabella." His eyes are hard on me. "Show me what you can do."

We've been sparring for the last hour, and it just doesn't feel right attacking Demitri. After all, we're on the same side.

He lets out a breath, then says, "If you manage to hurt me, it's my own fault for not blocking you. Give me your all."

"I need to know you can hold your own against Demitri, or I won't risk taking you with me," Alexei suddenly says.

I glance over my shoulder as he walks toward us. Crossing his arms, he stops on the side of the sparring mat, raising an eyebrow at me as if he's daring me.

"Okay," I mutter. Another thing that's frustrating is that I can't remember the training I received. I have no idea what I can and cannot do.

Suddenly Dimitri lunges at me, and twisting his body into the air, his leg darts out. Automatically, I dart forward, and grabbing hold of his leg, I pull my body up and manage to wrap my legs around his neck. I twist myself and flip him, and then we both crash to the floor, Demitri's full weight knocking the air from my lungs.

"Fuck yes!" Alexei shouts. "Now that's what I'm talking about."

Demitri rolls off me, letting out a chuckle. "Good move."

I let out a groan as I peel myself off the mat. "You weigh a ton."

"Again," Alexei orders.

Glaring at him, I say, "It's easy to stand there and give orders."

He tilts his head and then begins to remove his coat. "Okay. You and me."

I let out a burst of laughter. "Actually, I meant you should go find something else to do."

Alexei shakes his head as he removes his boots, and then he steps onto the mat. "Come on, babe. Dance with me."

"Rules first," I say as I keep my eyes on him. "Not the face."

"And not between the legs," he adds.

"Deal."

I dart forward and take a swing at Alexei. He blocks the blow, and then his fist connects with my right shoulder. Knowing he didn't use his full strength, it still stings.

Jumping back, Alexei shakes his head at me. "Come on, *little* princess. You can do better than that."

I run, and jumping at the last minute, I grab hold of Alexei's shoulder, but as I swing myself into the air, he turns around and grabbing hold of my arm, he yanks me down, causing me to fall to the mat.

Rolling over, I push myself into a kneeling position, and then I use the back of my hand to wipe the sweat from my forehead.

Alexei crouches in front of me with a bottle of water. "Take a break. Demitri and I will spar. Watch us and memorize the movements."

I take the bottle from him and nod, not feeling half as badass as he's made me sound. Climbing to my feet, I walk to the side of the mat.

Demitri and Alexei face-off, and then Alexei smirks at his custodian. "It's been a while."

Demitri smiles. "Take it easy on me." And then he attacks.

The bottle of water is forgotten in my hands as my eyes move to keep up with the two men. Neither's getting a blow in. It seriously looks like they're completely in sync with each other. I focus on their actions, and they feel familiar.

God, the fight will keep going until one of them grows tired. Only then will the other be able to get past the blocks.

They're equally good.

Suddenly, Alexei manages to wrap his arm around Demitri's neck, and twisting his body, he slams Demitri down on the mat.

Speed. Alexei's faster.

The two men chuckle as they climb to their feet, and then Alexei asks, "What makes you stronger than your opponent?"

"Speed."

"Good girl," he says with a wink.

I toss the bottle of water at him. "Get off the mat so I can train with Demitri."

Alexei catches the bottle then gives me a fake hurt look. "Why not train with me?"

"You're faster. I'd like to actually train instead of being on the defense all the time." Then I smile at Demitri. "Demitri's also more patient than you."

"I'll leave the two of you to train then," Alexei chuckles as he walks to where his coat and boots are.

I wasn't lying, Demitri's much more patient than Alexei. Plus, he's a good trainer, and his energy is calm.

We practice for another hour, and with Demitri's guidance, I start to move faster, feeling more confident with every move.

When we take a breather, Demitri smiles at me. "You'll get there, Isabella. You did well for your first day."

"Thanks," I say breathlessly.

"Same time tomorrow?"

I nod at him. "Okay."

When Demitri begins to walk away, I say, "Thank you." He stops, and when our eyes meet, I add, "For training me. I really appreciate it."

"You're welcome. Take a warm bath to relax your muscles."

As he walks away, I stare after him before turning my attention to Alexei, who's been silently watching us.

"I like my instructor," I tease Alexei.

Instead of getting jealous, he gives me a pleased smile. "I'm glad to hear that. Demitri's very important to me."

"You're the best assassin and clearly trained in fighting. Why did you get a custodian?"

Alexei glances to the doorway where Demitri disappeared through. "I needed someone I could trust one hundred percent."

Frowning, I say. "But you have Carson."

Alexei shakes his head. "Even brothers can turn on each other. A custodian is loyal until death."

Nodding, I walk closer to Alexei. "Well, I'm glad you have Demitri." I smile up at him. "And me."

He just stares at me for a moment. "Do I?"

The smile fades from my face. "Of course."

Alexei holds the bottle of water out to me. "Drink before you dehydrate."

I take it from him and swallow a couple of sips while a weird feeling slithers through my heart.

Alexei doesn't trust me.

Chapter 20

ALEXEI

I've placed orders with Lucian, Semion, and Lev for weapons. Everything from RPGs to incendiary grenades.

I also invited everyone I'll need for the attack to attend the engagement party. After we're done celebrating, I'll meet with them.

Five days until the celebration.

I have to get everything ready for the meeting. I managed to get plans of the castle in Geneva from before Madame Keller purchased it. She didn't change the primary structure during the remodeling.

I've also gotten my hands on satellite images of the grounds, and I'm busy comparing the old plans with the new layout.

Demitri and Nikhil are busy on the computer, merging the old and new information to create a holographic image for us to work with for when we go ahead with the final stage of planning.

A tumbler of vodka is set down in front of me, and then Isabella presses a kiss to the side of my neck. "Take a break," she whispers. "You've been in here since dawn."

Picking up the tumbler, I take a sip, then point to the east of the property on the satellite images. "Take a look at this."

Wrapping her arm around my waist, she leans her cheek on my shoulder, then she murmurs, "That's easily a couple of miles from St. Monarch's."

"That was only built two years ago," I say. "It's too close to St. Monarch's."

Demitri moves in on the other side of the table and looks at the image. "These old castles have tunnels. Where's the old map?"

I pull it out from beneath the pile of sheets and then lay it out in front of us.

I point to the basement and tunnel section. "There isn't one leading to the east. Also, I'm sure Madame Keller had them all sealed off." Then, lifting my gaze to Demitri, I say, "Unless she made her own after the attack on Lucian while he was there. It could lead to the new building as an escape route."

Demitri nods in agreement. "Let's assume that's what it is, so we're not caught off guard. I'll add it to the holographic image."

When I reach for the satellite images again, Isabella places her hand on mine. "Take a break. Just ten minutes."

Grabbing hold of the tumbler, I take a deep sip as I walk out of the security room. As I pass through the foyer, I stop at a side table to fill my glass, then I head up the stairs. Walking into our suite, I open the glass doors and step out onto the balcony, rolling my neck and shoulders to loosen the knots as I close my eyes.

When I take a deep breath, Isabella's hands slide over my shoulders, and she begins to massage the tense muscles, slowly moving down my back.

"How're the plans for the party coming along?" I ask, just focusing on her touch.

"Good. Ariana helped a lot. We've booked a catering company." Her voice sounds sultry, and it makes me turn around.

Leaning back against the railing, I take another sip of the vodka as my eyes settle on Isabella. She steps up to me, desire making her look like a cat stalking her prey.

Isabella places a hand on my thigh and pressing a kiss to my neck, her palm moves an inch up until she brushes over my cock.

Gripping me through my cargo pants, she begins to rub me until I'm hard as fuck.

I bring the tumbler to my mouth, my eyes locked on Isabella as she begins to undo my belt. I reach behind my back, pulling my personalized gun out, so it doesn't drop to the floor.

I watch as Isabella shoves my pants open, and then she sinks down in front of me. Her fingers wrap around me, and the moment her breath fans over my cock, pre-cum begins to form in anticipation.

When her lips part, I hold my breath, and then my eyes drift shut from how fucking amazing it feels as she sucks me into her mouth.

Her tongue snakes around the head of my length, and the pleasure makes me tighten my grip on the tumbler. My fingers flex around the handle of the gun, and I let out a satisfied groan.

Then she sucks me deep, and an intense heat spreads through my cock and to my balls. My muscles tighten, and my lips part, my breaths growing faster.

I lower my eyes to Isabella and watch as she takes half of my length, her fingers wrapping around the base and squeezing hard.

"Harder," I order, my voice low and commanding.

She increases her grip, and then she sucks fucking hard. Letting out a pleasure-filled groan, I watch the woman who's managed to capture my heart, her lips growing swollen from the friction.

Isabella takes me deep, and then she fucking hums. I toss the tumbler to the side and drop the gun to the floor, and then I grab hold of her hair. Fisting the strands, I begin to thrust inside the heat of her sinful mouth.

She relaxes her tongue, and then I'm able to stroke deep into her throat. My lips pull back from my teeth, and when she raises her eyes to mine, I fucking explode.

Intense ecstasy washes through my body, my muscles tightening until they feel like they might tear. My cock pulses as I sink as deep as she can take me.

Emptying myself down her throat, I watch as tears form in her eyes from the lack of air. I bring a hand to her neck and wrapping my fingers around her silky skin, I pull out and thrust back in, feeling how my cock fills her throat.

My cock pulses again and fucking again until the orgasm reaches its peak, and only then do I loosen my grip on Isabella's throat. Pulling out of her, I watch as she desperately sucks in a breath of air, a tear spiraling down her cheek.

Fucking perfect.

Leaning down, I grab hold of Isabella, and then I toss her over my shoulder, carrying her to the bed to repay the favor.

ISABELLA

After doing my makeup and curling the tips of my hair, I step into the black dress I've chosen to wear for the engagement party.

It has a low plunging neckline, and my back is exposed, the rest of the fabric falling elegantly to my feet. A slit on the right side reveals my leg all the way to just beneath my hip as I step into the stilettos.

Walking back to the dressing table, I squirt on some perfume before placing my ring back on my finger. I add diamond teardrops to my ears and check my reflection in the mirror, satisfied with what I see.

Alexei comes into the room and stops behind me. Placing his hands on my hips, his eyes rove over my reflection before he presses a kiss to my neck. "You look beautiful, my goddess."

I turn around, and adjusting the lapels of his suit jacket, I say, "You're devastatingly handsome. Tonight we look like a power couple."

The corner of his mouth lifts, pride shining from his dark eyes, and then he presses another kiss to my forehead. "You ready?"

"I just need ten minutes." I need to gather myself before I meet all the guests.

"No rush. I'll welcome everyone," he murmurs.

When Alexei leaves the room, I walk out onto the balcony and stare down at all the tables and decorations. Staff rush around, tending to last-minute details as the first guests start to mingle.

A chopping sound draws my attention, and glancing up, I watch as a helicopter approaches the mansion. When it begins its descent at the back of the property, there's a flash of a memory rippling through my mind.

My heart's pounding against my ribs. Hanging onto the landing skid, pain tears through my left shoulder. I pull the trigger, and there's a moment's satisfaction as I watch the bullet hit Hugo.

Then he fires back, and a stabbing ache rips through my chest. I lose my grip on the landing skid while more bullets spray the helicopter, and then I fall.

Slamming my eyes shut, a veil lifts in my mind, and for a moment, the world spins around me, making me stumble backward.

I grab hold of the glass door, an intense shivering spreading through my body – then my mind clears, and everything falls into place.

I gasp through the shock rippling through me.

Fuck.

Shit.

Lifting my head, anger bleeds into me at the speed of light, my hands trembling.

Holy. Fucking. Shit.

It takes me a moment to process everything, to align the before and after.

Fucking Alexei.

Fuck.

My rage bubbles over into an inferno as I realize what Alexei has done. How he deceived me.

Alexei Koslov spun his lies around me.

God.

He used me.

My eyes lower to my left hand that's shaking like a leaf in a shit storm, and I look at the engagement ring.

He tricked me into an alliance with him.

Oh, God.

Closing my eyes, I take deep breaths to try and calm down. I need to focus.

Focus, Isabella.

The memories of the past clash with the memories of the last five months, and it forms an explosion inside of me.

Remembering how I fell for the lies. How I believed them, not knowing any better. How they became my entire world.

How I fell for the façade Alexei put up.

Fuck, he's good. He really had me believing he loved me.

Enraged, I fight the urge to scream as I turn away from the balcony and stalk back into the room.

God, just the other day, I was on my knees, sucking him off.

Calm down.

Shhh...

On. My. Fucking. Knees.

Deep breaths.

Humiliation mixes with the deadly chaos in my chest, closing a tight fist around my breaking heart.

I lift a hand and press down on the spot where Hugo shot me. Sucking in deep breaths, I try my best to not lose my shit.

Heartache rips through the lie that was spun around me, tearing the webs to shreds.

I believed Alexei.

I fell for the act.

I loved him.

My eyes begin to burn, and I take quivering breaths, fighting back the urge to cry.

Thank God I didn't say the words to him. That would've made my humiliation a million times worse.

Then the thought of Ana stuns me, and I inhale sharply.

Oh my god.

Ana.

What happened to Ana and the girls?

I lift my trembling hand to cover my mouth as worry for my friend pours ice through my veins.

My head begins to pound from the overwhelming moment, and just then, there's a knock at the door.

Ariana comes in, smiling at me as if we're fucking friends. She takes in my state, then concern tightens her features. "Are you okay?"

"Just a bad headache," I barely manage to bite out, humiliation and rage making every muscle in my body tense.

"I'll get you something," she offers, rushing back to the door.

"Don't tell Alexei," I think to say, then add, "I don't want to worry him. It will ruin the party."

"Okay."

The moment I'm alone again, I begin to focus on the problem at hand.

There's no way I can fight my way out of this mansion tonight. Not with Alexei and Demitri… Carson, Damien… Winter… fuck… there's an army of elite assassins and custodians on the property. I won't make it out alive.

Okay. Think.

My breathing begins to calm down, and my heart slows down to a steady beat.

You're going to be the happy fiancée tonight. Just get through the party in one piece, and then you can reassess this fucking shit show.

Ariana comes rushing into the suite, carrying a bottle of water and a couple of painkillers. "Here you go," she says as she hands them to me.

I swallow the painkillers, then sit down on the side of the bed. "I'll be out in ten minutes."

"Okay." She gives me a concerned look.

"I'm fine. Go back to the party." I somehow manage to add a smile.

Ariana looks convinced, and my vengeful gaze follows her as she leaves the room again.

I just need to get through tonight. Tomorrow I'll figure out a way to escape, and then I'll go to Panama and check if Ana's at the rendezvous point.

One step at a time.

Rage keeps boiling inside of me, and my thoughts turn to Alexei.

I have to hand it to him; it was a clever move. Brilliantly played.

Bastard.

My gaze goes over the bedroom where I've let him fuck me. More than once.

God, he must be laughing his ass off at me – the Princess of Terror moaning for his cock.

I'm going to fucking kill him.

I look down at the engagement ring again, and all I want to do is rip it off my finger and shove it down Alexei's throat.

God help me.

I agreed to an alliance with Alexei Koslov, and there's no way out of it. Not in our world.

You don't just break an alliance. The only way out is death.

Either him or me.

Chapter 21

ALEXEI

Wondering what's keeping Isabella, I take the stairs two at a time and walk down the hallway. Just then, she comes out of the bedroom.

Her eyes land on me, and taking a deep breath, she begins to walk toward me.

"You okay?" I ask.

"Yes."

I hold my hand out to her, and when she reaches me, her fingers interlink with mine.

Something's different, and it has me staring at Isabella. "Sure?"

A smile spreads over her face. "Just anxious."

I tug her closer to me, and leaning down, I press a tender kiss to her mouth. When I lift my head, I say, "Don't be anxious. I'm here, and I won't leave your side."

Isabella stares deep into my eyes as if she's searching for something, and it has me saying, "I love you."

Instead of saying the words back to me, which honestly, I'm hoping I'll get to hear soon, Isabella murmurs, "Lucky me."

I tighten my hold on her hand. "I'm the lucky one."

We walk back to the stairs, and I keep my pace slow for Isabella to keep up.

My eyes roam over the hot as fuck dress she's wearing. "You look stunning."

A flattered smile graces her lips. "Thank you."

When I lead Isabella through the glass doors and out onto the veranda, pride fills my chest as all eyes turn to us.

Carson is the first to approach us. His alert gaze moves from me to Isabella, then he says, "Welcome to the family, Isabella."

She smiles at my brother. "Thank you. Who would've thought, right?"

"Right," Carson chuckles, then he turns to Hailey, who takes a step closer to Isabella.

Leaning in to give Isabella a quick hug, Hailey says, "Congrats. I'm sure the two of you will share many years of happiness."

It's only then I remember Isabella doesn't know who Hailey is. Leaning into her, I murmur, "Hailey's Carson's girlfriend. The woman behind her is MJ, her custodian."

Isabella nods, and as Lucian and Elena come toward us, I say, "Lucian and Elena, his wife."

Slowly we keep moving through the guests, taking time to welcome everyone personally. Finally, we reach Damien and Winter.

I watch as Isabella's smile widens when she says, "It's good to see you again, Winter."

"Likewise," Winter replies.

"I've always wanted to tell you," Isabella continues, "what a huge impact you had on my life."

"Oh?" Winter lifts a questioning eyebrow at Isabella.

"Watching you eliminate our enemies was inspiring. You gave me the courage to stand my ground."

A genuine smile spreads over Winter's face. "Wow… ah… I don't know what to say."

Isabella shakes her head. "You don't have to say anything. I just wanted you to know."

"How's the blood diamond business?" Isabella asks.

I press a kiss to Isabella's neck and then leave her with Winter so I can talk to Lucian about the shipment of weapons I've ordered.

When he sees me coming, a smile spreads over his face. "No business talk. It's your engagement, Alexei."

I let out a chuckle. "Did you get the RPGs?"

He shakes his head at me. "Do you ever take a break?"

"I'll rest when I'm dead," I joke.

His expression turns serious. "I've managed to get half of the order filled. The rest should reach me in two weeks."

"Good," I murmur, pleased to hear that.

Lucian's eyes sharpen on me. "Do you really want to do this?"

Nodding, I say, "There's no backing down."

I've saved Lucian's life more than once, so I'm not surprised when I see the loyalty on his face. "Then we go to war."

Elena joins us, and I drop the business talk. "Motherhood agrees with you, little one."

A happy smile settles around her mouth. "Luca keeps me busy."

"If he's anything like his father, I'm sure you have your hands full," I joke.

"Of course, he's the spitting image of me," Lucian grumbles.

I let out a chuckle, and patting my friend's shoulder, I say, "Excuse me, I need to get back to my fiancée."

When I'm close to Isabella and Winter, I hear them talking about Winter's wedding.

Christ, that was the quickest I've arranged and planned a wedding. I had Damien and Winter engaged and married in a matter of forty-eight hours.

Just then, Winter spots me and jokes, "Back then, Alexei still put the fear of God in me."

I wrap my arm around Isabella's waist. "Intimidation gets things done."

"Try that shit with me now," Winter says playfully.

Chuckling, I shake my head. "Too busy taking over the world, little one."

The relaxed atmosphere disappears as Winter frowns at me. "We're really doing this?"

Meeting her eyes, I nod. "We are."

She lifts her chin. "Okay."

I glance over the guests, the people who've each, in their own way, helped me to rise to the top. The ones I call family and friends.

This is what loyalty looks like.

Today they're celebrating my happiness, and soon they'll go to war for me.

When I turn my attention back to Isabella, she's staring up at me, her eyes sharp as if she's trying to figure something out.

"What's that look for?" I ask.

"Just wondering what you're thinking," she replies, and as a waiter passes us, she reaches for a flute of champagne, taking a sip of the bubbly drink.

She gives me a questioning look, and it has me answering, "I'm thinking about my family and friends and how far I've come because of them."

"From what Winter told me, I'm sure a couple of them hated you in the beginning."

I let out a burst of laughter. "Hate's a strong word. Winter, Elena, and Ariana needed some time to get used to me."

"Why?" Isabella asks.

I shrug. "I'm overprotective of those I love."

"In other words, you gave them hell?"

Shaking my head, I say, "No, I just warned them to not betray my friends."

"No warning for me?" Isabella asks, her voice becoming sensual.

My eyes drift over her beautiful face. "No need to. You know what will happen."

"You'll kill me?" she asks, lifting her chin.

Would I?

If Isabella betrayed me, would I be able to take her life?

It would fucking rip my heart out. "Yes."

Slowly, she nods. "Same goes for you, Alexei."

This conversation has quickly turned way too fucking serious.

Lifting both my hands, I frame her face and look deep into her eyes. "I'll never betray a loved one, especially the woman who holds my heart." Pressing a kiss to her forehead, I pull her against my chest.

ISABELLA

Bastard.

Asshole.

A string of curses runs on repeat through my mind as I walk with Alexei to the security room.

God, the party was such a sham. Luckily I've perfected the art of being a socialite, and it was easy to pretend I was enjoying myself.

My fingers tighten around Alexei's as the desire to punch the living shit out of him courses through me.

Alexei mistakes it for affection, and he squeezes my hand back.

Once we're in the security room, we all gather by the round table.

Now that I have my memory back, and I remember how I've fought against my mother, I really want to be there when she falls.

But I need to find Ana first. I need to know she's safe.

Demitri brings up the holographic image of St. Monarch's.

Carson lets out a heavy breath. "Christ Almighty."

Lucian shakes his head. "Yeah, now's a good time to start praying."

Alexei lets go of my hand, and then he begins to move around the table.

With his shoulders squared and his expression merciless, I see the powerful man he's become in the last four years... now that the rose-tinted glasses have been removed.

God, it was so easy to be swept up in his charm. But this man... the one in front of me right this instant – is the ruthless devil I have tied myself to.

As Alexei begins to share all the information we've gathered, my thoughts turn to the sparring session between Alexei and Demitri.

The corner of my mouth lifts at the valuable information I learned that day.

I now know who's the more significant threat between Demitri and Alexei.

And I've learned Demitri's moves.

My smile grows.

"Isabella?" Alexei suddenly interrupts my thoughts.

Shit.

My gaze darts to Alexei, where his eyes are narrowed on me, his head slightly tilted.

"Are you okay?" he asks, his gaze sharpening on me.

"Yes, just thinking how I can't wait to see my mother fall."

Alexei stares at me for a moment longer before he finally nods.

Fuck he's perceptive.

I focus on the holographic image as Alexei points to the west side of the castle. "We'll have to blow this side, and with a little luck, it will give us access to the office they'll be taking cover in."

"I've been in that office," Lucian says. "The walls are reinforced."

"Fuck," Alexei mutters. He thinks for a moment, then asks, "Are there any vents?"

Lucian nods. "Want to smoke them out?"

Alexei nods. "Which means one of us will have to crawl into the ventilation system."

"I'm the smallest. I'll do it," Winter offers.

Alexei's eyes touch on her. "Thanks." He looks at Damien, Carson, and Lucian. "The three of you will breach from the back of the property, along with Nikhil and Sasha."

The men nod their agreement.

"I'll have Semion and Lev enter from the front," Alexei continues. Then he looks at me. "You'll be with Demitri, Winter, and me."

I nod. "Okay."

"We'll breach from the west."

"Men?" Lucian asks.

"I'm looking into recruiting mercenaries," Alexei answers. "It will take a couple of weeks."

The meeting continues for another hour, and the moment I get to leave the security room, I head up the stairs and straight to the suite.

God, it's going to be a long night. I'll have to fight the urge to kill Alexei in his sleep because I need him to destroy my mother.

Grabbing a pair of leggings and a t-shirt from the closet, I hesitate, and then I toss the clothes back.

I'm taking control of tonight.

I step out of the heels and dress, then walk to the bathroom to shower. I take my time, and once I'm done, I walk back into the bedroom. Butt. Fucking. Naked.

Alexei's just unbuttoned his shirt, and pulling it off, he glances at me. "I have to say, I prefer that look over the dress you were wearing."

I stop next to the bed. "I want you naked on the bed."

His eyebrow lifts, and as he begins to undo his belt, he slowly stalks closer to me.

"Is that an order?"

I lift my chin. "Yes."

He lets out an amused chuckle as he pulls the leather belt through the loops. I watch as he steps out of his pants, and then he places a knee on the mattress before lying down on his back.

"You want control, little princess?" he asks, looking unbelievably hot as he smirks at me.

Bastard.

"Yes," I answer as I climb onto the bed and crawl over him.

Deceiving asshole.

I straddle his thighs and reaching to the bedside drawer, I take out a condom. The last thing I want is to fall pregnant.

I just want to be the one to fuck him the way he fucked me. I want to make him lose control because of me, so I can regain some of my hurt pride.

I rip the foil packet open and roll the condom onto Alexei's cock. Meeting his eyes, I begin to stroke him.

The amused smirk is still around his lips, a daring light shining from his eyes.

Slowly, apprehension begins to mix with anticipation, and the tiny hairs on the back of my neck rise. I lean forward, and with our eyes locked, my teeth tug at his bottom lip.

When he moves a hand to my hip, I shake my head. "My rules. No touching."

His smile grows, and the fucker places his hands behind his head as if he's planning on taking a nap.

Gripping hold of his cock, I position it at my opening, and then I lower myself, taking him all the way.

Sensually, I swivel my hips. It's all I do, not stroking his cock, but instead rubbing my clit against his pelvis.

Alexei doesn't break eye contact as I increase my pace, working myself toward an orgasm.

Smug bastard. Just you wait.

Lifting my hands, I bring them to my breasts, and then I let out a moan. I move faster, the friction quickly making my orgasm built.

Just as I'm about to come apart, Alexei grabs hold of my hips and lifting me off him, he rolls us over, and then he's hovering over me.

His features are tense, the veins snaking up his arms as he keeps himself braced over me.

"Two can play this game," he murmurs, making it sound more like a threat.

You fucking started it.

Grabbing hold of my wrists, Alexei pins my arms down on either side of my head, and then he slams back into me, making my body arch and my breath leave me in a rush.

He begins to move like a force, hammering into me while his eyes hold mine captive. His body rolls against mine, his skin setting mine on fire, and I fight the urge to lose myself in the moment.

His power rages against my strength as he takes me hard, making my muscles strain as my body tenses beneath his.

Alexei's so rough, causing my clit to feel overly sensitive with a weird mixture of pleasure and pain. A cry escapes me, and breaking eye contact, I turn my head and sink my teeth into his forearm.

It's too intense. Everything in me tightens, and then Alexei rips his arm away from me, and pushing his hand between us, he pinches the shit out of my clit.

Pleasure and pain explode through me, and I can't stop the whimpers from escaping me. I'm overcome, and they quickly turn to sobs. Not from tears but from how goddamn intense it is.

Suddenly Alexei stops, and then he lowers himself on me. He begins to gently rub my clit, sending involuntary spasms through me.

"Shh..." he whispers, his gentle touch soothing the ache and transforming it into ecstasy. "I've got you, baby." He starts to thrust into me again, this time keeping the pace slow and deep.

Alexei presses a kiss to my throat, and then he licks his way up to my ear. "No one makes you come but me."

And then his cock hits deep, colliding with a spot that unravels me at the speed of light. The orgasm sweeps through me like a tsunami, robbing me of my ability to breathe.

Alexei brings his hand up, and then he coats my lips with my wetness glistening on his finger before his mouth crashes against mine. His tongue takes my mouth the way his cock is owning my pussy, and I'm carried away in a rush of ecstasy.

Alexei lets out a grunt, and then he jerks against me as he takes his own release.

I lose sense of time until his movements slow down. When he stills deep inside me, he breaks the kiss, and then he captures my gaze.

"You're mine, Isabella."

It feels as if he's silently adding, *'No matter what.'*

With our breaths rushing over our lips, our bodies slick with sweat, and our hearts pounding, our eyes stay locked.

I hope you enjoyed your last fuck, Koslov.

Chapter 22

ALEXEI

When Isabella comes into the gym, I continue with the pull-ups I'm doing until I've completed the set.

Dropping to my feet, I glance to where she's standing next to the sparring mat.

"Training with Demitri?" I ask.

"No, I'm waiting for you," she says. "Thought we could spar today."

My eyes meet hers as I walk toward the mat.

Since yesterday I've had a weird feeling in my gut. There's something different in Isabella. The way she looks at me. The double-meaning in her words. The sex last night.

My gut instinct has never been wrong before.

Sweeping a hand over the mat, I say, "Let's spar."

I step into position, my muscles tense, just in case. I'm on edge from the shit with Sonia and St. Monarch's, and could totally be reading this wrong.

Isabella lunges at me, and I block the kick. Then I have to fucking move and block as she goes into full attack mode.

This isn't like any of the sparring sessions Isabella's had with Demitri. Her movements are planned and on point.

Fuck. If her memory's back…

Fuck.

My heartbeat speeds up as the thought that I can actually lose Isabella crosses my mind.

I begin to attack back, still careful not to hurt her, and a moment later, she tries to go for my throat. Grabbing hold of her arm, I turn into her, and then I send her flying over my shoulder. The second her back slams into the mat, I'm on top of her and locking my arms and legs around her, I force her to stop.

Our breaths explode into the air, and then Isabella lets out a dark chuckle. "Fucking bastard."

She begins to wrestle, trying to free herself from my hold. I have to duck to the side when she slams her head forward.

Letting go of her, I roll away and dart to my feet, ready for anything.

Just then, Demitri comes into the gym, and I shout, "Stay back. Isabella's memory has returned." Demitri stops, his eyes instantly locking on Isabella.

She lets out a burst of enraged laughter as her eyes lock on mine, cold and wild. "I'm going to fucking kill you."

I hold up a hand. "Calm down. Let's talk."

"Talk?" she hisses. "TALK?"

Isabella lunges at me again, and I allow her to take a swing at my jaw to let her blow off some steam. She packs one hell of a punch, my head turning as the ache spreads into my ear.

The next swing, I block and grabbing hold of her arm, I twist it behind her back. I lock my other arm around her neck, and then I tighten my grip to ensure she can't move.

"You fucking played me," she grinds the words out, and when I hear the heartache, the humiliation, the rage, I let go of her again.

Stepping back, I hold a hand up as she turns to face me. "You can't beat me, Isabella. Give me a chance to explain."

Her hands fly to her hair, and she lets out a frustrated scream, and then she glares murderously at me. "You can be glad I don't have a gun on me."

"Not everything was a lie," I say, wanting to get it out in the open.

My words only make her laugh, the sound filled with her need for vengeance.

"I. Love. You," I enunciate every single word. "I didn't lie about that." She shakes her head, her hair falling wild around her shoulders.

"I could've left you for dead, but I didn't. I could've taken what I wanted, but I gave you a choice. Don't forget that. Don't forget what I said to you on that cliff."

Isabella stalks toward me, her features unforgiving. She stops right in front of me, and I can only see hatred in her eyes as she says, "You. Betrayed. Me." She jabs a finger at my chest. "I was vulnerable, and you took advantage of the situation. You played me like a fucking puppet…" Her anger makes her eyes shimmer as if she's about to cry, and her voice hitches, "until I trusted you." Gasping, Isabella steps back as if she can't stand to be near me.

And it fucking guts my heart.

I shake my head. "I didn't play you. The only thing I lied about was how we met and that we were in a relationship. Everything else was real."

"Am I supposed to believe you?" she shouts, twin flames burning in her cheeks. "I'm the Princess of Terror, and you humiliated me as if I was… nothing." Her voice hitches again, and unable to keep my distance, I dart forward and wrap my arms around her.

Isabella fights me with a frustrated growl.

"I love you," I say as I tighten my hold on her. "I didn't lie about my feelings."

"I don't care about your feelings," she cries as she slams a fist against my neck. Before her other fist can connect with my face, I let go again, darting back.

Fuck. There's no calming her down.

But then Isabella sucks in deep breaths, and somehow she actually manages to calm down. Her face goes blank, all emotion draining from her features. When she lifts her eyes to me, they're empty. Even the rage is gone.

"I'll help take down my mother. After the attack, we'll meet, and only one of us will walk away alive because there is no way I'm honoring the alliance."

When she turns around, I ask, "Where are you going?"

"None of your fucking business," she bites out as she stalks toward the door.

My feet begin to move on their own, following after Isabella. When she walks into our bedroom, I watch as she changes into one of the leather outfits.

"For what it's worth, I never meant to hurt you," I say.

Isabella doesn't respond as she pulls on a pair of boots. Then she comes toward me, and stopping a couple of inches from me, she demands, "I want the motorcycle and a credit card."

Reaching into my pocket, I pull my wallet out and hand the black card over to her.

Isabella shoves it into her pocket, and for a moment, we stare at each other.

"Please be careful." I swallow hard on the fact that the woman I love doesn't love me back. If she did, she'd be able to forgive me. "If you need anything, let me know."

"I won't," she mutters, and giving me a glare, she walks out of the room where I worshiped her body.

Something in my chest snaps, and swinging around, I run after her. I grab hold of her shoulder and yank her body to mine, my arms engulfing her.

"Don't do this."

"Let go." Her voice is filled with warning.

Pulling back, I frame her face and look deep into her eyes. "Remember what I said on the cliff." I press my mouth hard to hers, savoring her taste just in case it's the last time I get to kiss her.

Let her go, Alexei. You can't tame her wild spirit. It's what you love most about her.

My hands fall away from her face, and I take a step back, and then I watch as Isabella walks away from me.

ISABELLA

It's late at night when I finally get to the rendezvous point, a house I purchased under Sofia Rojas, Ana's second and last name.

Please let her be here.

Grabbing hold of the wall, I hoist myself over, and then I drop down in the backyard. I walk to the security door, but before I can verify my identity on the biometric scanner, the door's yanked open.

"Isabella!" Ana cries, and then she throws her arms around my neck.

I engulf her in a tight hug, my soul sighing with relief.

Thank God.

Ana's body begins to jerk, and then she cries, tightening her hold on me.

"I'm sorry I took so long," I whisper as tears fill my eyes. When they fall, they're filled with intense relief that Ana's safe.

Overwhelmed, I lose control over the tight grip I had on my emotions, and I cry for the love I felt for Alexei and how he used it to humiliate me. The heartache threatens to eat me alive.

Somehow, I think to move us inside the house, so I can shut the security door. Then we sink to the floor, clinging to each other.

"I was… so worried," Ana sputters. "I thought… I lost you."

"I'm not that easy to kill." I try to chuckle, but it's smothered by a sob. "I got a little delayed."

Ana pulls back and wiping her cheeks with the back of her hands, sobs shudder through her. Then she looks at me, and her face crumbles again as she reaches for the scar that disappears into my hairline. "What happened?"

"It's a long story." I climb to my feet and help Ana up, and then we walk into the living room. When my eyes fall on the shrine Ana made for me, I feel the punch in my soul. "God, Ana." I pull her to me, not able to imagine the heartache she had to endure thinking I died.

"I never stopped praying."

I close my burning eyes, and then I just hold the only person who's ever given a damn about me. "I'm so glad you thought to come here."

Ana pulls back. "Men came to the safe house right after the attack on the mansion. I grabbed the girls and used the underground tunnel to escape."

A frown forms on my forehead. "What did the men look like?"

Ana begins to walk toward the basement. "I have them on the security footage."

When I walk into the room, a smile tugs at my mouth because Ana set the security systems up exactly like I showed her.

She brings up the footage, and then I watch as Carson and Damien sniff around the house. I let out a breath, feeling relieved that it was them.

Ana glances at me. "Also, I have this." She presses play, and I have to lean closer because the footage is grainy and dark. Suddenly the two older girls dart forward, and for a moment, Alexei steps into the light. He watches the girls, probably to make sure they reach me safely, and then he disappears back into the dark.

So it was him.

Alexei went after the older two girls.

Straightening up, my eyes meet Ana's. "The two men came to the house to get the girls because I got hurt. I don't think they knew about you and wanted to help the girls."

"I managed to help them return to their homes before I came to Panama," Ana says, erasing the worry I felt for the girls.

Then there's a stabbing ache in my heart because I don't want to think of Alexei doing something good. It will make me soften toward him, and he doesn't deserve that.

"Are you okay?" Ana asks, getting up from the chair.

I nod. "Yes." I gesture to the stairs. "Let's go up to the living room and get rid of that shrine. Then I'll tell you what happened."

While I clear out the table with the candles, rosaries, flowers, and photo of me, Ana gets us something to drink.

When we're comfortable on the couch, I take a sip of the water, then say, "Hugo shot me, and I fell from the helicopter. Alexei took me to LA."

Ana's eyes scour over me. "You must've been hurt badly if it took you this long to recover."

I shake my head. "I had amnesia."

Shock ripples over Ana's face. "What?"

"I lost all my memories of the last four years." I take a deep breath, my heart aching. "Alexei lied and said we were in a relationship. I didn't know any better, so I stayed with him."

Ana shakes her head, her features tightening as if she can feel my pain.

I lower my eyes to the glass in my hand. "He fooled me, Ana. I fell in love with the act and really thought he loved me back."

"Isabella," she murmurs, and then she takes the glass from me as I begin to fall apart.

I break down in my friend's arms, knowing it's a safe place. "I feel so humiliated," I cry against her shoulder.

"I know," she whispers, rubbing a hand over my back. "I'm sorry."

"I really… loved him." Sobs tear through me as I let the heartache bleed through me while admitting my true feelings out loud.

"Shh…" Ana gives me the comfort I need, and when the last tear falls, she pulls back and wipes the wetness from my cheeks. "This will only make you stronger. Okay?"

I nod as I let out a shuddering breath. "I just needed to let it out so I can put it behind me."

She nods. "I know."

We stare at each other for a moment, and then a breathtaking smile spreads over Ana's face. "I'm so glad you're back."

Her smile revives my broken and trampled heart, and it shines a light through the darkness.

"Ana," I whisper in total awe, "you're smiling."

She lets out a sputter and then hugs me again. "Of course. I have my friend back. You're my only family, and I was so lost without you."

Ana's my family.

"From now on, we stick together," she adds.

I nod. "Just the two of us. Always."

I don't need Alexei.

Chapter 23

ALEXEI

Standing in front of the window in our bedroom, I check the tracking device I had slotted between the diamond and the band of Isabella's engagement ring. It shows she's in Panama.

She hasn't taken the ring off.

"What's in Panama, baby?" I whisper as I watch the dot flash. It hasn't moved for the last twenty-four hours.

Letting out a sigh, I shove my phone back in my pocket and stare out at the garden as the sun rises.

What a fucking mess.

My teeth tug at my bottom lip as I try to come up with a way of convincing Isabella not everything was a lie.

There's a soft tap on the bedroom door, and when I glance over my shoulder, Demitri comes in.

"How are you holding up?" he asks as he comes to stand next to me.

"I'll survive."

Somehow.

The thought of Isabella not being a part of my life is too unbearable to even consider.

"I'll find a way to get her back."

"You might not be able to," Demitri warns.

"I'll find a way," I say with certainty. "She can't hate me forever."

"How would you have reacted if you were in her position?" Demitri asks, crossing his arms over his chest.

"I didn't force her," I mutter.

I'm not my father.

"Answer the question."

Letting out a sigh, I try to put myself in Isabella's shoes. Then I shake my head and glare at Demitri. "I wouldn't be as pissed about it as she is."

Demitri lifts an eyebrow at me. "What if you were in Isabella's position, but instead of it being Isabella, your memory returns, and you come face to face with Sonia."

"What the actual fuck," I snap at him. "That's just twisted, brother. Anyone else but Sonia."

"Isabella considered you the enemy, and then she spent two months falling for the charismatic version of you while you had your way with her. I can only imagine what a fucking shock it must've been for her. I told you not to do it."

Rage explodes through my veins. Turning to face Demitri, my features tighten. He assumes the same position, and then we stare at each other, tension building between us.

Then my body shudders as the memories from my past crawl to the surface like rotten corpses.

I can hear Papa slapping Mama. It's the only sound echoing through the house because she never cries out loud.

I glance at my baby brother, glad he's asleep, and then I sneak out of the room. As I creep closer to the stairs, the awful sounds of Papa hitting her become louder. Reaching the railing, I crouch and peek down.

Papa has his favorite gun in his hand, using it to hit Mama. I bite my bottom lip when I see all the blood.

Stop.

My face crumbles, and I almost cry out to Papa to stop, but then he points the gun at Mama. She turns her face toward me, and it hurts to see how badly Papa has beaten her.

"Close your eyes," she cries, her eyes locked on me.

I can't, Mama.

A bang makes my body jerk, and then my heart pounds out of my chest as I watch Papa glare up at me.

"You never hesitate to pull the trigger, Alexei. When someone betrays you, you kill them. Got it?"

I can't nod as my eyes move to Mama.

"Do you understand?" Papa shouts.

My movements are jerky as my head bobs up and down.

I understand that Papa killed Mama.

I return from hell with a shuddering breath, and my eyes focus on Demitri's concerned face.

He didn't just say what I think he did.

Demitri knows my past.

"Not once did I force, Isabella. And let's not forget the attraction was there before she lost her memory," I bite the words out, the rage tightening my voice to breaking point. "I lied about one thing. Don't make it sound like I fucking held her here against her will, tied her to my bed, and fucking raped her."

My body begins to tremble uncontrollably from my temper shooting into outer-fucking-space, and my breaths speed up.

Demitri takes a step back, realization flickering in his eyes. "I never said that. Calm down." The concern quickly deepens on his face. "That's not what I meant."

Not able to think straight, I walk away before doing something I'll regret and blindly head out of the house.

"Alexei!" Demitri shouts behind me.

Climbing into one of the SUVs, I start the engine, and then I floor the gas, fishtailing it out of the driveway.

I push the SUV as fast as it will go while everything in me trembles as if a fucking earthquake is ripping through me.

Is that how Isabella feels?

Is that how she sees it?

I didn't.

I wouldn't.

Only when I bring the SUV to a skidding stop do I realize where I am. I shove the door open and walk up the trail until I reach the top of the cliff, and then I sink to my knees.

'Close your eyes,' I hear my mother whisper.

Lifting my hand to my chest, I grip the fabric over my heart as unbearable pain rips through me.

Our mother was a sex slave, and when she was done giving birth to Carson and me, my father shot her like she was nothing more than a sick dog that had to be put out of its misery. All because she tried to escape. My father saw it as a betrayal.

It was the first death I witnessed, and I was the last thing she saw.

At seven years old, I was old enough to understand what happened. Luckily Carson was too young to remember anything about her. I've protected him from it all his life.

And when I turned twenty-one, I killed my father.

These are my darkest secrets only Demitri knows. The skeletons in my closet, demanding I live by a strict code of honor.

We don't force women.

This is why I fucking hate Sonia more than anything. It's why I'm willing to die as long as I take her with me.

My body shudders as I bend over, my fingers grasping at the grass beneath me.

If Isabella feels that I violated her, then there's no way I'll ever get her back.

The thought tears mercilessly through my heart, and when it's done shredding it to pieces, it moves onto my soul.

Because that's how deeply I love her.

I begin to shake my head, refusing to accept the possibility that she won't be able to forgive me, that I'm no different from my father.

Christ. No.

I begin to gasp for air as the most profound ache seizes my chest.

Fuck.

I suck in a strangled breath and slam a fist into the ground, and then the first tear falls, and it feels as if it's coated in my mother's blood, leaving a trail of betrayal over my cheek.

I'm sorry.

I'm so fucking sorry.

Hearing footsteps behind me, I dart up and spinning around, it's only to see Demitri walking toward me.

When he stops in front of me, he takes hold of my shoulder and pulls me into an embrace. "I'm sorry. That's not what I meant. Don't even think that."

I suck in a painful breath of air. "What if that's how she feels? Then I'm no better than him."

Demitri shakes his head hard, tightening his arms around me. "You didn't force yourself on Isabella. Just take a moment and calm down. You can't think clearly when you lose your shit."

It doesn't happen often, but when it does, it's hard to calm down.

Closing my eyes, I listen to my friend. I focus on taking deep breaths.

"You're a good man," Demitri murmurs.

I nod, taking another deep breath.

"You're nothing like your father."

Bringing my arms up, I grab hold of Demitri, the ghosts of the past refusing to let go of me.

"You're nothing like your father," Demitri repeats.

I shake my head, just trying to even out my breathing.

Demitri pulls back and placing his hands on the sides of my neck, his eyes lock with mine. "Listen to me, Alexei. You didn't force Isabella. Yes, you lied, but you didn't force her to do anything she didn't want to."

I just stare at the only person who truly knows me.

Then he continues, "You're a good man. I wouldn't risk my life for you if you weren't." I lower my eyes from Demitri's, but then he says, "You have my loyalty and love because you are nothing like your father. The day you killed him, I vowed to be your custodian because I knew there wasn't a man alive more deserving of my protection than you."

I nod, swallowing hard on the turbulent emotions inside me. Turning away from Demitri, I focus my eyes on the ocean.

He moves in next to me, and then silence falls between us as he gives me time to push the past back into the shadows.

I didn't force Isabella.

Slowly, I blink as I cling to the thought for the sake of my sanity.

ISABELLA

I drag my body out of bed and get ready for the day.

The strength that used to flow through my veins feels like it's been sapped from my body. The anger has given way to raw heartache, and as much as I hate to admit it, I miss Alexei.

I miss his playful smile.

I miss the way he looked at me… as if he really loved me.

I miss feeling his strong arms around me.

I even fucking miss the way he walks.

Ugh.

Shaking my head, I try to force Alexei from my mind, and after putting on my boots, I leave the bedroom.

I find Ana in the kitchen, where she's preparing a cup of coffee. "Want some?"

I nod and take a seat at the table.

"We don't have to go today," she says. Ana's made it clear she's not happy about us going back to Columbia to get my motorcycle and weapons.

I've spent the past week watching the area around the safe house and the other property to make sure it's clear. Which it isn't. My mother's men are watching it, which tells me she's figured out what I was up to.

"I have to. I can't leave them there."

She sets a cup of coffee down in front of me and takes a seat across from me. Her eyes drift over my face, then she pats her heart and asks, "How are you feeling?"

"Raw." I shake my head. "It's hard to think it was all an act."

"Maybe it wasn't," Ana mentions.

I let out a bitter chuckle. "Alexei Koslov does nothing unless he's going to gain from it. The most important thing to him is power." I take a sip of the beverage, then add, "And loyalty." I let out a sigh.

Ana gives me a comforting look.

Shaking my head, I continue, “I’m still trying to put all the pieces together, and there’s one thing I’m not clear on. Why fake a relationship between us? What would he stand to gain from it?”

Ana shrugs. “It’s not like he can get to your mother through you.”

“Exactly. That’s the confusing part.” We sit and think for a moment. “Alexei wants my mother dead. To think he lied about a relationship just to form an alliance with me… that’s seriously too extreme, even for him.”

Ana sets her mug down on the table. “You said you hooked up with him. Maybe it was love at first sight for him.”

I let out a burst of laughter. “No.”

“Why won’t you consider it?” Ana asks.

“Because it’s ridiculous. Alexei Koslov doesn’t fall in love.”

“He’s human, Isabella. Even your mother fell in love. It happens.”

I stare down at the caramel liquid in the cup, considering what Ana just said.

Remembering how Alexei looked at me like I was everything he ever wanted stabs at my crushed heart.

Was it all an act?

'I. Love. You.'

'I could've left you for dead, but I didn't. I could've taken what I wanted, but I gave you a choice. Don't forget that. Don't forget what I said to you on that cliff.'

Closing my eyes, my mind goes back to when Alexei proposed to me.

'Whatever happens in the future, I want you to remember this moment. I mean everything I'm going to say,' Alexei takes a deep breath, and then his eyes lock with mine. 'I love you.'

God, it felt like he meant what he said. I remember how the words hit, making me feel emotional.

'I fucking love everything about you. I could spend the next hour going into detail, but I won't. I want you. All of you. I want you next to my side. I want to wage wars with you. I want to build empires with you. I want you in every new memory I make because there isn't a woman on the face of this planet I respect more.'

The heartache becomes too much to bear, and shaking my head to rid myself of the memories, I get up. I grab the cup and empty it into the sink. "We leave in five minutes."

"Isabella," Ana calls after me. I stop and glance over my shoulder. "It does get easier with time."

"It does?" I ask, wondering if she's referring to what happened to her.

Ana nods. "Yes, especially when you have someone to lean on."

"Did I make it easier for you?" I ask, needing to know if I made a difference in her life.

"I wouldn't be sitting here if it weren't for you," she admits, then she gets up and comes to stand in front of me. "Not because you saved me, but because you gave me a reason to live."

Emotion wells in my chest. "I really needed to hear that."

Ana's mouth lifts slightly. "Sorry I haven't said it before."

I shake my head, then I meet her eyes. "You never talk about what happened."

Pain flashes over her features. "I can't."

"Okay."

Ana takes a deep breath, and then she steps around me. "The five minutes are up. I guess we should get going."

I follow Ana out of the house, thinking how she's changing day by day.

Maybe that's all it will take to get over Alexei – time.

Chapter 24

ALEXEI

"This feels familiar," Demitri mutters as we sit in the safe house in Columbia again.

I held out a week before I followed Isabella, and now I'm back to square one, watching her.

I'm staring at the tracker that shows Isabella's at her own safe house. Suddenly the marker begins to move, and I dart to my feet. "She's on the move."

Demitri gets up and follows me out of the house. He's been glued to my side since I lost my shit, watching me like a damn hawk.

"I can go by myself," I mention even though I know it's pointless.

Demitri shakes his head and opens the passenger door. Once we're inside the vehicle, he says, "Not with Sonia's people crawling all over the place."

Even though Sonia's in hiding, business is continuing as always. She's put a man named Oscar in charge. He's the usual scum of the earth.

"You can't throw a stone without hitting a cockroach around here," I mutter.

I start the engine and then steer the SUV toward the vacated house where Isabella seems to be heading.

I park down the road from the vacated house where Isabella keeps her motorcycle so she won't see us. We only have to wait a couple of minutes before a van pulls into the driveaway.

"That's the same van we've seen at her safe house," Demitri mentions.

Then both our heads tilt to the side as we watch two people get out of the vehicle. I grab the binoculars and bringing them to my eyes, I get a better look at the other person.

"Woman. Either late teens or early twenties," I murmur. "Also Latino."

Just then, a car turns up the street and dims its lights. "Fuck."

Demitri and I move, rushing out of the SUV, and then I'm running straight for the car as I yank my gun from behind me. I raise my arms, and stopping in the middle of the road, I take aim. As soon as the fuckers are close enough, I fire a shot that shatters the windscreen.

Men spill from the vehicle, scattering like roaches. My barrel tracks the driver, and then I pull the trigger, dropping him to the pavement.

Demitri guns two down.

"Is that all of them?" I ask.

"Yes, but yours is still moving."

"Just like a fucking cockroach. Chop off the head, and the fuckers still keep going," I mutter as I stalk to where the man is trying to drag himself into the shadows. Coming up to him, I fire two more shots. "Die already."

When I turn around, it's to see Isabella walking into the road, her gun drawn and ready at her side. Seeing her is a sucker punch to my heart as I tuck my weapon into its place behind my back.

"What are you doing here?" she calls out, her voice sounding tense as fuck.

"Making sure you're safe," I answer honestly.

"You tracked me?"

I begin to walk toward her and only stop once I can see her clearly and am close enough to touch her. It doesn't escape my attention that I don't have a gun pointed at my chest, and I'm totally taking it as a win.

Then a breeze picks up, and her scent washes over me, making my heart constrict.

"If you don't want me knowing where you are, you should take off the engagement ring," I say, praying she won't.

Isabella lifts her left hand and looks at the ring. "Should've known."

"And don't forget the tracker on the motorcycle," I add.

Isabella's eyes snap to mine, and then we stare at each other.

"You look good," I murmur.

"It's only been a week."

"A week too long."

Isabella shakes her head at me. "You should leave."

"Who's the woman?"

"None of your business," she bites out, instantly going on guard and giving me a look of warning.

Okay, it's someone who means a lot to Isabella.

"I'm not leaving," I say. "Sonia's men know you're here."

"I can take care of myself."

I nod. "I know, but it doesn't change the fact that I'm not leaving."

Isabella glares at me. "You're infuriating."

The corner of my mouth lifts. "So I've been told."

She turns away from me and begins to walk back to the house.

For a moment, I hesitate, but then I call after her, "Isabella."

She stops and gives me an annoyed look. "What is it now?"

Pushing through, I ask the question that's been gnawing at my soul, "Did I force anything on you?"

Her gaze narrows on me, and it makes my heart stop, then she says, "You wouldn't be alive if you did."

My eyes drift shut as intense relief spreads through me.

"Go home, Alexei. I'll meet you there before the attack."

Opening my eyes, I focus on Isabella, and then honesty spills over my lips, "It's not home without you."

She looks at me for a moment longer, and then she disappears behind the van.

As I pass the house, I glance at the property, but there's no sign of Isabella or the other woman.

When we get back to the SUV, I pick up the binoculars and scan over the property.

"She better get out of there before the cops come," Demitri mentions.

"She should have another five minutes," I say, and just then, the shed door opens, and Isabella pushes the motorcycle out. It takes her a while to kickstart the engine, and then she climbs on.

The van starts, and it has me saying, "I wonder who the other woman is. Isabella had a strong reaction when I brought her up."

"Could be her partner," Demitri guesses.

"Would explain what happened to the girls. The woman probably moved them before we got to the safe house."

I begin to smile because it's good to know Isabella's not alone out there.

"Feel better?" Demitri asks.

"Yes. I needed to hear that from her," I admit.

It also means I still have a chance to get Isabella back.

ISABELLA

It's been an agonizingly long week since I unexpectedly saw Alexei in Columbia.

'It's not home without you.'

I stare at the engagement ring on my finger. I've tried to take it off but couldn't. My heart wouldn't let me. No matter how much I want to hate Alexei, I can't because when all is said and done, I love him.

My thoughts are inundated with Alexei.

Who is he?

The ruthless head of the bratva? The assassin who kills without a second thought?

Or the man who looked at me with devotion while he worshipped my body?

I'm still struggling to align the devil with the man I fell in love with.

Maybe it wasn't all a lie?

Maybe… just maybe, Alexei does love me?

What will you do then, Isabella?

I shake my head.

"Let's go for a walk on the beach," Ana suddenly says. "The fresh air will be good for you."

Nodding, I climb to my feet, and as I leave the house with Ana, the thoughts of Alexei follow me.

It's time for Ana and me to head to LA. The shipment of weapons Alexei ordered must've arrived by now.

As we reach the stretch of sand, I don't even glance at the waves lapping at the shore.

"We need to travel to LA," I say.

Ana's quiet for a moment. "Are you sure we can trust them not to kill us the moment we're there?"

I think for a while, and no matter what scenario runs through my mind, the end is always the same. "Alexei won't hurt us."

"He's already hurt you," she mutters.

"Not physically." I glance at Ana. "We'll be safe. I won't let anything happen to you."

A smile tugs at her lips. "I know."

For a while, we walk in silence until Ana picks a spot to sit down. I make myself comfortable next to her and glance around us to make sure we're safe before I turn my gaze to the clear blue water.

Ana begins to draw random patterns in the sand, and keeping her eyes lowered from mine, she admits, "I thought you were an angel."

I frown, but she doesn't see it.

"When you… when you pulled him off me, I thought you were an angel that came to take me to heaven."

Goosebumps spread over my skin as my eyes lock on Ana's face.

This is the first time she's brought up that night, and I'm holding my breath, hoping she'll continue and purge the burden weighing so heavy on her.

"I lived with my mother in San Antero. Men broke in, and… they just shot my mother before we even had time to process they were in the house." Ana's voice lowers to a whisper. "That's when I was taken."

Feeling Ana's sorrow, I want to hold her, but I keep still, not wanting her to stop talking.

She lets out a sigh. "It feels like another life… the time I had with my mother."

Unable to stop myself, I place a hand on her back. Ana leans into me, and resting her head against my shoulder, she stares at the ocean.

"I didn't know this part of the world existed. I didn't know there was such horror out there."

I move my hand to her arm and give her a squeeze.

Then Ana's body shudders, and she lets out a sob. When she turns and buries her face against me, I wrap my arms around her and press my mouth to her hair.

"I can't… I can't even think of it," she cries.

"Shhh… it's okay." I brush a hand up and down her back.

Ana pulls away, and her tearful eyes meet mine. "I can't lose you, Isabella. You're all I have, all that stands between me and the demons."

I lift my hands to her cheeks, framing her face, and then I look deep into her heartbreaking gaze. "You won't lose me. I'll always protect you."

Ana hugs me, and then she whispers, "I love you."

My eyes drift shut as her words piece some of my heart back together again. "I love you too."

It's the first time I've said those words to a person, and no one's more deserving than the woman I call my sister.

"If we really need to go to LA, I'll go. I'll follow you wherever you go," she says as she wipes her cheeks. Then, taking a deep breath, she admits, "I trust you."

My lips curve into a smile, and then a weird sensation skitters down my spine. I glance around us for the source.

It could be Alexei.

Not wanting to take the chance, I get up and help Ana to her feet. "Time to go back. We've been out here for too long."

I keep glancing around us as we quickly walk toward the house.

"Something wrong?" Ana asks, her eyes darting around us.

"No, I'm just being careful," I answer. "Don't worry." As I say the words, I move my right hand behind my back, and my fingers wrap around the hilt of the gun.

I place my left hand on Ana's back so I can grab hold of her if we're suddenly attacked.

My senses are on high alert until I finally push Ana into the house, sealing the security door shut.

"What's going on?" Ana asks.

I shake my head. "I'm not sure. It could just be Alexei watching us." I head to the basement and bring up the security cameras we have around the property.

Ana and I take a seat, and then we wait to see if anyone approaches the house.

Not even seconds later, a car slowly passes by the front of the house, and then three men approach from the back of property.

Ana stiffens next to me, her voice fearful as she whispers, "Isabella."

I get up, pulling my gun from behind me. "Secure the door behind me."

"Wait!" Ana points at the screen.

My eyes snap to the monitor. One man's already down, and I watch as another drops. The third begins to run but doesn't make it far before he slumps to the ground.

Alexei.

Just then, movement by the sidewall grabs my attention, and I watch as Alexei jumps over, running for the security door.

My body moves, and I race up the stairs. I slam into the security door, then quickly put in the code to open it, and then Alexei fills the narrow hallway, shoving the door shut.

His eyes lock on mine. "We have to move. Now. Demitri's holding them off."

"Ana!" I shout as I turn to run back to her. "We need to leave. Wipe the systems."

Alexei grabs hold of my arm, and then I'm yanked to his chest, his arms wrapping around me. I hear him take a deep breath, and he presses his mouth to my temple. Precious seconds pass before he lets go of me.

His hand lingers on my arm as our eyes meet, and the sight of him alone rips through my heart, never mind feeling his touch.

Then he gently nudges me. "Go, baby."

I dart away from him, and as I race down the stairs, Ana looks at me, stark panic on her face as she feverishly types to wipe the computers clean.

"It's going to be okay," I assure her as I grab my backpack, shrugging it on. I check the clips of my Heckler

& Koch and Glock, then set the timer for a device that will initiate a fire to burn the house down.

"What can I do?" Alexei suddenly asks, and Ana startles so bad, she forgets about the system and jumps up from the chair.

I hold up a hand to stop Alexei from moving and approach Ana. Her eyes dart to my face. "It's okay. Alexei won't hurt you." I pat against my chest. "I'm here."

Ana darts away from the wall toward me, and a second later, she comes to a skidding stop next to me, grabbing hold of my shirt at my side. Her fingers dig tightly into the fabric while she apprehensively watches Alexei.

Tugging Ana along, I walk to the system and finish the shutdown procedure, then I turn to Alexei. "You just startled her."

Alexei's eyes move to Ana. "Nice to finally meet you, little one."

Ana just nods, her eyes locked on me.

"We really have to get out of here," Alexei reminds me.

I activate the timer, then help Ana put on her backpack. "Stay behind me," I say, and she nods. "If anything happens to me, you run as fast as you can."

Ana's face pales, and then she meets my eyes and shakes her head.

I don't have time to argue with her as we rush to follow Alexei back to the security door. "Is it clear, Demitri?"

I can't hear Demitri's response, but a second later, Alexei gestures to the door. "Open it."

I do as he says, and as we abandon the last safe house I had, the realization hits that even after everything, I still trust Alexei.

Chapter 25

ALEXEI

'Clear,' Demitri murmurs.

"Over the wall," I order the women.

Isabella begins to help Ana up, but then I step in and, taking hold of Ana, who doesn't look a day over twenty, I push her onto the top of the wall.

Isabella's up next to the girl before I take another breath. Then, hoisting myself over, the three of us drop to the ground.

'Run. More cars are approaching,' Demitri's voice comes over the earpiece.

"Run," I bark. "Toward those apartments." I point to where Demitri's taken up a sniping position.

The women dart forward, and I'm right behind them.

When we're near the building, I hear a bullet hitting metal behind me.

'Faster,' Demitri growls.

Darting forward, I grab hold of Ana, and tossing her over my shoulder, I shoot past Isabella. She quickly catches up and sticks to my side as I race for the spot where the SUV is parked.

Reaching the vehicle, I yank the back door open and toss Ana inside. "Isabella, get in the back," I shout, and then I climb in behind the steering wheel. "Demitri."

'Go. I'll catch up.'

"Fuck!" I start the engine and floor the gas, knowing Demitri can follow the tracker I have in the tag I never remove from around my neck.

As I steer the SUV through traffic, I bring up Demitri's tracker on my phone.

When I see he's still in the snipping position, I order, "Move, Demitri!"

'Five seconds.'

"Fucker!" I snarl, and then I pull up the handbrake and yank the steering wheel, making a U-turn. "Get your ass to the street. I'm coming."

'You never fucking listen to me,' he mutters.

As I approach the building, I say, "Get ready, Isabella. I need you to provide cover. Move in behind me."

"Down," she instructs Ana, and then she opens the back window and moves in behind my seat.

"Ready?"

"Yes," she breathes, and I glance in the rearview mirror for a moment. Seeing she has a gun in each hand, I focus on the road ahead.

Just as Demitri jumps to the ground, I pull the steering wheel to the right. "Cover!"

Isabella opens fire as the SUV skids to the side, and then I lean over and throw the passenger door open.

A bullet slams into my door as Demitri darts into the vehicle. Pressing on the gas, the SUV shoots forward while Isabella keeps firing behind me.

When I've put some distance between Sonia's men and us, Isabella slumps back against the seat and reloads her weapons.

"Hi, Demitri," Isabella says. "Miss me?"

He lets out a chuckle. "No, but thanks for the cover."

"Just repaying the favor."

The corner of my mouth lifts, then I say, "The little one behind your seat is Ana. Ana, this is Demitri."

"I figured as much," Ana says, not sounding as fearful as she did earlier.

"Stay down," Isabella tells Ana, then she grabs hold of my seat and leans forward. Her scent drifts to me as she asks, "Where are we going?"

"Airfield and then home," I answer.

I keep glancing behind us to make sure we don't have company until we reach the airfield. I stop the SUV in a hanger, and we all pile out of the vehicle.

Ana sticks slightly behind Isabella as we all walk to the private jet.

Climbing the steps, I wonder how Isabella and Ana met. I'm guessing she's one of the girls Isabella saved, but I can't figure out why she kept her.

Demitri secures the door behind us before going to the cockpit.

Isabella and Ana take off their backpacks, and taking a seat, they strap themselves in. I sit down opposite Isabella, and my eyes settle on her.

Christ, it's fucking good to have her so close to me.

When she glances up and sees me staring, she gives me a *what now* look.

"Still hate me?" I ask.

Her eyes narrow on me.

"You know there's a thin line between love and hate," I tease her. My eyes slant to Ana. "What do you think, little one. Will Isabella forgive me?"

Ana meets my eyes for the first time, just giving me a shrug.

I see I have my work cut out to win Ana's trust.

My gaze goes back to Isabella. "There's an even thinner line between the truth and a lie."

"Clearly. You've mastered the art of that," Isabella mutters.

"Just like you have," I say, and it makes Isabella stare at me.

What matters right now is that I'm taking Isabella home.

One win at a time.

As Demitri flies us back to LA, I alternate, staring out of the window and looking at Isabella. My eyes keep finding their way back to her.

Three hours into the flight, Ana finally seems to relax, and she begins to nod off. Isabella presses Ana's head to her shoulder and whispers, "Sleep a little. I'll wake you when we land."

I watch the two women interact, and seeing how protective and loving Isabella is with Ana, once again warms my heart.

Life is so much easier when you have someone you can call family.

ISABELLA

The flight to LA messed with my head.

By the time we reach Alexei's mansion, I feel drained and frazzled. I'm holding Ana's hand, more for myself than to give her support.

I'm using Ana as a shield to keep Alexei at a distance, and it makes me feel like a rotten friend.

Then I remember the fact that Alexei came for us. We would've been attacked, and there's no telling if I would've been able to get us out of the house alive.

Alexei could've left me to my own defenses, but he didn't. That has to mean something. Right?

Then the thought crosses my mind that Alexei charges a substantial amount for his protection, and my eyes dart to him.

"How much do I owe you?" the words burst from me as we walk into the house.

Alexei lets out a chuckle. "Hmm… I'll let you know."

I shoot him a glare. "Don't play games with me."

Alexei stops walking and comes to stand right in front of me. His stare is intense as his eyes meet mine.

It's different meeting his eyes after my memory returned, knowing the power he holds. It's intimidating, making me feel awkward instead of strong.

Ana's fingers tighten around mine, and I give her a reassuring squeeze.

"How much?" I demand. I have twenty million that I've stolen from my mother over the past two years. I'll pay everything if it means I'm not in Alexei's debt.

He tilts his head. "I want time as payment."

A frown forms on my forehead. "How much time?"

The corner of his mouth lifts in a hot smirk. "An hour alone with you."

Ana grips my hand tighter, and it has me asking, "Only to talk?"

"Of course," Alexei mutters, and then there's a sudden flash of anger in his eyes. "I'm offended that you even have to ask."

Instant regret ripples through my heart because I know Alexei won't demand anything intimate. Taking me by force won't be a turn-on for him.

To Alexei, it's all about me submitting willingly and the power he gains from it.

"I didn't mean to offend you," I say, then I agree, "One hour."

"Now," he demands, and then he heads up the stairs. "Get Ana settled in one of the guest rooms."

I tug Ana up to the second floor and watch as Alexei goes into his suite while I head to the guest room next to his.

When I shut the door behind us, I turn to Ana. "We'll be safe here."

Ana nods as she glances around the room.

"Go take a shower while I talk to Alexei."

Her eyes dart to mine. "Will you be okay?"

I nod. "It's better to get the talk over with as soon as possible." I open the door then say, "Try to relax."

Ana nods as she sets her backpack down.

I shut the door behind me and walk to Alexei's suite. When I step inside, Alexei's standing out on the balcony, his back turned to me.

My gaze roams over the room, and I notice everything I used while I lived here is exactly where I left it.

Alexei turns to face me, and then a sad smile tugs at his mouth. "Do you feel violated?"

The question catches me off guard, and I frown at Alexei. Shaking my head, I admit, "Humiliated. Angry as hell. Hurt." I move closer. "The list goes on, but no, not violated."

Alexei looks relieved, taking a deep breath and letting it out slowly. Then he sets the timer on his watch. "One hour, starting now."

I nod, and lifting my chin, I brace myself.

Alexei doesn't say anything but just stares at me. When minutes start to tick by, I ask, "You wanted to talk?"

"I'll get to that. But, first, I just want to look at you."

Lightly shaking my head, I take a seat on the side of the bed, and then I stare back at Alexei.

I take in the man that's upended my world while making me feel safe at the same time. It's something to get used to.

I'm torn between how I felt during the two months I stayed here and not knowing what to believe.

Chapter 26

ISABELLA

The longer my eyes are on Alexei's face, the more the ruthlessness fades until all I see is the man I fell in love with.

I search for the anger inside me, but I'm not able to find it. All that's left is the hurt.

Suddenly Alexei nods, and as if he just read my mind, he murmurs, "I never meant to hurt you."

"But you did," I say, rising to my feet. "You could've told me the truth from the beginning."

"I didn't want you to leave," he admits.

Frowning, I ask, "Why? I can't figure that out. What do you want from me, Alexei?"

"Everything," he answers. The possessiveness lacing the word sends shivers rushing over my skin.

God, he still has the power to cloud my better judgment. His presence makes it hard to focus on the fact that I should be spitting angry with him.

Alexei begins to move toward me. "I want you and everything you have to offer." He stops in front of me, and lifting his hands, he frames my face. His eyes bore into mine as he says, "I just want you, Isabella."

I search his eyes for the truth, but doubt makes it impossible to read them. Something's holding me back, and I can't figure out what it is.

I pull his hands away from my face, and stepping around him, I walk out onto the balcony. With my back to Alexei, I say, "I have no idea what's the truth and what's a lie when it comes to you."

I feel Alexei as he comes to stand behind me and my eyes drift closed.

I might be angry and hurt, but at the end of the day, Alexei still has the power because I can't stop loving him.

Just a couple of minutes alone with him, and even the heartache is starting to ease.

I shake my head, wondering if I even stand a chance against him. Or has he already taken ownership of me, and I just need to come to terms with it?

Alexei places his hands on my shoulders, and then his breath fans over my skin right before he presses a kiss to the side of my neck. "When I brought you to the hospital, I just wanted time so you'd be open to an alliance between us."

I turn around, coming face to face with him. I'm so tired of putting up an act that I don't think to wear a mask. Looking at Alexei, I don't think to hide what I feel. "If you only wanted an alliance, why did you make me fall for you?"

Emotion washes over his face, and then his features become predatory. "You fell?"

"That's not what's important," I argue. "Why did you do it? Why humiliate me in the process?"

Alexei shakes his head. "I didn't do it to humiliate you." He looks sincere as he says, "I did it because I love you."

My eyes search his, and then I ask, "Who are you, Alexei? I can't put the two versions of you together. All I've ever known of you is how calculating and ruthless you are. You're the devil, the only person my mother fears." I shake my head. "But during the two months I stayed here, you were caring and so attentive…" I shake my head again.

Lifting his hands, he places them on the sides of my neck, and then he moves closer until his cologne is all I breathe. "I'm both men, Isabella. I don't show everyone the person I am when I'm home. That would be fucking stupid and suicidal."

"God, it's hard thinking Alexei Koslov is playful and caring," I mutter.

He lets out a chuckle. "I'm full of surprises."

"You can say that again."

His expression turns tender, and it makes a wave of emotion wash through me. "If I didn't lose my memory, would I still be here now?"

Alexei nods. "Definitely. I would've found a different way to convince you to form an alliance with me." He lets out another chuckle. "Besides, after the hot hook-up we had in the club, I knew the attraction was there. I just had to build on that."

The blood drains from my face as the realization slams into my heart.

Oh. My. God.

I forgot about our initial attraction.

Concern flashes over Alexei's face. "Isabella?"

My heartbeat speeds up. "You're attracted to me."

Alexei nods. "I thought I made that clear?"

"You really love me?"

A smile curves his lips, and his eyes soften. "More than anything."

Holy shit, how could I forget?

It means not everything was an act like I thought. The initial attraction was there from the first moment we laid eyes on each other.

Lowering my gaze, I close the distance between us and press my forehead to his chest.

He really loves me?

Alexei Koslov really loves me.

I suck in a deep breath, the realization overwhelming me and making me feel emotional.

"I'm sorry I lied to you," he murmurs as he wraps his arms around me and presses a kiss on my hair. "But I'd do it again if it meant I got you at the end."

I think that's what I've been struggling to accept – that Alexei Koslov has fallen – for me. Love is rare in our world, and men like Alexei… they don't love anything but power.

"I'm processing," I whisper as I take a deep breath, "the fact that you actually love me."

He pulls a little back and leans in to catch my eyes. "Why?"

"Because we were supposed to be sworn enemies."

Alexei begins to chuckle. "That was until I watched you risk your life to save the innocent."

"Why did that make such an impression on you?" I ask.

A shadow moves over Alexei's face. "That's a story for another day."

"You're assuming there will be another day?" I tease him.

"Damn right I am." Wrapping an arm around my waist, he yanks me against his chest, and then he gives me the possessive look I love so much. "Are we done fighting, Isabella?"

"For now."

"What do you mean for now?" he asks.

"Until you do something to make me angry or vice versa."

A hot smirk tugs at his mouth. "We can always end our fights with sex. It's a great way to let off steam."

As he begins to lean down, I arch back to tease him. "Oh, is that so?"

Alexei's hand fists in my hair to keep me in place, and then he crushes his mouth to mine just as his watch begins to beep, indicating the hour is up.

ALEXEI

Isabella laughs as I silence the timer I set on my watch, then she says, "One hour. Was it worth the amount you would've charged under normal circumstances?"

I press a kiss to her mouth. "Yes." My teeth tug at her bottom lip, and I feel a relieved groan build in my soul. "Definitely."

She's back. I didn't lose the love of my life.

Thank fuck.

As my tongue drives into her mouth, and I taste her again, I know I'd pay a hell of a lot more than the ten million I would've charged just for the chance to kiss her like this.

Before I can take things further, Isabella breaks the kiss and leans backward. "I have to get back to Ana."

Oh. Right.

Reluctantly I let go of her, then I ask, "Is Ana one of the girls you saved?"

Isabella nods.

"Why did you keep her?"

A protective look settles on her face. "She had nowhere to go, and… she needed me."

Searching Isabella's eyes, I say, "You love her a lot."

"Ana's my family," Isabella admits. "I trust her."

A smile curves my lips. "She's to you what Demitri is to me."

Nodding, she says, "Yes." She hesitates for a moment. "Ana's been through a lot. She's… sensitive." Regret flashes in Isabella's eyes. "I was too late."

I stare at Isabella as I realize what she's trying to tell me. Nodding, I say, "I'll tell everyone to be careful around Ana."

"Thank you." Isabella swallows before she adds, "It will take her a while to get used to everyone. It took a year before she was comfortable with me. She'll probably keep to herself."

Knowing how much Ana means to Isabella, I ask, "What does she like to do?"

"Security. She handled the cameras and system for me."

Drawing my bottom lip between my teeth, I try to come up with a plan. "That's Demitri's area. Ana will probably freak out if I stick her in the security room with Demirti and Nikhil."

Isabella nods. "Maybe at a later stage." Taking hold of my hand, she gives me a sincere look. "Thank you for wanting to make her feel at home. I think she should take a break and just be a normal nineteen-year-old."

My eyebrow lifts. "Ariana will be perfect to help her with that. Will Ana be okay with her?"

A smile tugs at Isabella's mouth. "I'll ask Ana." Then she presses a kiss to my lips.

As she starts to walk to the door, I ask, "Why didn't you take the engagement ring off?"

She glances over her shoulder and smiles at me. "How else would you find me?"

"You wanted me to watch you?"

"I used you for the protection you provided," she teases as she opens the door.

"You're sleeping here tonight," I say, my tone clearly stating it's not negotiable.

Still, Isabella defies me as she murmurs, "We'll see."

I follow her out of the room and smile when she glances at me before opening the door to the guest room. Heading downstairs, I go to the security room.

When I walk inside, Demitri turns his attention to me. "No black eye?"

"And I even got a kiss," I joke.

He lets out a chuckle, shaking his head at me. "Lucky fucker."

"About Ana. Tell everyone not to approach her. She's a survivor and still dealing with things."

Demitri nods. "I'll take care of it."

"We'll let Ariana bond with her first and then take it from there."

"Okay."

Just then, my phone begins to ring, and pulling it out of my pocket, I see it's Lucian. "Give me good news," I answer.

"Your shipment is ready."

"Thank you," I say, grinning from ear to ear. "Today is a good day."

"When will you arrive?" Lucian asks.

I think for a moment. "Three days."

"See you then."

Ending the call, I meet Demitri's eyes. "Have you told Ariana she'll be staying with Cilian?"

"I'll take care of it tonight."

I nod. "I'll text to remind Carson to do the same with Hailey if he hasn't yet. I'm going to leave MJ on the island to help Cillian guard the women."

Relief flashes in Demitri's eyes. "That's a good idea."

When I walk out of the security room, Ariana comes toward me. "It's almost time for dinner."

"Fuck, I forgot about food," I say, and then I glance to the second floor. "Let me check with Isabella, but I get a feeling they'll eat in the bedroom."

"Okay."

Meeting Ariana's eyes, I say, "I need a favor from you. Ana's been through a lot of shit, and she's sensitive. Will you try to form a bond with her?"

Compassion washes over Ariana's face. "Definitely."

"Thanks." I head up to the guest room and softly knock on the door. I'm surprised when Ana opens the door a couple of inches and peeks at me.

"Where's Isabella?" I ask.

Ana pulls a little back behind the door, looking skittish as fuck. "She's showering."

"You want to eat in the dining room, or should I bring your food up here?" I ask, giving Ana a choice.

"Ah…" she glances to the bathroom, then back at me.

The fear and pain in her eyes is a punch to my gut, and I crouch down, so I have to look up at her, hoping it will give her a false sense of strength.

"You're important to Isabella, so I really want us to get along."

Ana just stares at me as if she's waiting for the other shoe to drop.

Taking a deep breath, I say, “When I make a promise, I keep it, so I don’t make them often. But, Ana, I promise you’re safe with me. I won’t touch you unless it’s to save your life. I’ll respect your boundaries. I love Isabella, and I plan on marrying her, which means the two of us will become family. I always protect my family.”

“Do you really love her?” Ana asks the question I least expected.

“With everything I am.”

Ana nods, then she swallows hard. “Can you bring the food up here?” I nod and straighten to my full height, then she adds, “And maybe you can eat with us?”

A smile spreads over my face. “I’d like that, little one.”

When I glance over Ana’s head, my eyes connect with Isabella’s. Her features are tight with emotion from watching Ana and me, and then she mouths, *‘Thank you.’*

“I’ll be right back.”

Chapter 27

ISABELLA

When I overhead Alexei talking to Ana, it sealed the deal for me. He didn't have to do that, but still, he tried to set her at ease.

"So?" Ana asks. "How do you feel?"

"About Alexei?" I ask as I take a seat next to her on the bed after getting dressed.

"Yes. He looks like he really meant what he said."

"Yeah," I murmur, still trying to come to terms with the fact that he really loves me.

"He said he's going to marry you." Ana's gaze searches mine.

"I agreed to an alliance with him. The only way out is death." Ana frowns, obviously not liking the sound of that, and it has me saying, "Besides the alliance, I do love him, or at least the part of him I got to know." I let out a sigh. "It's weird. It's as if the Alexei I've heard horror stories of in my past and this Alexei are two different men. I have to get used to both sides of him."

Ana thinks for a moment, then she says, "He seems nice."

I let out a chuckle. "Nice is not the word I'd use to describe Alexei."

"Well, he was nice to me."

I raise an eyebrow at Ana. "Are you boasting right now?"

She shrugs, and then there's a knock at the door. "You sure about letting him eat with us?" I ask as I slip off the bed.

"Are you going to marry him?" Ana asks.

I stare at her for a moment. "Yes."

"Then I have to get used to him as well."

"Thank you. I know it's not easy," I say as I walk to the door. Opening it, Alexei walks in with one plate of food, and then Ariana appears in the doorway with two more plates.

She gives me an apologetic smile. "Hey, I come bearing a peace offering."

I return her smile, knowing people don't have a choice but to go along with things once Alexei's decided to do something. "It's okay."

I watch as Ariana steps into the room, and then she smiles at Ana, who's standing near the bed. "Hi, Ana. I'm Ariana, Demitri's better half."

Alexei lets out a chuckle.

"Hi." Ana returns the greeting, her features tense.

Alexei holds the plate of food out to her, and she takes it while keeping her eye on Ariana instead of Alexei.

Ariana hands the other plates to Alexei. "Let me go feed my man. Enjoy dinner."

Once she's out of the room, I shut the door, and when I turn around, Alexei's taking a seat on the floor, leaning back against the bed.

"Wow, now this is a sight to behold," I tease him as I sit down beside him.

He hands me a plate. "Just want to keep things casual."

Ana sits to my right, and crossing her legs, she looks down at the roast chicken and vegetables, silently saying a prayer of thanks.

Only when she looks up again does Alexei pick up his fork.

We eat in silence for a while before Alexei asks, "How old are you, little Ana?"

"Nineteen."

He nods as he shoves the broccoli on his plate aside before spearing a carrot.

Bringing my food closer to his, I scoop the broccoli onto my plate and give him the rest of my carrots, and then I lean back again and continue to eat.

Ana lets out a chuckle, and my eyes snap to her, but she's staring at Alexei. When I turn my gaze to him, he's staring at me.

"What?" I ask.

"That was such a couply thing to do," he says, sounding a little surprised.

"So?"

"Oh, you're admitting we're a couple?" he asks, a playful grin forming on his face.

"We're engaged," I state the obvious.

Alexei nods, his grin growing. "Good to know you're aware of that fact."

I hold up my left hand. "Never took off the ring. Oh, and by the way, your wedding band better have a tracker in it."

"I already have a tracker," Alexei says, using the back of his fork to point at the tag hanging from a chain around his neck. Then he gives Ana a pointed look. "I'll ask Demitri to have one made for our Ana."

Our Ana.

Warmth spreads through my heart that Alexei is making such a huge effort with her.

"Do you track everyone?" I ask.

"Only those I call family."

My food is forgotten on my lap as I stare at Alexei. "You already consider me family?"

He meets my eyes. "From the moment I put that ring on your finger."

A feeling I've never felt before creeps into my heart. Having someone stronger than me care enough to call me family makes me feel protected in a way I've never been.

I've always had to be the strong one, watching my back, skirting around the depraved. I always had to fight for myself.

But now that I have Alexei, it feels like I can take a moment to be a woman and not just a fighter.

Nodding, I swallow hard and then focus on the food.

Alexei nudges his shoulder against mine. "Did I say something wrong?"

I shake my head. "Just nice to know there's someone stronger than me I can lean on."

Alexei leans over and presses a kiss to my temple.

Yeah, so much for being the Princess of Terror. Give me a man to love, and I'm the same as any other woman.

Then again, I'd kill for mine.

ALEXEI

It's already past one in the morning, and I'm still fucking hoping Isabella will come to me.

Turning away from the window, I walk to the bed, and just as I toss the covers back, the door opens, and Isabella comes in.

"You're still up?" she asks.

"Someone kept me waiting," I say, just happy she came.

"I waited for Ana to fall asleep," Isabella explains as she walks to the middle of the room. Glancing into the walk-in closet, she says, "You didn't move any of my things."

"Of course not."

She turns to face me, and then she smiles. "Always so sure of yourself."

"Thank you," the words spill from me. "Thank you for coming back."

Her eyes lock with mine. "Did I make the right decision?"

I nod as I begin to slowly walk toward her. "You did." When I reach her, I lift a hand and brush a lock of hair away from her temple. "When did your memory come back?"

"Right before the party when Lucian's helicopter landed on the grounds."

I thought so.

I take a deep breath and let it out slowly. "What did you want to prove that night?"

A slight frown forms on her forehead. "When we had sex?" I nod, and it has her answering, "I wanted control."

"Hmm…" I step closer and press a kiss on her forehead. "I'm a bit of a control freak."

"I've noticed," she murmurs on a light chuckle. Her gaze drifts over my face, and I can see she's thinking about whether she should ask me something or not. "Sonia Terrero is my mother. How can you look past that?"

"I never judge a child for the sins of their father, or in your case, mother."

I bring a hand to her face and brush my knuckles over her cheek and down her neck, relishing in the feel of her silky skin.

"Why didn't you follow in Sonia's footsteps?" I ask, wanting to know why Isabella turned on her mother.

"Seeing the depraved horror..." she shakes her head, the ghosts of her past shadowing her eyes, "someone had to try and put a stop to it."

Another reason I want Sonia dead. She's repeatedly tried to kill the woman I love, and Christ only knows what Isabella has seen growing up in the cartel.

My goddess with a will of steel that's been forged in the bowels of hell.

My eyes caress her face. "So fucking brave."

"Is this really who you are?" Isabella asks.

I nod. "Unless I lose my temper."

"Does that happen often?"

The corner of my mouth lifts. "No."

Isabella places her hands on my sides, and then she looks up at me. "What are triggers for you so I know to avoid them?"

"I only have two triggers," I admit. "If someone goes after one of my loved ones and people preying on the innocent."

Isabella nods. "We're the same."

I lean down. "That's why we belong together." Pressing my mouth to Isabella's, my tongue sweeps into her heat. I wrap an arm around her waist and pull her tightly against me as I deepen the kiss.

I take my time reclaiming her mouth until her lips are swollen, and pulling back, our breaths mingle as our eyes lock.

"After the attack, we'll marry."

Isabella lifts her arms, wrapping them around my neck. "Okay." She presses a kiss to my throat and then to my jaw. "I want to feel you deep inside me."

I lift her against my body and carry her to the bed. Shoving her back onto the mattress, I say, "What my woman wants, my woman gets."

She lets out a sinful chuckle. "Hmm… I love the sound of that."

Taking hold of her waistband, I begin to undress her before stepping out of my sweatpants.

I spread Isabella's legs wide open, and crawling over her, I lower my head and suck one of her nipples hard. I take hold of my cock and begin to rub it against her clit, coating myself with her wetness.

As I position myself at her entrance, I lift my head and meet her eyes. "I just want to feel you bare, and then I'll put on protection."

Isabella nods, and as I push inside her, I wrap my arms around her and hold her body to mine. I still once I'm all the way in and drink in the moment of having absolutely nothing between us.

Christ. She's mine.

When I start to pull out, Isabella's hands grip my ass, and then she shakes her head. "I don't want anything between us."

"You might get pregnant," I state the obvious.

"You have a problem with me bearing your children?" she sasses me.

I quickly shake my head, and the image of Isabella pregnant with my child almost makes me lose control. "Hell fucking no."

"Then fuck me, Alexei."

My mouth slams down on hers, and I begin to move, my pace instantly unrelenting and hard. Isabella's hands roam up my back, her nails leaving trails, before moving down to my ass. Her fingers dig into my skin as she opens her legs wider, giving me complete access to her body.

Knowing she's submitting to me sends me into a frenzy, and I brand her mouth while pounding harder into her.

She whimpers into my mouth, and it has me framing her face, my body pressing hers into the bed. Her nails dig deeper as she whimpers again, and it only makes me increase my pace until sweat beads on the back of my neck.

I feel her clench tightly around my cock, and only then do I push a hand down between us, rubbing her sensitive clit.

Isabella cries into my mouth, and I swallow the sound as I force her to the edge. When I'm sure she can't take anymore, my touch turns tender, and a moment later, her body begins to convulse. She starts to sob against my lips from the intense orgasm tearing through her.

Pulling my hand from between us, I slow my pace, and locking eyes with Isabella, I fill her deep.

"I love you," I breathe as I lose myself in every thrust. "So fucking much." My body keeps moving while my mind's consumed by this woman who cast a spell on me.

Isabella moves her hands up to my back, and then she holds me tightly, as devotion shines from her eyes.

"I love you, Alexei."

The words I've been dying to hear wash through me, and then my orgasm hits, taking me higher than I've ever been.

Isabella's eyes are glued to mine while I'm at my most vulnerable, and when the pleasure fades, I still inside her.

"Say it again," I demand breathlessly.

Isabella knows what I want because, without hesitating, she murmurs, "I love you."

Since my mother died, I've never heard those words from a woman. Emotion fills my chest and pulling out of Isabella, I move a little down and rest my head on her breasts.

Her hands find my hair, and she trails her fingers through the strands, then she asks, "What are you thinking?"

I take a deep breath. "I want to share something with you."

"Okay."

I move off Isabella, and we turn on our sides, facing each other. I take hold of her hand and press it over my heart.

"I've only told Demitri."

She nods at me. "I'll take it to my grave."

Swallowing, I stare into her eyes as I admit my darkest secret, "My mother was a sex slave."

Isabella's eyes widen, and her lips part.

"When she tried to run, my father shot her. I was the last thing she saw."

Isabella brings her other hand to my jaw, her eyes reflecting the pain that's ingrained in my soul.

"That's one of the reasons why I have to kill Sonia."

She nods. "I understand."

Turning my face, I press a kiss to her palm.

"Is that why you asked me whether I felt violated?" Isabella asks.

I nod as I turn onto my back, pulling Isabella against my side. "Are you still angry because I lied to you?"

When she takes too long to answer, I glance down at her. She turns her head, resting her chin on my chest. "I was hurt, but we talked about it."

"You sure? Because you looked pretty pissed off when you punched the shit out of me before leaving."

She lets out a chuckle. "You let me have that punch." Then she tilts her head. "It's not a known fact that you can fight. Why do you hide it?"

"It's so my enemies will underestimate me. It's always a good thing to catch the fuckers off guard."

I nod. "You're such an enigma," she says as she lays her cheek on my chest. "Every day, I learn something new."

"I like keeping things interesting," I chuckle.

Chapter 28

ALEXEI

After stopping in Italy, we fly to Damien and Winter's island.

Stepping off the plane, I glance around, and then I hold my hand out to Isabella. Her fingers interlink with mine, and I tug her right to my side.

Looking at Ana, I say, "Beautiful, isn't it?"

Ana nods as she takes in the island, partially covered by a forest.

When Demitri and Ariana join us with the other women, I say, "Can you take the women inside?"

He nods. "Sure."

I watch as Carson and Lucian's women follow Demitri to the house, and I pray I'll be able to return their men to them.

I turn to Ana. "Will you be okay here?"

She takes a deep breath before answering, "Yes." Then she glances at the house, and her chin begins to quiver.

Ana's still a child in so many ways, and it makes me feel protective of her. I let go of Isabella's hand and crouch down in front of Ana. "Hey, no tears, little one."

She tries to reign in her emotions but fails, and a tear rolls down her cheek. "Bring Isabella safely back to me."

"I'll make sure she returns to you," I say.

Then Ana adds, "And you."

Our eyes lock, and I tilt my head as Ana creeps into my heart. This time I only nod.

"Promise," she demands, her silent tears falling faster.

"I promise." *I'll do my best, little Ana.*

She wipes the tears from her cheeks then lifts her chin. "I'll be okay here."

Just then, Cillian and MJ walk toward us, and I stand up, turning to Isabella. "You two go ahead."

Isabella places her hand against my chest, right over my heart, and presses a kiss to my mouth, and then she walks away with Ana.

When Cillian and MJ reach me, Cillian nods at me. "Alexei."

I glance between the two people who'll guard the women. "Ana's sensitive. She'll need her own space." They nod, then I add, "Let MJ deal with her."

"Okay," Cillian agrees.

I take a deep breath and then order, "Shoot down any unauthorized aircraft or watercraft. No one sets foot on this island."

"Of course," Cillian replies.

I take another deep breath. *Christ.* "If we don't make it back, I've made arrangements with Demitri and Damien's uncle. He'll be in touch."

Cillian's features tighten because that includes him losing Winter, who's like a daughter to him.

Patting him on the shoulder, I say, "I'll do my best to bring everyone back in one piece."

Cillian nods, then gestures to the group of men he managed to gather for me. "I trained them myself."

"And they can be trusted to do the job?" My eyes stop on each man, knowing most of them won't make it out alive.

"Yes. They know their families will be well compensated," Cillian answers.

"Good."

I turn my attention to MJ, the custodian Carson got to guard Hailey. "I know Hailey's your first priority, but I need you to protect Ana."

MJ nods. "I'll guard them both with my life."

I hold MJ's stare for a moment. "The payment will be made no matter what happens to me."

MJ nods again.

Placing my hand on Cillian's shoulder, I say, "Tell the men to board the plane. I'll send out Winter for you."

I walk to the house, and when I step inside, Damien's waiting for me. "Ready?"

"I just need a moment."

He nods and gestures to the living room, where everyone's gathered. When I walk inside, I place a hand on Winter's back and lean into her. "Cillian's waiting outside for you."

When she leaves, I turn to the women and make eye contact with each of them, and then I stop on Ana. "Come with me."

I go to the dining room, and then I turn to face Ana.

She instantly begins to shake her head. "You already promised."

I step closer to her and then catch myself before I place a hand on her shoulder. Crouching, I look up at her. "Just in case I can't keep my promise, I've made arrangements for you with Ariana. There are funds so you can study or start something of your own. Until you're twenty-five, Ariana will help you with the trust fund that will be set up."

"Don't say that," Ana bites out, her face a second away from crumbling.

I take a deep breath, and meeting her shimmering eyes, I say, "I'm sorry for what happened to you. We're not all monsters."

"Then come back and prove it to me yourself," Ana demands.

I nod, praying I'll get the chance.

Standing up, I let out a heavy breath, and then I go back to the living room and hug Ariana. "Take care of Ana."

She nods against my chest.

I press a kiss to Ariana's forehead, then pull away and walk out of the house.

ISABELLA

Dressed in red leather, I feel weirdly calm. Today the red represents the blood I will spill to take revenge for all the innocent lives my mother has destroyed.

With all the mercenaries that have been hired, we have sixty trained men. The bratva, Semion and Lev, arrived with twenty more.

And then there are the nine of us.

"Semion and Lev, you'll breach the front with your men plus ten of ours," Alexei says one final time. "Carson, Damien, Lucianm Nikhil, and Sacha will enter from the south with thirty men. Winter, you're with us, and then the vent is your baby. Demitri, Isabella, and I will move in from the west with the rest of the men. Once I launch the RPG, it will be a free-for-fucking-all. Be ready."

Everyone murmurs their understanding.

Just then, Alexei's phone begins to ring, and taking it out of his pocket, he puts it on speaker. His features are unforgiving as he answers, "Madame Keller."

'Mr. Koslov, I hear you'll be paying St. Monarch's a visit?'

"There's still time for you to send Sonia out," Alexei replies.

'Reconsider your actions, Mr. Koslov, or I'll be forced to place an open contract on your head.'

Alexei lets out a dark chuckle. "Don't let me keep you."

'Alexei...'

Placing his hands on the table, he stares down at the phone. "Get out of there, Madame Keller. I only want Sonia."

He cuts the call and tucks the device back in his pocket, then he says, "Final weapons check."

I begin with the KA-BARs tucked in my right boot and strapped to my left forearm, then I check the clips in my Heckler & Koch and Glock. A sub-machine gun hangs over my shoulder, and I have a backpack with more ammo.

I tug at my armored vest to make sure it's secure.

Alexei stares down the engraved steel of his gun, then slowly, his eyes lift to the people who are willing to die for him. He takes a moment to look at each one, and then his eyes lock with mine before settling on Demitri.

He tucks his gun behind his back, then lets out a deep breath as he adjusts the black coat he always wears. "If any of you want to leave, do so now. I won't hold it against you."

Not a single person moves. "Where you go, we go," Lucian replies.

Alexei takes another breath. "If any of you come across Madame Keller and she wants to leave, give her safe passage. I only want Sonia. As soon as Sonia's confirmed dead, we pull out."

There's a moment's silence, and then Alexei says, "Let's hunt."

Semion and Lev file out of the building with their men, but before Carson can leave, Alexei grabs hold of his shoulder, yanking his brother into a tight embrace.

"Stay alive," Alexei murmurs.

"You too." The brothers let go of each other while Damien and Winter take a moment to say their goodbye.

Winter's the one to push Damien back. "Go, I'll be fine."

Damien takes one last look at his wife, and then he leaves with Carson, Lucian, and their group of men.

Winter comes to stand next to me, and then Alexei locks eyes with her. "As soon as you've dropped the pepper grenade, I want you to get your ass off the grounds."

"What?" Winter gasps, frowning at Alexei.

"I won't risk Nickolai losing both parents. It is not negotiable. You leave the moment you're done in the vents."

"Alexei!"

Demitri steps toward his sister-in-law and snaps, "Winter, think of Nickolai!"

Winter pauses, and then she reluctantly nods, clearly upset.

"Time to leave," Alexei orders, and then we walk out of the building.

When we reach the SUV, Alexei slides in behind the steering wheel, and Demitri takes the passenger seat while Winter and I climb in the back. The rest of the men load into the other vehicles, and then Alexei steers us away from the building.

As we head toward St. Monarch's, I think how much everything's changed.

Six months ago, I was fighting a losing battle against my mother.

Six months ago, Alexei was the devil I heard horror stories about. He was my enemy, not because of my mother, but because I thought there wasn't an ounce of good in him.

Boy, was I wrong.

Turns out Alexei's everything I stand for.

I close my eyes, wanting one last moment to relish in the fact that he loves me.

I love him.

And we might both die today.

At least I got to taste some goodness in this life. I got to feel intense raw passion from a man who protected and adored me.

I got to make a difference.

My life might end today, and I'm okay with that – as long as my mother joins me in hell.

Then I allow the horrors I've seen to flash through my mind. The broken bodies and destroyed souls. The depravity and unspeakable agony.

It sets fire to my soul, and when I open my eyes, I'm ready to end my mother's reign of terror.

Chapter 29

ALEXEI

Stopping the SUV to the west of St. Monarch's, the castle towers on the other side of the wall.

When everyone gathers behind me, I say, "Team one, earpiece check."

'In position,' Semion's voice sounds in my ear.

'Ready,' Lev replies.

"Team two."

Carson, Damien, and Lucian take turns to mutter, *'Here.'*

Then Damien asks, *'Princess, you there?'*

"I'm here," Winter replies.

'Be careful,' he tells her for the hundredth time. The man's going to give himself a heart attack from all the worrying.

"Damien, cut it out," I snap. "Winter will be fine."

He lets out a huff.

"Remember, Madame Keller is not to be killed unless absolutely necessary," I remind everyone.

Then I glance at Demitri on my right. "Ready, brother?"

He nods, and our eyes hold for a moment before I turn my head to Isabella on my left.

"I'm ready," she says, looking like an angel of death.

I lift my hand behind her head and press a hard kiss to her mouth. For a moment, her palm settles against the armored vest covering my chest. I take a deep breath of my woman and then pull back.

Lifting the grenade launcher to my shoulder, I say, "Breach in three… two…" I fire the grenade, and then my eyes follow it as it whistles through the air.

I hope Madame Keller left.

The grenade strikes, blowing a hole near the armory and dropping the launcher, I run for the wall. Lodging a foot against the solid wall, I push my body hard, and for a split-second, I'm airborne, and then I grab hold of the top and pull myself up. I jump over and land in a crouching position.

Demitri drops next to me, and as I dart forward, I hear my team behind me. Grabbing the sub-machine gun at my side, I bring it up, and when the guards open fire on us, I pull the trigger.

I don't take in faces as my group's bullets spray St. Monarch's guards while we close in on the side of the building that's been blasted open.

Nearing the rubble, I let go of the sub-machine gun and, reaching beneath my coat, I pull the two Heckler & Kochs from behind my back.

I bring my arms up, and instinct takes over as I take out one after the other target. The popping and rattling of gunfire fill the air around St. Monarch's.

As we reach the rubble, we're slowed down, having to pick our way through bricks and mortar scattered on the ground.

'Entering,' Carson's voice sounds in my ear.

Smoke plumes hang heavy in the air as we step into what's left of the hallway, the armory's one wall down.

Thank God for small mercies.

My eyes dart up to the second floor, a gaping hole giving me a slight view of what used to be a suite.

It's eerily quiet on our side, and it only sharpens my senses as we slowly creep forward.

Reaching the nearest vent, I say, "Winter, you're up."

Demitri grabs hold of Winter's waist, lifting her into the air while Isabella and I watch their backs. Winter uses a small power drill to take care of the screws, and then the cover drops to the floor. Demitri gives her a shove, and Winter grabs hold of the hole in the ceiling, hoisting herself into the ventilation tunnel.

"Good luck, little one," I say as I watch her disappear.

The three of us begin to move down the hallway, and when we reach the armory, there's no sign of Miss Dervishi, the trainer of the assassins. Hopefully, it means she left along with Madame Keller.

Demitri throws an incendiary grenade into the armory, and then we hightail it down the hallway. The explosion shakes the floor beneath my feet, and then guards dart from the rooms used for training.

Sonia's men.

A bullet whistles past my head, and I take down the man responsible before he can get another shot in.

Reaching the archway where the hallway splits, I order the men that are still left from my group, "Spread out." Then, taking a moment as the men scatter deeper into the castle, I ask, "Winter, update?"

'Another five minutes,' she grunts.

I glance at Demitri and Isabella, making sure they weren't hit, then say, "Winter, let me know as soon as you've delivered the package."

Taking a deep breath, I move into the hallway leading to the office where Sonia will likely be. Carson's team will move to the second floor to check the suites in case I'm wrong.

The first stretch to the medical section is way too quiet for my liking. When we round a corner, and there are no custodians stationed outside the office door, apprehension trickles into my veins.

"Something's not right," I advise the others.

Just then, the castle shudders and deafening blasts make my ears ring. The ground behind us crumbles away, exposing a gaping hole with fire, smoke, and debris beneath. I fight to keep my balance while it feels as if the rest of the hallway will give way at any moment.

Fuck, Madame Keller blew the basement and cellars.

I shake my head to try and lessen the ringing in my ears, and then the door to the office opens, and fucking Hugo sprays a round of bullets our way.

In a matter of seconds, I drop my guns and grab hold of Demitri and Isabella, yanking them down, and then one bullet after the other slams into my armored vest, forcing me backward and robbing me of my breath. Intense pain radiates through my chest, most likely from a couple of ribs being cracked or broken.

Demitri swings, trying to grab hold of my left arm, but he falls to the side and slides over the edge of the hole torn in the floor. A gasp of horror shudders from me, but then he manages to grab hold of an exposed rod, stopping his fall.

I take a shot to my left arm, and then I lose my footing.

As I fall backward, I see Isabella delivering two shots to Hugo's armored vest, and then Winter drops from the vent behind him, burying a KA-BAR in his skull.

Throwing my right arm out as I fall, I grab hold of the torn-up concrete, and the momentum of my body slamming into a solid wall slices my palm open. I bring up my left arm, but the fucking thing is useless from the bullet I took, sending white-hot pain tearing through my shoulder and rib cage.

Blood flows from my palm, making it hard to hold on so I can pull myself up, and then I begin to slip.

'Alexei,' Demitri breathes hard in my ear. *'Hold on.'*

Unable to, I try to get a foothold against the wall as I brace myself for the fire and shards of concrete below.

"Fuck," I whisper, and as my hand slips from the edge, Isabella falls half over, grabbing hold of my wrist.

My fingers tighten around her slender wrist, and our eyes lock.

"Left arm!" she shouts at me as my weight begins to drag her over the edge. When my feet grapple for purchase against the wall, I pull Isabella another couple of inches over the ledge and immediately stop.

My body stills and panic floods me, my heart stuttering in my chest. "Let go."

Isabella frantically shakes her head, and as our eyes lock, I see the future we could've had flickering in her brown irises.

Then she grabs hold of my right arm with both her hands, giving her zero leverage to stop herself from falling over. My body jerks as she slips again, and then she lets out a scream as she fights the inevitable.

Christ, have I ever loved her more?

"Let go, baby," I breathe. I try to twist my wrist free from her hold. "It's okay." I give her a pleading look. "Let go."

"Shut up! I'm not losing the man I love," she snaps angrily.

"Isabella," I say, accepting my fate, "Let go. You need to kill Sonia."

"Shut up," she cries, and then she puts all her strength behind her and pulls hard, letting out another scream.

Winter grabs hold of Isabella around the waist, helping her pull, and they actually manage to get me close enough. Forcing myself through the pain, I grab hold of the ledge with my left hand.

Then Demitri appears next to Isabella, and grabbing hold of my coat by my neck, he yanks me onto the ledge, the concrete taking a slice from my thigh.

I fall partially over Isabella and Demitri and suck in a painful breath of the dust-filled air.

Then Isabella delivers a punch to my shoulder. "Asshole!"

I let out a relieved chuckle as I push myself up until I'm in a kneeling position. Glancing over my shoulder, I look at the fire below.

Fuck, that was close.

Wrapping my left arm around my waist, I breathe through the deep ache in my ribs, and then I climb to my feet.

Winter waits beneath the vent for us, and I let out an inward groan, knowing this is going to fucking hurt like a mother. Unfortunately, there's no other way out of this side of the castle, so I suck it up and begin to walk toward Winter, not sparing Hugo's body a glance.

ISABELLA

Demitri climbs up into the ventilation system, and then he reaches down for Alexei.

We've wrapped one of the sub-machine gun's straps around his right hand to try and stop the bleeding. A frown settles on my forehead when Alexei gives Demitri his right hand instead of his left.

My eyes scour his left side, and then I see the blood dripping to the floor. "Alexei!"

The two men freeze, and Alexei's head snaps to me. "What?"

I dart forward and begin to inspect his arm, finding a bullet wound just above his elbow. "Fucking asshole! You got shot and didn't tell us?"

"It's nothing," he says, then he looks up at Demitri, "Are you going to pull me up?"

Demitri tugs hard, yanking Alexei up into the vent. For a moment, there's a flash of pain on Alexei's face, and it makes anger and worry bubble in my chest.

So fucking reckless! The man will be the death of me today.

Because Winter is shorter, I grab hold of her hips, and then I shove her into the air. Demitri grabs hold of her hand and quickly pulls her into the vent. Then he leans down again, holding his hand out to me.

Jumping, my fingers wrap around his wrist, and then I'm tugged up.

It's one hell of a tight fit for the men, and I have to leopard crawl over Demitri's back until I come up behind Winter. Demitri brings up the rear as Alexei takes the lead.

The crawl goes slow, especially when we reach a corner. The men struggle through the tight space, but I'm just glad no one's claustrophobic.

With every vent opening, Alexei checks if we can go down into a room or hallway, but most of the ground has been blown away.

"Check-in," I hear Alexei say, his breathing labored.

'No sign of Sonia,' Carson replies.

When there's silence following his report, Alexei asks, "Semion? Lev?" No reply comes from the two Russian men. "Fuck," Alexei curses.

'We're near the front. I'll check on them,' Carson's voice comes over the earpieces.

Suddenly there's a spray of bullets where Winter is, and then the ceiling gives way, and she drops.

My breath rush over my lips as I bring my gun up, and then I inch forward.

"Careful," Alexei whispers.

I peek over the hole and then pull the trigger, hitting Oscar, one of my mother's men, in the collarbone. I fire another shot, and giving him a third eye, I watch as he falls forward and into the rubble beneath.

I lean over and glance around. Not seeing anyone else, I say, "Clear."

"Winter?" Alexei calls, then he asks, "Can you see her?"

I search for her between the rubble. "No. I'll go down."

"No!" Alexei orders.

'What happened?' Damien asks.

"Nothing," I answer him, not wanting to cause him worry. "Winter just took a detour."

'Princess?' His voice is tight. *'Winter!'*

"We're still assessing the situation," Demitri tells his brother.

'Your fucking position. Now,' Damien demands.

I glance around again as I pull myself forward, bracing against the sides. "Looks like the dining room. I'm going after Winter."

"No!" Alexei snaps, unable to turn around to stop me.

I let go of the sides and drop down.

"Mother fucking Christ," Alexei's shout follows me down.

My feet hit a slab of concrete, and then I have to move, jumping from one piece of debris to the next until I'm able to stop the momentum the drop gave me. Crouching down, I take a couple of breaths, my heart pounding in my chest. "Made it."

'I'm going to fucking tan your ass!' Alexei hisses in my ear.

'Keep the kinky talk off the earphones,' Lucian says with a chuckle.

Demitri thinks to ask, *'Can you see Winter?'*

I start to inch my way deeper into the rubble, and then I see a flash of red hair. "I have eyes on her."

'We're moving forward to find a place where we can get out of this fucking ventilation tunnel,' Alexei says.

"Don't get yourself killed," I mutter, and then I slip down the concrete pieces until I finally reach Winter. She's covered in a grey layer of dust, but then she blinks at me and lets out a groan.

"Winter's conscious."

'Thank fuck,' Damien breathes.

When I move in next to Winter, she starts to push herself into a sitting position. "My leg."

I glance down and see that her left leg is wedged between two slabs of concrete. Placing my hands against the one slab, I push it away from her, and then I take in the huge gash on the side of her shin. I take my jacket and armored vest off, then pull my shirt over my head. After putting the armored vest and jacket back on, I remove my belt and wrap the t-shirt around her leg, securing the fabric with the belt. Winter clenches her teeth, letting out a pain-filled groan.

"Are you hurt anywhere else? Gunshot?" I ask.

Winter shakes her head. "I lost my earpiece."

Taking mine from my ear, I place it in Winter's. "Tell your man you're okay."

"Damien. I'm fine," Winter says.

"My fucking heart!" His voice sounds somewhere above us.

"Damien?" I call out.

"I'm coming down."

"No. Wait up there. I'm going to need you to pull Winter out."

Wrapping an arm around her back, I pull Winter up against my body, and it has her letting out another pain-filled groan.

I give her a moment, then ask, "Ready?"

Winter nods, and then I begin to climb over the debris with her. It takes longer than I'd like, but finally, Damien comes into view.

Tired, I push Winter up the last part. Damien grabs hold of her hands and yanks her to him, embracing her tightly.

I pull myself over the edge and into the foyer and climbing to my feet, I glance around at the bodies and destruction.

"No sign of my mother?" I ask.

Damien shakes his head.

Where the fuck is she?

"She's fine, Alexei!" Winter hands me my earpiece back. "Your turn to talk to your man."

Placing it back in my ear, I say. "I'm going after my mother." I jog to the entrance of the Castle. "Are you still in the vents?"

'So help me, God!' Alexei rages. *'We're on the south side.'*

"I'm at the front, moving around the left side of the castle. I'm coming to you."

As I round a corner, a palm slams into my nose, and I stagger backward, and then my tearing eyes focus on my mother.

Chapter 30

ALEXEI

'Sonia,' Isabella's voice comes through the earpiece. *'East side.'*

My already simmering anger explodes like a volcano as I break out into a run with Demitri by my side. My chest is on fucking fire as if molten lava is filling my torso, but I push through the pain.

When I round the west corner, it's to see Sonia kick Isabella's in the chest. Isabella drops, and as she tries to sweep Sonia's legs from beneath her, Sonia jumps, almost delivering a knee to Isabella's chin.

Isabella flips back and onto her feet, and then she storms Sonia, getting in a strike to her mother's shoulder.

My heart leaps from my chest when Sonia grabs the gun from behind her back, and then Isabella struggles with her mother to keep the barrel pointed away from her.

My pain takes a back seat as I push forward, leaving Demitri behind. Jumping, my feet hit the wall, and then I spin into the air, the heel of my boot connecting with the side of Sonia's head. The gun flies to the side as she drops to the ground.

As I land on my feet, a relentless ache vibrates through me. Sonia darts up as I pull a KA-BAR from the holder by my belt, and then I lunge for her.

As I strike at her, she blocks the blow, her palm connecting with my left shoulder. It sends a searing ache through me, which Sonia notices.

Turning sharply, I avoid a hit from her while managing to slice her across the chest.

Fucking armored vests.

Isabella gets in a kick from behind, but Sonia uses the momentum to swing at me. I lean back, the move taking its toll on my injured ribs as I narrowly avoid the blow.

Isabella lunges onto her mother's back, her arm wrapping around Sonia's throat.

Darting forward, I plunge the knife deep into Sonia's side. I come face to face with my enemy, our rushing breaths mingling. She lets out a manic, strangled chuckle. "Koslov."

"Terrero," I hiss as I pull the blade out so her blood can flow freely. "You never stood a chance." I bury the KA-BAR into her side, where her lung is. "I'm marrying your daughter. Isabella is mine." I watch as her eyes widen for a moment, filling with rage. "Fucking die."

Isabella tightens her hold, letting out a growl as she yanks back, and then there's a sickening crack as she snaps her mother's neck.

When Sonia's body drops between Isabella and me, I suck in a labored breath, the ache in my chest returning with a vengeance.

I wrap my left arm around my waist, and then I just stare at the woman who's been the bane of my existence.

It's done?

Relief floods my veins.

It's done.

I drop to my knees, finally defeating the greatest enemy I have… had.

Looking up at the sky and the smoke billowing into the air, a smile spreads over my face.

Now there's no one left to challenge me.

Then Isabella comes to stand in front of me, smiling triumphantly down at me.

"Hi, baby," I murmur.

She leans down, and framing my jaw, she presses a kiss to my lips. "Hi, baby," she echoes my words.

"Let's get out of here," Demitri says.

Isabella takes hold of my right arm, helping me up. I wrap my arm around her shoulders, then say, "We'll talk about the stunt you pulled as soon as we get home."

She lets out a chuckle. "You're in no condition to give me a spanking."

"Then we'll talk after I've healed."

She smiles up at me as we walk toward the front of the castle, leaving Sonia's body behind.

"Can't wait," Isabella says.

As my people gather at the entrance, I take in the wounded and the losses we've suffered.

Damien supports Winter while Carson helps Lucian, who seems to have taken a bullet in the leg.

Semion's standing by Lev's body, and I shake my head, feeling the loss deeply. I glance at Nikhil and Sacha. "Help Semion with Lev's remains."

Even though most of us are injured, we move as fast as possible to get to the vehicles.

Demitri has to drive because my left arm and chest are fucked. As he steers us away from St. Monarch's, I rest my head back against the seat and close my eyes.

Thank God Madame Keller wasn't there.

Thank God.

I'll have to face her at some point, but not today.

"Where else are you hurt?" Isabella asks.

"Sounds like broken ribs," Demitri mutters. "And a gash to his right thigh."

I let out a tired chuckle. "Not bad for a day's work."

"Only you'd say that," Isabella huffs from behind me.

When we reach the building we're operating from, it's clear everyone's exhausted and hurting.

I should've brought Dr. Oberio, but at least Demitri has medical experience.

Turning to Demitri, I say, "First, take care of the other's bullet wounds and injuries."

His eyes settle on my left arm. "And yours?"

"I'll dig it out myself."

"Like hell," Isabella mutters. "I'll do it."

The corner of Demitri's mouth lifts. "Good luck."

As Demitri walks away to tend to the wounded, Isabella asks, "Was that meant for me or you?"

"Me. I've seen what it looks like after you've removed a bullet," I joke.

She slants her eyes at me. "One more comment like that, and I won't give you any painkillers."

Not caring about the blood, I lift my right hand to her neck, and then I stare at her. "You were amazing. Reckless, but amazing."

Taking hold of my hand, she leads me to a chair and table. "Sit."

My eyes settle on the woman I love as she begins to remove the strap around my palm.

"You okay?" I ask.

"Better than you," she says, her focus on the cuts.

"I meant, are you okay after killing Sonia?"

Isabella lifts her eyes to mine. "There was only hate between her and me. I don't feel anything but relief."

My lips tug up into a smile. "Thank you."

A slight frown forms between her eyes. "For?"

"Saving my life." It's proven to me Isabella is one hundred percent mine.

I can trust her.

With her gaze on mine, she smiles at me. "Of course. If anyone's going to kill you, it will be me and on my terms."

"You love me too much," I tease her.

"Lucky for you."

ISABELLA

When I step off the plane after Demitri landed us safely on Winter's island, I brace myself as Ana runs to me.

"Isabella!" she shrieks, and then she throws herself at me.

My arms envelop her, and then we just hold each other. I know it's only been hours, but it feels so much longer.

"Told you I'd come back," I whisper.

Ana nods against my shoulder, then she pulls back, her eyes searching behind me. "It's done?"

I nod. "She's dead."

The corner of Ana's mouth lifts slightly, then she walks around me, and I turn to see where she's going.

Alexei stops a couple of steps from Ana, and they stare at each other.

Ana's chin begins to quiver, then she says, "Thank you for keeping your promise."

Alexei nods. "Couldn't let you down."

Ana lets out a sputter, and then she moves closer. Alexei lifts his bandaged hand and pauses midway to touching her. When Ana nods, he places it on her shoulder, and then she closes the last of the distance.

"Careful, Alexei has broken ribs," I warn her.

She pulls back, but then Alexei tugs her against him, wrapping his right arm around her.

Emotion wells in my chest, and my eyes begin to burn, knowing the significance of this moment. Alexei's the first man to touch Ana since she was raped and almost killed.

Ana only lets him hold her for a couple of seconds before she moves away, wiping the back of her hand over her cheek. "Now, I can hold you to your other promise."

Frowning, I ask, "What promise?"

Alexei chuckles. "Wouldn't you like to know?"

I narrow my eyes at him. "You still have a couple of body parts I can break."

He moves in behind Ana. "You need to get through our Ana first."

Letting out a burst of laughter, I shake my head at them.

Winter comes to stand next to me. "Can I talk to you?"

Nodding, I follow her a short distance. "What's up?"

Winter's eyes meet mine. "I just want to say thank you for coming after me when I fell."

"Of course."

She shakes her head. "You didn't have to, Isabella. It means a lot to me."

Nodding, I accept her gratitude.

Lifting her hand, she gives my arm a squeeze. "It's nice to know there's a woman I can count on. If you ever need me, I'll be there."

Hearing the words from the woman who inspired me so much brings tears to my eyes. "That means a lot coming from you."

She smiles and then slowly makes her way to where Damien is waiting with their son.

I head back to where Alexei and Ana are waiting. Throwing my arm around Ana's shoulders, I tug her against my side, and then the three of us walk to the house.

Ariana runs toward the plane, and I glance over my shoulder, watching as she jumps in Demitri's arms, kissing the living hell out of her man.

Letting go of Ana, I glance up at Alexei. I lean closer and whisper, "You're going to be out of action for at least six weeks."

"Action?" he asks.

'Sex,' I mouth the word.

"Hell fucking no. You haven't seen me heal. With enough motivation, I'll be good to go in a week."

I let out a burst of laughter. "What kind of motivation?"

He winks at me. "I'll tell you when we're alone."

We head into the house where Cillian's wife, Dana, prepared a feast.

The atmosphere is joyful and full of bantering as we all help ourselves to the food. I fix a plate for Alexei and take it to where he's sitting in the dining room, staring at the table.

I set the food down, along with the utensils, then take a seat on one of the chairs. "What are you thinking?"

"St. Monarch's," he murmurs. "I need to reach out to Madame Keller."

"You don't have to do that today," I say. "Eat something so you can shower and get some rest."

Alexei's gaze lifts to mine. "Where's your food?"

"Here," Ana says as she brings me a plate. She sits down next to me with her own food. "I helped with the mash."

Raising an eyebrow at her, I ask, "You did?"

She lets out a chuckle, then shrugs. "I peeled the potatoes."

"Still counts," Alexei says as he scoops some mash onto his fork.

We dig in, and silence falls in the house as everyone eats. As soon as Alexei's done, I take our plates to the kitchen. When I get back to him, he rises from the chair, a flash of pain tightening his features.

Glancing at Ana, I ask, "Will you be okay on your own?"

She nods. "I'll help Dana clean up."

I follow Alexei out of the dining room, and he stops by Damien, "Which room can I use?'

"First on the left," Damien answers as he gestures up the stairs.

Alexei's much slower as we climb the stairs, and it tells me just how much pain he's in. I follow him into the room and shut the door behind us.

Walking to the bathroom, I say, "All you have to do is stand in the shower. I'll be quick, so you can get to bed."

Alexei still manages to chuckle. "Damn, my first shower with you and can't do shit."

I shake my head as I shoot him a smile before turning on the faucets. While I strip out of the armored vest and my clothes, Alexei asks, "What happened to your shirt?"

"I used it as a bandage for Winter's leg." Turning to Alexei, I'm careful as I help him out of his clothes. Once I have him naked, my eyes scour his body, assessing all the bruises. "God, Alexei."

He moves in beneath the spray and then leans back against the tiled wall.

Grabbing the body wash and a loofah, I begin to gently clean his body. I avoid his chest because the bruises look feverish and painful.

I take a moment to quickly wash myself, and then I turn off the faucets. I grab a towel and pat Alexei dry before taking care of myself.

When I glance at his face, he's grinning at me.

"You're liking this way too much," I mumble.

"Of course. I can get used to you tending to me."

"Just don't make it a habit of getting yourself shot," I warn him.

When I finally have Alexei sitting on the bed, I walk to the bags we left here when we dropped off Ana and take some clothes from them.

I help Alexei into a pair of sweatpants, and throwing the covers back, he eases down onto his back.

"One week?" I tease him. "I don't see that happening."

His eyes roam over my body. "With the kind of motivation I'm looking at right now, give me seventy-two hours."

"In your dreams, lover boy," I taunt him as I put on a pair of leggings and a t-shirt. I crawl onto the bed, and lifting a hand to Alexei's face, I brush my fingers over his jaw.

He turns his head, and we stare at each other.

"Sonia's dead," he whispers as if he only realizes it now.

"One down, many more to go," I say with a heavy breath.

Alexei frowns at me. "Many more? How many enemies do you have?"

I let out a burst of laughter. "Ohhh… just every flesh peddler in the world."

Admiration shines from his eyes. "You're going to continue freeing girls?"

I nod. "It feels like I'm actually making a difference. Doing something good to balance out the bad."

"Kiss me," Alexei orders.

I lean over him and press a quick kiss to his lips. "It also doesn't hurt that I have a badass fiancé to save my butt when I get in trouble."

"Your badass fiancé will be right by your side whenever you find a shipment to free."

A smile splits over my face. "You want to help?"

Alexei nods. "I'll always have your back, Isabella. We're a team."

Chapter 31

ALEXEI

As soon as we're back home, I head to the security room.

I haven't been able to stop thinking of Madame Keller and St. Monarch's.

Taking a seat behind the security system, I make a couple of calls to government officials in Switzerland that are on my payroll. It takes me three hours and a substantial amount of money to sweep everything under the proverbial carpet.

When I let out a sigh, Demitri looks at me. "This couldn't wait?"

I shake my head as I dial Madame Keller's number.

'Mr. Koslov.'

"Thank you for leaving the premises," I say, needing to get it out of the way.

'You didn't give me much choice in the matter,' she replies, her voice tight.

"I'm calling to make a deal," I get to the point.

Madame Keller lets out a burst of laughter. *'For entertainment value, I'll listen.'*

"I've already covered things in Switzerland. I'll rebuild St. Monarch's and reimburse your losses while the doors are closed."

There's only one thing on this planet Madame Keller is interested in, and that's money.

A chuckle sounds in my ear. *'Add a one hundred percent fine, and we have a deal.'*

I pull a pained face. "What amount are we looking at?"

'How long will it take you to rebuild St. Monarch's?'

Christ, probably a year at the quickest.

"A year?"

'You don't sound certain.'

"A year, Madame Keller," I repeat.

'I expect a payment of a hundred million for the loss of income and another hundred for the fine.'

I take a deep breath that makes my ribs ache and let it out slowly. That's one hell of a blow to my bank account. "Deal." I glance at Demitri. "Transfer two hundred to St. Monarch's."

"Thousand?" Demitri asks.

"Million. Euros."

Demitri gives me a look, silently asking if I'm crazy.

"Do it."

He shrugs, then turns to the system, and after making the payment, he nods at me.

"Done. Is there anything else I can do to apologize?" I ask.

'Hmm... a partnership, so something like this never happens again. You just bought a ten percent share in St. Monarch's, Mr. Koslov. Congratulations.'

I let out a soft burst of laughter. "There's always a plot twist when it comes to you."

'Of course, at my age, I have to get my kicks where I can.'

"So the war is over?" I ask to make sure.

'It's over. I trust you'll make every effort to rebuild St. Monarch's to its former glory.'

"I will."

'Will there be anything else, Mr. Koslov?' Madame Keller asks.

"No. Thank you for your time and leniency," I reply, and then she ends the call.

"Care to explain?" Demitri asks, leaning back in his chair.

I set the phone down on the desk. "I just bought ten percent's shares in St. Monarch's, and we have to rebuild the castle."

"Doesn't explain shit," he mutters.

I lock eyes with him. "Madame Keller is old, Demitri. She's making sure there's someone who will take over St. Monarch's once she's gone."

Demitri begins to laugh. "And that someone is you? Christ. God help everyone."

I shake my head, and it has him saying, "I'm not fucking taking over St. Monarch's."

"Not you. Carson. He hates being an assassin, and he has a fondness for Switzerland."

Demitri's eyebrow pops up. "That's actually a good idea."

I give him a scowl. "Do I ever have bad ideas?"

Demitri starts to laugh. "You? Never."

"Fucker."

Climbing to my feet, an ache spreads through my chest.

"Where are you going?" Demitri asks.

"To get some sympathy from my fiancée," I mutter as I walk out of the security room to go look for Isabella.

I find her in our bedroom, where she's pulling clothes from the walk-in closet.

"What are you doing?" I ask as I gingerly sit down on the edge of the bed.

"I don't need these," she says, pointing to the bunch of dresses. "I only wore them to fool my mother. I'll get dresses that are more to my taste."

Tilting my head, I ask, "Why do you call Sonia your mother?"

Isabella glances at me. "Because she is… was."

"Did she do anything to deserve the title?"

Isabella drops a dress on the pile. "You have a point."

"Of course," I smirk.

She walks toward me, and pressing her palm to my jaw, she leans down and kisses me, then she asks, "How do you feel?"

"Like I need tender, loving care," I say as I scoot back on the bed. Lying down, I watch as Isabelle begins to pull off my boots.

You'd think it would be degrading to have her tend to me, but it's not. I fucking love that she's doting on me.

Isabella comes to sit on the side of the bed. "Is there anything I can get you?"

I shake my head. "Come lie down next to me."

She gets up and moves around the bed, then lies down facing me.

We stare at each other for a moment, and then she asks, "When did you fall in love with me?"

A smile spreads over my face. "The moment I learned my party crasher was the goddess of mischief and chaos."

Her lips curve up. "You really have a way with words."

"Is that why you fell for me?" I ask.

"No." Isabella scoots a little closer, careful not to jar my body. "I fell for you because you were my salvation."

I give her a questioning look, and it has her explaining. "I wouldn't have lasted long on my own. You might've taken me in the beginning, but in return, you gave me the freedom to be myself."

"Which is a badass woman who doesn't listen to me," I mutter.

Isabella lets out a huff. "You're back to that again? Winter needed my help."

"I know, but as soon as I can move without feeling like I'm dying, I'm still going to spank you for giving me a heart attack."

Grinning, she leans closer, pressing a kiss to my lips. "That's if you can actually pin me down long enough to spank me."

"Is that a dare?" I ask.

"No, I'm just giving you some motivation to get better faster."

ISABELLA

Three months later.

"Where are we going?" I ask again as Alexei steers a speed boat across the water of Lake Superior.

"And people say I'm impatient," he chuckles.

As the sun begins to set, I glance around us, but I can't figure out where we're heading.

Soon enough, I finally get my answer as Alexei steers the boat into the private bay of an island.

"Really? You could've just told me," I say as I glance at the double-story house that has the same Mediterranean feel as the mansion in LA.

My gaze drifts over a helipad and pine trees. I notice half the island consists of rocks.

"Welcome to my home away from home," Alexei says as he steps off the boat. He holds his hand out to me and then helps me step onto the dock.

"It's beautiful."

"It's our safe haven," Alexei explains.

Liking the sound of that, I smile as we walk to the front door. Alexei keys in a code, and then the door swings open.

I step inside and look around at the lavish décor of the open-plan kitchen and living room.

"Did you purchase it like this?" I ask.

Alexei sets our luggage down next to a couch, then walks to a side table to pour two tumblers of vodka. "No, I had it built."

"It's impressive."

He comes to stand in front of me, handing me a glass, then he meets my eyes, "I have a fondness for beautiful things."

I take a sip of the vodka, then say, "I'm more of a tequila girl."

Alexei's eyebrow lifts. "I'll keep that in mind." He sets his tumbler down on the coffee table and picks up our luggage. "Let me show you upstairs."

I place my drink next to his and follow him to the upper level.

"These are guest rooms," he says as we pass closed doors. "Demitri's room." He gestures to our left, then he opens a door. "Our room."

Seeing it's black and silver, the corner of my mouth lifts. "It has a similar feel to our bedroom at home."

Alexei places the bag on the bed and zips it open, then he takes a box out of it and puts it on the covers. "Change into this, then come downstairs."

I give him a questioning look but answer, "Okay."

As soon as Alexei leaves the room, I lift the lid off the box. Taking hold of the shimmering black fabric, I hold it up, and then laughter bursts over my lips.

It's a replica of the dress I wore the night I crashed the party, and we hooked up.

I lay it down on the bed and walk to the bathroom to take a quick shower. When I feel refreshed, I take my makeup bag from the luggage and sit down by the dressing table.

I don't go overboard, even though I wish I could do the skull look myself.

I slip into the risqué dress, sans underwear, and step into a pair of stilettos. When I leave the bedroom, my heartbeat speeds up, excited to find out what Alexei has planned.

Coming down the stairs, I don't see Alexei. I begin to look through the rooms, and when I step into an entertainment room, it's dark, except for the light shining on Alexei, where's he's sitting on a chair as if he's a king on his throne. Music is softly playing as I walk to the middle of the room, and then I stop. My eyes lock with his. "You'll do."

"I'd fucking hope so," Alexei says as he rises to his feet.

"That's what I thought when I saw you at the club."

His lips curve up as he slowly walks toward me. "My party crasher."

"My devil," I murmur as he stops in front of me.

Alexei takes me in his arms, and then we slowly begin to dance. Soon intimacy weaves a spell around us, and everything else fades away.

Alexei's eyes hold mine prisoner, and then he says, "Whatever happens in the future, I want you to remember this moment. I mean everything I'm going to say."

I smile, remembering the words he said to me on the cliff. "Okay," I murmur.

Alexei stops moving and lifting his hands, he frames my face. Then, staring deep into my eyes, he says, "I love you so fucking much, Isabella."

Emotion warms my chest. "I love you, too, Alexei."

He lets out a chuckle. "Shit, you weren't supposed to say that right now."

"Oh." I raise an eyebrow. "I must've missed the script."

"Don't sass me, woman. I'm trying to be romantic," he chastises me.

"I'll give you an A for effort."

"I was hoping for a BJ."

I let out a burst of laughter. "Of course you were."

His features grow serious again. "I trust you with my life."

This time his words hit me right in the heart, knowing how rare trust is in our world.

"I trust you too."

A smile tugs at his lips, and then he lowers himself onto one knee. Taking hold of my left hand, he rubs his thumb over the engagement ring. "Isabella Terrero, will you marry me?"

And then I finally get it. Alexei is proposing to me – the me with all of my memory intact.

God, can I love this man any more than I already do?

Clearing my throat, I say, "I accept all of you, Alexei. Your devil's side, your ruthlessness, your amazingly big heart, and your demons you hide from the world. I love everything about you. There isn't a man on this planet I respect more."

Absolute devotion shines from Alexei's eyes, then he grins, "Is that a yes?"

"Get up," I mutter, and once he's standing in front of me, I wrap my arms around his neck. "That's a hell fucking yes."

Lifting myself on my toes, I crush my mouth to his – the man who stole my heart and saved my life in more ways than one – the man who turned out to be my salvation.

Epilogue

ALEXEI

Three years later.

Demitri and I are sitting in an SUV, parked down the road from a warehouse where a shipment of girls is being held.

I hear a motorcycle, and glancing in the side mirror, I watch as Isabella parks behind us. Opening the door, I climb out and walk to my wife.

"Ready?" I ask as I reach her.

Isabella takes off her helmet, then climbs off the motorcycle. "Yes. Ana's in place."

Demitri joins us. "I'm going to head up."

"Okay." I watch as he jogs to the side of a warehouse, and then I turn my attention back to Isabella. "Let's do this."

She grins at me as we walk in the direction of the shipment.

"Don't be greedy tonight."

I raise an eyebrow at her. "Me? I let you kill more than half every time." I wink at her before I continue, "It's a turn-on to watch you go all badass on the fuckers."

'Ugh,' Ana mutters over the earpiece.

'How about we focus on the job?' Demitri joins in.

Isabella lets out a burst of silent laughter, and then she pulls her gun from behind her back.

I do the same, and as we round the corner, we pull our ski masks over our faces.

Isabella raises her arm as we approach two guards, and then I call out, "Surprise, motherfuckers." She pulls the trigger, burying a bullet in the one guard's head.

I take aim, killing the remaining guard just as the warehouse's door rolls open. More men spill out, and then it's fun and games.

When we're close enough, I cover Isabella as she darts forward. It gives me an instant hard-on as she jumps into the air. Kicking a guard square in the chest, she rides him like a fucking surfboard as he falls backward, and then she plants a bullet between his eyes.

"That's my girl," I boast to no one in particular.

'The whole fucking world knows,' Demitri mumbles under his breath, making me chuckle.

As we walk into the warehouse, I scan for threats while Isabella runs to the girls.

And then my good mood fades.

Fucking cockroaches.

The girls have been squashed into animal cages, and knowing we don't have a lot of time before reinforcements might arrive, I walk to the nearest cage.

Usually, I leave it to Isabella to deal with the girls, but seeing as we're tight for time, cautious and caring will have to take a back seat.

"Come," I say to the girl as I open the door.

"It's okay," Isabella begins to coo. "We're here to help you."

I move along the cages, opening the doors, and then say, "Ana, we need you here. The shipment's bigger than we expected."

'On my way,' her voice sounds over the earpiece.

"Demitri, any movement?" I ask.

'Nothing. It's too quiet, though. Hurry.'

A couple of minutes later, the van pulls up, and we herd the eight girls out.

"It's going to be a tight fit," I mention to Isabella.

"Doesn't matter." She opens the side door and then gets the girls to climb inside. "We're taking you to a safe place."

My gut instinct kicks in, telling me something's off. "Wait," I say as Isabella begins to shut the door. I step closer, and then I take a good look at the girls.

Suddenly one of the girls pulls out a weapon, and my arm flies up. Without hesitating, I pull the trigger, dropping her.

The remaining seven pile from the van, my eyes scanning over each one.

"A mole?" Isabella asks.

I nod. "Probably to track us."

"Good thing you caught that," Isabella says as she takes hold of the dead girl's feet, pulling her from the van.

"My gut instinct's never wrong."

'Okay, move. Two incoming jeeps,' Demitri warns.

Isabella piles the rest of the girls back into the van while I search the body of the woman that's no older than twenty.

I'll never understand flesh peddlers. But, working with Isabella over the past three years has taught me they come in all forms.

Isabella shuts the door and bangs a fist against the metal. We watch as Ana drives off, and then Demitri mutters, *'One mile out.'*

"We're coming," I reply, and taking hold of Isabella's hand, we start to walk back to where we parked the vehicles.

'Sure, take a stroll. There's no hurry whatsoever.'

"Take out the tires if you're so worried," I say, enjoying fucking with Demitri way too much.

"Come on," Isabella says, taking pity on Demitri. She pulls her hand from mine and begins to jog.

'Thanks, Bella.'

Demitri and Ariana started calling her Bella right after the wedding. I tried it once and almost got my ass kicked. I'm only allowed to call her Isabella, baby, and my goddess.

Reaching the SUV, I watch as Isabella puts on her helmet, and only when she rides off do I climb behind the steering wheel.

The passenger door opens, and Demitri slips inside the vehicle. "Fucker."

"You love me," I taunt him.

Shaking his head, a grin tugs at his mouth.

I make a U-turn and then floor the gas to catch up to Isabella.

When I flash the headlights, she opens the throttle, and then she speeds away like a bullet.

"So fucking hot," I chuckle as we fall in behind Ana's van while Isabella takes the lead.

ISABELLA

Four years later.

Sitting outside on the patio, I watch as Mariya scowls at Viktor, Demitri and Ariana's son. "Be nice," I call out to our daughter. Lately, she's been giving Viktor hell.

"Leave her," Alexei says. "She's just going through a phase."

"Don't take her side when she does something wrong," I chastise him.

"I'll take her side even if she wipes out a small country," he chuckles as if that would be something funny.

"I can't win with you. Mariya has you wrapped around her little finger."

"As it should be," Alexei murmurs while looking at our daughter with all the love in the world.

Demitri sits down in one of the chairs. "Don't worry about them, Bella. Kids will be kids."

Ariana comes out of the house and sets a salad down on the table, and it has me asking, "Need any help?"

"Nope, I've got this. You watch the kids and make sure they don't kill each other."

Ana places a garlic bread next to the salad, and then she walks to where Mariya and Viktor are sitting in the sandbox.

"Want me to build you a castle?" Ana asks the kids.

Mariya turns her head away, pouting. As Alexei moves to get up, my hand darts out, and grabbing hold of his arm, I say, "Wait."

"She's angry because I won't be her prince," Viktor mutters while digging a finger into the sand.

Mariya's chin begins to quiver, and she crosses her arms over her chest.

I have to tighten my grip on Alexei's arm as his body tenses.

"My heart hurts," Mariya sniffles, making my heart squeeze.

Viktor glances at her, and then he scoots a little closer. Leaning forward, he stares at Mariya's face. "Why are you crying?" he asks, his voice sweet as pie.

"Because you're mean."

Viktor wraps his arm around Mariya's shoulders, then he says, "Okay, I'll be your prince."

Instantly a triumphant smile spreads over Mariya's face, and I slump back in my chair, shaking my head. "She takes after you," I blame Alexei.

"So fucking cute," Demitri murmurs.

Alexei grins at his friend. "I know."

"Fucker. I meant the kids."

"Of course."

Ariana drops down on the chair next to me, shaking her head. "It feels like Bella and I have four kids. Would be nice to have husbands once in a while."

"Amen, sister," I agree.

The End.

Published Books

STANDALONE NOVELS
Mafia / Organized Crime / Suspense Romance
(Can be read in this order or as standalones)

MERCILESS SAINTS
Damien Vetrov

CRUEL SAINTS
Lucian Cotroni

RUTHLESS SAINTS
Carson Koslov

TEARS OF BETRAYAL
Demitri Vetrov

TEARS OF SALVATION
Alexei Koslov

Men of Honor

Organized Crime / Suspense Romance

Predator
Redemption
Legacy

Enemies To Lovers

College Romance / New Adult / Billionaire Romance

Heartless
Reckless
Careless
Ruthless
Shameless
False Perceptions
(Spin-off Military Romance)

Trinity Academy

College Romance / New Adult / Billionaire Romance

Falcon
Mason
Lake
Julian
The Epilogue

The Heirs

College Romance / New Adult / Billionaire Romance

Coldhearted Heir
Arrogant Heir
Defiant Heir
Loyal Heir
Callous Heir
Sinful Heir
Tempted Heir
Forbidden Heir

Stand Alone in The Black Mountain Academy Series
Not My Hero
Young Adult / High School Romance

The Southern Heroes Series

Suspense Romance / Contemporary Romance / Police Officers & Detectives

The Ocean Between Us
The Girl In The Closet
The Lies We Tell Ourselves
All The Wasted Time
We Were Lost

Connect with me

Newsletter

FaceBook

Amazon

GoodReads

BookBub

Instagram

Acknowledgments

Jenika, thank you for including me in the Underworld Collaboration!

My Readers; You are by far the most amazing. Thank you for reading the words I write. Because of you, I'm able to see my dreams come true.

To my alpha and beta readers – Leeann, Sheena, Sherrie, Kelly, Allyson & Sarah, thank you for being the godparents of my paper-baby.

Candi Kane PR - Thank you for being patient with me and my bad habit of missing deadlines.

Yoly, Cormar Covers – Thank you for giving my paper-babies the perfect look.

My street team, thank you for promoting my books. It means the world to me!

A special thank you to every blogger and reader who took the time to participate in the cover reveal and release day.

Love ya all tons ;)